Lace AND Blade

Edited by

Deborah J. Ross

LACE AND BLADE

Edited by Deborah J. Ross

Copyright © 2008 by Deborah J. Ross
Cover Design Copyright © 2008 by Vera Nazarian
All Rights Reserved.

Cover Paintings:
"Hippolyte-François Devillers," by Jean Auguste Dominique Ingres, 1811
"Landscapes with Wild Beasts" by Roelandt Jacobsz Savery, 1629

ISBN-13: 978-1494488161
ISBN-10: 1494488167

Trade Paperback Edition

February 14, 2008

A Publication of
Norilana Books
www.norilana.com

ACKNOWLEDGMENTS

Introduction © 2008 by Deborah J. Ross
"Virtue and the Archangel" © 2008 by Madeleine E. Robins
"The Crossroads" © 2008 by Diana L. Paxson
"Touch of Moonlight" © 2008 by Robin Wayne Bailey
"Lace-Maker, Blade-Taker, Grave-Breaker, Priest" © 2008 by Tanith Lee
"The Beheaded Queen" © 2008 by Dave Smeds
"The Topaz Desert" © 2008 by Catherine Asaro
"Night Wind" © 2008 by Mary Rosenblum
"In the Night Street Baths" © 2008 by Chaz Brenchley
"Rule of Engagement" © 2008 by Sherwood Smith
Editor's Note © 2008 by Deborah J. Ross
Publisher's Note © 2008 by Vera Nazarian

ANTHOLOGIES

Edited by Roby James:

WARRIOR WISEWOMAN, 2008
WARRIOR WISEWOMAN 2, 2009
WARRIOR WISEWOMAN 3, 2010

Edited by Deborah J. Ross:

LACE AND BLADE, 2008
LACE AND BLADE 2, 2009

Edited by Elisabeth Waters:

SWORD AND SORCERESS 22, 2007
SWORD AND SORCERESS 23, 2008
SWORD AND SORCERESS 24, 2009
SWORD AND SORCERESS 25, 2010
SWORD AND SORCERESS 26, 2011
SWORD AND SORCERESS 27, 2012
SWORD AND SORCERESS 28, 2013

CONTENTS

INTRODUCTION

by Deborah J. Ross

"The wind was a torrent of darkness among the gusty trees.
The moon was a ghostly galleon tossed upon stormy seas.
The road was a ribbon of moonlight over the purple moor,
And the highwayman came riding—"

Alfred Noyes, *The Highwayman*, 1906

Something in these deeply romantic words tugs at our imagination, stirs our dreams. Is it a yearning for adventure and passion in our own lives? Do we resonate with the underlying mythic images? Is it pure escapism? Or . . . do we, in some wordless manner, recognize the truth that our hearts whisper if we can but listen: that life itself is filled with mystery, with wonder, with paradox that can be lived but not analyzed?

The book you hold in your hands began thousands of years ago, when Homer sang of the anger of Achilles and Odysseus matched wits with Circe. It owes a debt to the many writers and editors who, over the centuries, translated eternal archetypes into exciting, engaging stories.

In putting together this anthology, I was amazed and

delighted by the richness and variety of the stories. Yes, there are highwaymen here, although not always of the conventional variety, and rogues, and moonlight, and damsels fully capable of rescuing themselves. What struck me was the depth of the stories, the recurrent themes of compassion, of the importance of being true to one's self, of the ways in which we belong to one another and to the world around us. They are stories of love both conventional and utterly unexpected, of the limitless capacity of the human spirit.

> *"While the Blood Moon shines above,*
> *"I deal out life and death and love. . . ."*
>   Diana L. Paxson, *The Crossroads*, 2008

Come with us, then. Venture into the moonlight, but one word of caution: be sure to keep your wits about you, for nothing here is entirely predictable, and you may lose your heart before you know it . . . .

VIRTUE AND THE ARCHANGEL

by Madeleine E. Robins

Madeleine E. Robins is a native New Yorker, a sometime fencer and stage combatant, and has been, in no particular order, a teacher, an editor, an administrator, an actor-combatant, a nanny, and a repairer of hurt books. She's the author of ten books (including *The Stone War*, a NY Times Notable book for 1999, and *Point of Honour* and *Petty Treason*, noir mysteries set in an alternate English Regency). Currently, she lives in San Francisco, working on another Sarah Tolerance book and a non-fantastic historical set in medieval Italy, and dealing with one husband, two daughters, and "the dog who is currently annoying me by wanting to go for a walk."

Said dog plays a prominent role in Madeleine's delightful blog: http://madrobins.livejournal.com/

Madeleine's stories always take me by surprise with their wit, elegance, and more than a hint of audacity. This one is no exception.

Velliaune meCorse left her virtue in the tumbled sheets of a chamber at the Bronze Manticore. This act, which would have licensed her parents to cut her off from family and fortune, was a grave error; but with her maidenhead, Velliaune also left the Archangel behind, and that was a calamity.

Velliaune had departed the inn before dawn, made her way through empty streets and back to her parents' home in the Vocarle district, slipped into the garden and thence through a window into the servants' hall, and finally to her room. There, happily unaware of the missing jewel, she had thrown herself upon her bed and considered the night just past.

She had gone to the opera. She had flirted dutifully in her mother's presence with half a dozen acceptable men. At the end of the intermission, she had pled a headache and been permitted to return home on her own; instead, she had gone to meet Col haVanderon for a private supper at the Bronze Manticore. She had not intended matters to progress to the point where her clothes were strewn across the room and her ankles crossed behind Col's back, but all in all, she was not unhappy. Recalling the event now, Velliaune's hands strayed across her pale breast, trailing a faint echo of sensation. If it had not been the rapturous experience romantic poetry led her to expect, it had at least been exciting.

Then her fingers reached the hollow of her throat. The Archangel, an enormous sapphire given by a long-dead king to some long-dead Corse forebear and, since then, the sign and magical underpinning of her family's power and position in Meviel, was gone.

Velliaune had begged to wear it the night before, noting how beautifully it would set off her gown, silver-blue silk chosen to complement her fair, blue-eyed beauty, the bodice cut low across the breast, tight-fitted from shoulder to hip, where the skirt blossomed in a froth of lace. Her mother had hung the jewel, set in a cunning filigree of gold, around Velliaune's neck, and the girl had sworn upon her life to guard it as she would her virtue.

About which the less said, the better.

Velliaune sat up and plunged her hand frantically into her bodice, hoping the jewel had simply fallen into the gown. Finding nothing, she began to shed her clothing—dress, undergown, stay-cover, petticoats one, two and three, stays, and chemise. When she stood naked in the ruins of her toilette, she had nothing to show for it but a love bite on one breast. Velliaune sank into the pile of fabric and despaired.

When she had cried her fill, she slept a little, having slept not at all the night before. Waking, hope and commonsense reasserted themselves. Col would have found the stone amid the sheets. He would keep it for her; he might even now be wondering how he might discreetly return it to her. She had only to write him a note, and find someone to carry it to him and bring the jewel back. Someone who could be trusted, both to return the Archangel to her and to keep her parents uninformed as to Velliaune's several lapses.

Velliaune rose up, fetched her dressing gown and writing desk, and wrote a note to an old schoolmate.

ങയ്യാഴ

To say that Nyana meBarso was surprised to hear from Velliaune meCorse understated the matter. Since leaving school, Nyana's path had so far strayed from that prescribed for young ladies that a continuing acquaintance between them would have been unlikely. Nyana's parents had died under an overturned carriage; a cousin had inherited the entire estate and Nyana, a resourceful girl, took rooms in the Dedenor district and learned to fence. She had progressed so far as to become an assistant teacher at a fencing studio where fashionable gentlemen found it agreeable to be coached by a pretty girl. As her livelihood was known by her former schoolmates, it was not surprising that they did not recognize her when they passed in the street. On the whole, Nyana preferred it that way.

The note delivered to the studio was on heavy rose-scented paper.

> *Dearest friend:*
>
> *I have a commission I can entrust only to you. Will you come to my house this afternoon? I shall be waiting; do not fail me!*
>
> *Velliaune*

Here's melodrama. Nyana wiped her blades and sheathed them. Of course, she remembered Velliaune meCorse, the prettiest and most desirable girl of her year. They had never been friends, let alone *dearest* friends. Still, Nyana was intrigued by the suggestion of mystery and desperation: if Velliaune had thought to summon Nyana and call her friend, her need must be dire indeed.

Nyana arranged to take the afternoon off. Since she was attired in her work garb—leggings, blouse, and leathern tunic—she went home to make herself suitable for the drawing room of a wealthy schoolmate. Some time after the fourth chime, wearing a plain walking dress of green twill, she presented herself at the Corse house. She was shown directly upstairs, not to a parlor, but into Velliaune meCorse's bedchamber.

Her schoolmate cast herself directly upon Nyana's breast. "My dearest, *dearest* friend, thank you!"

Nyana breathed in the lavender scent of the other girl's hair for a moment, then disentangled herself. "I was never your dearest friend before. What makes me your intimate now?"

Velliaune meCorse looked briefly disconcerted. Then, "You're quite right. I did not value you at school as I ought to have done. I tell you, if you will help me now, you will be my dearest, dearest, *dearest* friend forever!"

Or for as long as you remember, Nyana thought. "What help could I give you?"

"First, you must promise me you will tell no one! I know that sounds like something from an opera, but if my parents learn—"

Nyana found mild satisfaction in her schoolmate's anxiety, but thought it unfair to tease. "I'm unlike to meet your parents."

Velliaune shook her head. "No one," she repeated. "Not my parents, nor any of our friends from school—"

"I have no friends from school, Vellie. You're the first I have spoken to since my parents' funeral. But if it makes you feel better, I will vow silence."

"Thank you." There was no mistaking her relief, and as Velliaune began to explain her predicament, Nyana understood its reason.

"You wore that great vulgar sapphire to the opera and *lost it?*" Nyana reflected that the years since school had increased Velliaune's beauty but done very little for her sense. Or her parents', for that matter. What had they been thinking, to let Velliaune borrow the talisman of family power? "How do you expect I can help?"

Velliaune, who had stood throughout the embarrassing recital of her seduction and its result, dropped to her knees before Nyana. "I need someone to go to Col haVandron and retrieve the Archangel from him."

"He has it? And will give it to me?"

"Of course he will!" Velliaune looked shocked. "How could he not?"

"Is the sort of man who invites a young woman to a midnight supper and relieves her of her virtue likely to relinquish a famous jewel she dropped among the bedsheets?" Nyana's tone was dry.

Velliaune flushed. "I am certain that Col waits only for a way to return the Archangel to me. Please, Nya, will you help?"

Nyana considered. "What do you mean to pay me for this service?"

The expression upon Velliaune's face was comical. She was used to paying for bonnets and gloves, Nyana realized, but not for services done her. "What would it cost?"

"That rather depends upon how difficult your errand is. At least—" Nyana paused to calculate a day's wages. "At least 20 *senesti*, perhaps more." Then, in answer to Velliaune's moue of anxiety, "I shan't charge you more than you can pay, I promise."

The tiny crease between Velliaune's brows smoothed. "Will you do it at once? Mama thinks I'm abed with a headache and hasn't troubled me, but I can't play sick forever."

"You must write a note to Col haVandron; if I appear upon his doorstep asking for sapphires, I doubt he'll indulge me otherwise."

A short while later, Nyana meBarso left the Corse house, heading for the apartments occupied by Col haVandron. The rooms were in a large granite block that loomed blankly over its smaller brick-and-plaster neighbors, a modern building in an area otherwise known for charm, elegance, and the money of the past. She gave her name to the porter and was shortly ushered up the stairs to the third floor.

Nyana had never met Col haVandron. She had imagined height and saturnine charm; what she met was a fair, stocky, open-faced fellow with a cheeky smile and a look of bewilderment. The bewilderment was replaced by understanding when he read Velliaune meCorse's note.

"I cannot recall that I have ever heard your name," he said at last. "Yet Velliaune entrusts you with a delicate matter."

"We were at school together," Nyana said shortly. "The sapphire, sir?"

If her directness offended him, haVandron gave no sign. "I wish that I had it."

Nyana examined him, trying to gauge truth. "Do you know where it might be?"

HaVandron's brows drew together in a frown. "Do you think I slipped that great, heavy thing off the young lady's neck while we were—" he broke off with a suggestion of delicacy.

"I know nothing more than Velliaune told me, sir. Do you recall having seen the Archangel when Velliaune arrived for your supper?"

HaVandron appeared to think. "Yes, I noted it when she arrived, for the gem caught the light from the candles."

"And later, when her clothes were removed?"

"Oh, they were not all removed," he said genially. "She kept on her shift, at least half-way, and—" He broke off at Nyana's frown. "Yes, I recall that she wore it still. I was afraid it might gouge me when—" Again he stopped. The man was far too pleased with himself, Nyana thought.

"And after?" she prompted.

"I don't recall. She rose and dressed in a hurry, to get back to her parents' house before dawn. I went back to sleep for a time, then rose and went on my way. I did not," he added, "feel any lumps in the bed as I slept."

"How comfortable for you." He had not escorted his lover home, either. "You understand the importance of that gem to her family, sir. If I cannot return it to Velliaune, thence to her parents, your tryst with her will likely become public knowledge."

HaVandron shrugged. "It was a very enjoyable evening, a memory I shall cherish, but all I had for it was the pleasure of Velliaune meCorse's body. I do not have the Archangel, and while I would be very sad to hear of Velliaune's discomfiture over the gem, I cannot produce what I do not have."

Nyana rose. "That is your final word?"

"I have no others to offer. You might check at the inn; no chambermaid in her right mind would keep such a bauble as the Archangel; if the stone was found there, it is likely still in the possession of the innkeeper." Col haVandron bowed over his visitor's hand.

As she left the building, Nyana considered. She had done what she promised: taken the note to Col haVandron and attempted to gain the Archangel from him. She had been unsuccessful. She thought of Velliaune, sitting in her chamber awaiting the return of the sapphire. At last, and sighing, Nyana turned her steps in the direction of the Sign of the Bronze Manticore.

Houses of accommodation—particularly those as handsomely fitted out and expensive as the Bronze Manticore— were entirely outside Nyana's experience. She approached the place with her most respectable demeanor and asked to speak with the housekeeper.

"You wantin' a job?" the tapster looked her up and down. "We got none at the moment."

"No, I have other business. A matter of something left behind which I wish to retrieve."

"Huh." The tapster scratched the wen on the side of his nose with a thumbnail. "Then it's Jass you're wanting. Hey, boy, go fetch Jassie down. Tell her there's a woman here for something she left behind."

Nyana's reflex was to say that it was not *she* who had

been here, but she stilled it. If Col haVanderon had followed what she believed to be the usual protocol, he would have hired the room and the supper, then brought in Velliaune, as cloaked and hidden as a springtide priest. If playing a role would help get the Corse sapphire back, she could do so for a short time.

"Yah?" Jass was the tallest woman Nyana had ever seen, red-haired, red-faced and bony, wrapped in a vast canvas apron.

"I—I was here last evening, and I believe a . . . possession . . . of mine was left behind."

The tapster, having passed Nyana safely to her proper resource, turned away. Jass motioned Nyana to follow her to a small empty coffee room. "You hardly look the type. Wha's this youn lost?"

Did one just out and say *I've lost a spectacularly large sapphire, have you seen it?* Nyana did not think so. "I've lost a necklace of my mother's," she said at last. "I'd borrowed it, and it came off when I, when I went, when—"

"When yer man tuck the clos off you," Jass offered helpfully. "Well, I stript the beds this morn and found no necklaces. Wha rhum was you in? You mi go look."

Of course neither Velliaune nor Col haVandron had told Nyana which chamber they had occupied. "Might I?" she said, thinking quickly. "The problem is that I was, um, cloaked, and I don't recall—"

Jass shrugged. "Look n'em all, if you like. What's it look like, this necklace?"

"It has a big blue stone in a gold setting. There would be a reward," Nyana suggested, hoping Velliaune would agree.

"F'I see it I'll tell you."

Nyana spent an unprofitable hour looking through every empty chamber. She found three earbobs, an empty wallet, a small box of the sort made to hold sheepskins, and two opera playbills stuffed under mattresses. Of the Archangel, no sign.

As she was leaving the inn, she passed Jass dusting a bronze figure in the hallway: a manticore, of course. "Fin' your bit o' sparkle?" the maid asked.

"No, alas. I do not think anyone would have stolen it. It's quite remarkable, and anyone who tried to sell it would instantly be turned over to the magistracy." Nyana hoped the maid would remember this if the Archangel suddenly appeared. What else could she do now but leave?

House Corse was in the midst of preparation for dinner; Velliaune was being dressed, and Nyana—whose supper usually comprised a bowl of soup in her landlady's kitchen—was forced to sit through the dressing and combing of her friend's hair before they were suffered any privacy.

"At last! If Mama asks for the necklace—" Velliaune held out her hand to receive the Archangel. Nyana shook her head and braced herself: Velliaune, balked of a desire, had been known at school for her voluble tantrums. Instead, the girl turned milk-pale.

"You *must* have it," she wailed.

For the first time, Nyana felt truly regretful. "I wish I did."

Velliaune started to pace back and forth. After a dizzying minute of watching her, Nyana took one of the girl's hands in her own in an attempt to stop the pacing and make Velliaune focus. "Col haVandron says he does not have it. He may be lying, but I could not prove it. The inn says it was not discovered there; *they* may be lying, but I could not prove it. Think, Vellie. Could the necklace have fallen off at any time after you left the Bronze Manticore?"

"The clasp was quite sturdy enough for walking through the streets. If it *had* fallen off, it surely would have gone into my bodice or petticoat, or clattered on the ground so that I heard it." She faltered. "At the inn, the activity of—with Col—we were very *busy*, you see. Could not the *activity* have knocked the clasp open?" Her blush was so profound, it seemed to make her glow under the light, and her hand in Nyana's was hot.

"You would know that better than I."

"Nya!" Velliaune's tone was imploring. "If the Archangel is truly lost, I'll be cast out of the house in my shift! I'll starve! I'm not like you, I don't know how to do anything but marry well."

It's likely your night with Col haVandron has taught you some marketable skills. Nyana bit down hard on that thought; voicing it would not improve the situation, and she had promised to help.

"It won't come to that. We'll find the wretched sapphire and your parents will be none the wiser. Let us think. Both you and Col say that you wore the Archangel when you arrived for dinner; Col says you had it on *during . . . .*"

Velliaune choked. *How readily she blushes,* Nyana thought.

"You say the clasp was too sturdy to come undone while you were walking home."

"It was, I swear it."

"Then all I can guess is that it fell off, as you thought, when you were in bed with Col haVandron."

"Nya!"

"If you can bed the man, you can hear the words spoken! If you lost the Archangel in bed, then either it was lost in the sheets, and the inn has it, and that maid lied—" Velliaune nodded vigorously, "or Col managed to unclasp it while he was *clasping* you, and *he* has it." Velliaune shook her head. "In either case, someone has lied to me."

Nyana released Velliaune's hand and rose. "I suppose I had best find out who."

Nyana left the Corse house in perplexion. *I have no power, no authority, no money. A little wit, and some skill with a fencing sword, and that is the sum of it.* Well, she would have to use whatever came to hand.

Evening was drawing like an opera cloak over the city of Meviel. Torches glittered in doorways like inconstant gems. At the Bronze Manticore, the staff would doubtless be getting ready for that night's assignations. Nyana returned to her room long enough to change from the gown suitable to visiting the Corse household back into her breeches, leathern tunic and steel-buckled shoes. With her blades hung on her hip, she felt ready to proceed.

Nyana's route brought her first to the back of the inn, where she observed a figure sneaking—there was no other word for the posture and manner—in through the stableyard doors. Extraordinarily tall, female, red-headed: it was Jass.

Now that *is interesting.*

Nyana followed after the maid as stealthily as she might; the last thing she needed was to bring the tapster, the ostlers, or the owner of the inn into this discussion. She caught up with Jass in one of the dim service hallways between the stable and the kitchen.

"Wha? You agan?" The maid looked apprehensive. Why would that be, when she had been so casual in their last conversation? Nyana was inspired.

"I'm afraid I must ask you to turn out your pockets."

"Won't." The syllable was sullen, but Jass's eyes moved back and forth as if seeking a route of escape. "Can't make me."

"I see the matter thusly." Nyana smiled. "If you turn out your pockets, I shall not have to make a fuss. If you do not, the innkeeper will become involved, and when he learns that you were in league with Col haVandron to steal a very expensive piece of jewelry—"

"In league? I never!" Jass's eyes opened so wide they appeared to be in danger of rolling out of their sockets.

"Turn out your pockets," Nyana said again.

Jass dug a raw-boned hand into her apron pocket and produced, not the Archangel but a purse, which she held out. Nyana's eyes opened nearly as wide as the maid's when she saw how much money was inside.

"Where did you get this?"

"Woun't even gimme wha the sparkle was worth," the maid said resentfully. "When I foun it this mornin' I was gon to hide it from him, sell it or make him pay more. Then you said what about I coun't sell it safe, an I figurt it for a bad business, and tol him where—"

"Where?" Nyana said urgently. It was one thing to convince the maid to give up her secret; she was certain Col haVandron would be far more difficult.

"Upstairs. In the hall—"

Nyana turned. "When did you leave him?"

"Quarter hour, maybe. At the alehouse in Pastern Stre—"

Nyana did not stay. If she were lucky, she might reclaim the Archangel and see that Velliaune meCorse was never troubled by rumors of her night with Col haVandron. She left the inn at the back, circled around to the front hall, and there found a stool to station behind the drapery.

She watched as several couples arrived, intent upon an evening's pleasure, and a drunken blade was turned away when he asked the innkeeper to supply a woman ("The Bronze Manticore does not *procure*, sir!"). Just as Nyana had begun to lose her patience with waiting, the door arced open just wide enough to admit a man without setting the bells to clamor.

Col haVandron slipped inside and went at once, as Nyana had suspected he might, to the brazen manticore figurine on the trestle table opposite the door. She watched as he ran his hands up and down the figure, fingers seeking what the light was too dim to reveal otherwise: the hiding place of the Archangel. Nyana knew when he had found it, for his hands stilled and he made a noise in the back of his throat. He slid the sapphire out of its hiding place beneath the left-hand wing; the chain and stone caught the lamplight for a brief moment before Col pocketed them. Then, with the same care he had used minutes before, he slipped silently out of the door.

Nyana, behind him, followed with equal stealth.

The air had cooled and the last blue glimmer of daylight was gone. By the light of torches burning at each door, she saw the stocky figure of Col haVandron pause at the corner as if seeking a carriage for hire. When none appeared, he proceeded on foot, not toward his rooms, but toward the Dedenor district, where the fencing studio, her own rooms, and a sizeable number of Meviel's criminal populace were located.

He's mad, or as naive as Vellie meCorse! A gentleman, swordless, carrying a rock like that down Hangsaman Street after dark? Perhaps he doesn't like the throat Nature gave him and hopes someone will vent it for him?

Nyana put her hand on the hilt of her sword and followed.

The attack came just as Col haVandron turned the corner of Hangsaman Street onto the narrower Wattle Street. Three men, large, armed, and confident enough of a kill that they had not bothered to mask their faces, surrounded haVandron in the time it took him to take a pace.

"Stand!" the tallest man barked. Instantly, what foot

traffic there had been disappeared. If Col haVandron expected the folk of the Dedenor district to come to the rescue of an unknown gentleman, he was in for a sad correction. "You got somethin' we'm wantin'."

HaVandron stumbled slightly and eyed a blade that flashed up to stop any attempt at flight. *They're quick,* Nyana thought.

"Why, *gentlemen,*" haVandron drawled. "What can I have that you would want?"

"A bit o' sparkle," the man to the right said. He was the shortest of the three tall men, and his words came out with a shower of spittle that caught the torchlight.

"Shut it, Cheevie," the first man said. He reached forward to touch the tip of his blade to haVandron's top coat button. "Gimme the sparkle and you'll see the morra." A long few moments passed. Was haVandron trying to decide what he might offer these men in place of the Archangel? More interesting, to Nyana at least, was the question of how the men had known he had the sapphire in the first place.

The lead man pushed a little harder with the tip of his sword. HaVandron stepped backward and was prodded gently with the third man's swordpoint. His hand slid into his pocket.

"Well, since you must," he said.

Reluctantly Nyana realized that, if she were to reclaim the Archangel for Velliaune meCorse, this would be the moment. She drew sword and dagger, stepped out of the shadow, and within a moment had the tip of her dagger pressed against the nape of the third man's neck.

Matters became complex. The third man froze for a moment, then turned to face Nyana. The leader and Cheevie, momentarily shocked by the arrival of an unanticipated assistant to their quarry, raised their blades to chase her away, permitting

Col haVandron to step to his left, out of range of the two swords.

Col caught sight of her. "You!"

"I," Nyana agreed. She tossed her dagger, hilt first, to haVandron. "A loan," she said, and turned to deal with the third man. Despite the weighty blade in his hand, he was no swordsman. He waved the blade back and forth like a finger waggled at a naughty child; Nyana, in a move she had only practiced and never accomplished in good earnest, beat the blade away with a strong strike and hit true in the man's center, feeling her point cut into his chest, bounce along the side of a rib, then slide further. It was not a pleasant sensation.

The man cried in outrage, then was silent as blood bubbled up in the corner of his mouth and he crumpled. Nyana fought the urge to vomit and tugged her sword free—the muscle of the man's chest held tight to her blade—because the leader was coming at her now. Looking over, she saw Col haVanderon engaged in blocking Cheevie's cuts with her dagger; at least he was not dead already.

"Messing in business that's none of yourn, girl." The leader did not seem concerned by the sight of his companion dying upon the street.

"Whose business is it, then?" Nyana stood on guard, circling warily. This man looked far more comfortable with a blade than his companions had done.

"More none of yourn." He stopped and held his arm and blade straight out, pointing at Nyana's neck as if in warning. "You'd be wise to go home to your Mammy."

"Haven't one." The man appeared nonplussed by her air of unconcern. "If it's not *my* business, might it be Jass's?"

That startled him. The leader glanced from side to side as if the tall red-headed woman might appear from nowhere. "How d'you—"

"Who else would have known that Col haVandron had the jewel?" she said. Nyana beat his blade away. "I thought she'd sold the thing to him?"

The man grinned. "When we take the sparkle home, Jass'll turn it in for reward." He feinted broadly at her hip.

"Clever." Nyana parried again. "The problem is that I'm charged to bring the jewel home to its right owner."

A yelp from the left drew the leader's attention for a second; Col haVandron had pinked Cheevie in the arm and taken his sword from him. As Cheevie ran down the street, the soles of his boots pale in the torchlight, the leader turned back to Nyana.

"The odds have changed," she noted. "I think you should go home."

"And face Jassie without nothing to show for it? Not likely." The leader brought his sword up in a circling motion, cutting for Nyana's shoulder, but she had already dropped down on one knee and thrust her point deep into the man's underarm, the blade reappearing just below the shoulder. His sword dropped, he screamed, and it was the work of several minutes to disentangle her blade, wipe it down, confiscate the sword and bind the man's shoulder up so that he did not bleed to death on the way home.

"There. You have something to show Jassie. Now, will you please go?"

Nyana and haVanderon watched as the leader walked heavily away into the darkness. Then she turned to him.

"My dagger, sir?"

He handed her the dagger, which she slid at once into its hanger.

"And the Archangel."

Col haVanderon paused, calculation written upon his face.

"A man who comes into the Dederon without so much as a penknife to defend himself is not the man who can best me in a fight, particularly with an unfamiliar sword." She nodded at Cheevie's blade, which dangled in his hand. "I think the necklace simply fell off, was discovered by the maid at the Bronze Manticore, and offered by her to you. An unexpected gain, but not worth dying for. Give me the Archangel, sir. Or raise your weapon."

A moment more calculation, then Col haVanderon shrugged. "Right on every count." He slid his hand into his pocket and produced from it the Archangel, large, blue, glittering. Nyana put it into her own pocket.

"Well. Good night, sir."

໊ຕຽໜ

Velliaune meCorse had chattered throughout dinner in hopes of distracting her parents from the subject of the Archangel and now found herself in the parlor, singing, "So Gently Dies the Woodland Doe," for their pleasure. At the song's end, her maid whispered that Nyana meBarso was waiting.

As soon as she could depart from her parents' beaming presence, Velliaune joined Nyana in her bedchamber. The moment the door closed behind her, she wheeled round.

"Do you have it?"

"It took longer than I had expected, but—" Nyana held the Archangel out to her, "here."

Velliaune snatched the thing to her breast and held it there. "Praises!" She vanished from the room. This time, Nyana had to wait only a few minutes.

"I have given the wretched thing back to my mother, and hope never to wear it again!" She threw her arms around Nyana extravagantly. "Thank you, thank you, thank you! You have—I cannot tell you—if my parents had learned . . . I can breathe again!" Indeed, she felt as light as a breeze.

"Well, then, there's the matter of my payment."

Velliaune drew her head back. She had rather hoped Nyana would forget the matter of her payment, but her expression suggested that this was not likely. Gracelessly, she stepped away from Nyana, took up her purse, and counted out twenty *senesti*.

"Is that sufficient?" she asked sullenly.

"Almost." To Velliaune's astonishment, Nyana meBarso stepped forward and kissed her. It was no trivial embrace: her lips were soft and seeking, and one hand tangled itself in Velliaune's curls. After a moment of surprise, Velliaune relaxed, and returned the kiss, her insides fluttering.

It was Nyana who broke off the embrace.

"There. Your debt is paid. All through school, I wanted to do that, and now I have."

"All through school? But—" Velliaune held out a hand as if to draw Nyana back. "You're not going to kiss me like *that* and leave!"

"I believe I am, Vellie. Have you learned nothing about the wisdom of leaping into action you may later regret? If you want more, you may always find me in the Dedenor. But remember that price may be more than even the Archangel could buy you."

Nyana smiled, not unkindly, bowed, and was gone. Velliaune meCorse sank down to sit upon her bed, staring after her schoolmate in wonder and alarm.

THE CROSSROADS

by Diana L. Paxson

Diana L. Paxson is the author of many novels, most recently, *Ravens of Avalon* and *The Golden Hills of Westria*, and has contributed to many anthologies, including *Thieves' World* and *Sword and Sorceress*. She recently served as a judge for the Pagan Fiction contest. She is also a student of the Afro-Brazilian tradition of Umbanda. She lives in Berkeley, California. Read about her *Westria* books and more at http://www.westria.org/

Set in the lushly evocative world of colonial Brazil, Diana's tale unfolds on many levels: an adventure, a love story, a fantasy involving supernatural forces . . . but most of all, the struggle of a man to discover his true self.

Even before the ship entered the harbor, the scent of the new land reached out to enfold it, rich and fecund as the scent of a woman.

Brazil . . . . Claude took a deep breath. *My fortune . . . my destiny* . . . .

After so many weeks at sea, the colors were a shock to the senses; a wave of green washing against the immense gray knobs of stone that stood guard above the shores, vivid as emeralds from the mine that was all that remained of the family's fortune. The Emperor had made his grandfather a baron, but the DeLormes had suffered during the changes of regime that followed. There were times, this past year, when all that had kept Claude afloat was his skill at cards. To be poor was like living in a cage. But he was a gentleman. What choice did he have?

As the ship passed between the two forts and into the Bay of Guanabara, the wind brought a vibration deeper than the throb of the ship's engines, the sound of distant drums. Perspiration beaded Claude's upper lip beneath the short-clipped mustache, and a runnel of sweat snaked down his back beneath the white linen of his suit.

This land is a hot mistress, he thought, *but a rich one, if I embrace her boldly.* Memory shied away from the mistress he had left in Paris. If Manon had railed at him for lack of money, he could have shouted back at her. If she had wept, they could have mourned together. It was her sweet, civilized regret that chilled his soul. By now, she would have found another protector. He would return with a new fortune and a necklace of emeralds as green as her eyes, and smile politely when they met at the Opéra and she saw another woman wearing it, laughing as she clung to his arm.

They passed the shanty-town at the outskirts of the city, and beyond it, the ornate buildings erected when Rio de Janeiro had been the capital of the exiled government of Portugal during Napoleon's wars. The billow of steam from the funnels thinned and the ship eased smoothly toward the quay. People waited on the shore, in every shade from heat-flushed pink to ebony. One saw blacks in Paris of course, from the colonies, but the African influence in Brazil was much more clear. One of those people ought to be *Senhor* Hermilo Braga, who had been his father's agent, and who had been instructed to meet him here.

The ship jerked as first one, then a second line was tossed from the lower deck to the dock and tightened around the stanchions. Claude gripped the railing, for a moment overwhelmed by the barrage of noise and color.

Courage, mon ami, he clutched at calm, *you are a gentleman of France. You must not let these people think you are afraid . . . .*

⋙⋘

Music threaded the babble of conversation in the cabaret. Tres Rosas, it was called, a surprisingly elegant place to find in the *brega*, a decidedly declassé part of town. Claude felt the drumbeat beneath the civilized sweetness of the strings, persistent and compulsive, like the drumming he had heard the night before through the open window of his hotel. Or perhaps the throb in his temples was anger. He leaned across the round table, forcing Braga to meet his gaze.

"Monsieur, I have made a very long voyage to have this accounting. I *will* have truth from you!"

"But *Senhor* Barão, I have told you. It is God who set the emeralds into the ground, and luck alone that lets a man find them." The little man threw up his hands. In the flicker of the gaslight his round, perspiring face took on the hue of the crimson flocked wallpaper behind him. From the gaming tables in the room beyond came a shout as someone made a lucky throw.

Claude ground his teeth in frustration. "Do you blame the good God? I have seen the reports on other mines in the Serra das Equas. Until five years ago, the income from Santo Pedro was much the same. If the mine was playing out, the totals would not have gone down so suddenly!" he exclaimed. "No,

Monsieur Braga, it is not God whom I question, but men."

As Claude sat back, striving for control, the music ceased at last, leaving only the regular squeak and swish of the ceiling fans being pulled by dark-skinned boys. Despite the fan he could still feel the prickle of sweat beneath his clothes. People rose from their tables. The mix of respectably dressed gentlemen and women who, though equally fashionable, were hardly respectable, reminded him of the clientele at the Moulin Rouge. Even the man who leaned negligently against the piano was a familiar type, burly but elegant. They called him "Dom" Julio Carneiro, a prince of the *brega*, the quarter of whorehouses and cabarets.

"But I assure you, *senhor*, it is the truth! There has been no thieving!"

"Perhaps *you* do not understand. I must know whether the mine can still yield . . . ."

Claude paused as a bright swirl of women's garments caught his eye. Beyond them he glimpsed the musicians, sober black trousers setting off the brilliant red of the shirts they wore. An androgynous person in a pink gown bent to whisper something in the drummer's ear. White teeth flashed. For a moment his gaze held Claude's, amused and knowing, then he shook his head and laughed once more.

Claude blinked, and took another drink of the uncured rum they called *cachaça*. The harsh liquor burned in his belly, reigniting his anger. He glared at Braga.

"Will you guide me to the Serra das Equas?"

"If you insist," Braga shrugged. "But—"

Claude was no longer listening. In the open doorway of the cabaret stood a woman in a crimson silk gown. Carneiro was bowing over her hand. Claude glimpsed a dark, brilliant gaze, a complexion like creamed coffee, crimson roses nestling in waves of raven hair dressed high and falling in curls down her back. He raised one eyebrow.

"You are surprised?" *Senhor* Braga began to recover his self-possession as he followed Claude's gaze. "That is Corquisa. She was once a courtesan, very expensive. She owns the cabaret now."

"So I see," said Claude, watching as the lady took Carneiro's arm and moved among the tables to receive the homage of those in the room. Black lace framed an arresting decolletage. The smooth curve of the corset outlined a tiny waist. Below, the rich silk swept back to fall in a complicated swirl set with spangles over a tiered, lace-trimmed underskirt that flared to sweep the floor. As she passed, male eyes brightened, shoulders straightened, and paunches were sucked in. The reaction of the women was even more interesting, expressions and bearing shifting as if for a moment each became a mirror for Corquisa's beauty.

Silk rustled as the lady drew closer. Her scent, a hint of musk beneath attar of roses, awakened a throb of desire. Claude rose smoothly to his feet, bracing to make the most of what height he had. His shoulders might not be as broad as Carneiro's, but he could at least boast of superior, if somewhat dated, tailoring.

"*Senhora*, I am honored to present to you the *Senhor Barão* Claude DeLorme of Paris," said Braga, who had hauled himself to his feet as well. "He comes to see his family's emerald mine."

Claude had the impression that the little man had exchanged a glance with Carneiro, but he had eyes only for the woman.

"Enchanté, Madame." He bowed over her hand.

"The honor is mine," she responded in the same

language, her full lips parting in a smile. "Welcome to Brazil . . . ."

Even here, Claude thought in relief, French was the language of culture.

"*Senhora*—" Braga cleared his throat, "Will you join us in a glass of champagne?"

Claude glanced at him in surprise, having noted the lady refusing a number of other such invitations as she progressed around the room. Corquisa's dark gaze slid toward Carneiro, who smiled suddenly and signaled a waiter. In another moment, the bottle of *cachaça* had been replaced by one with a French label and four long-stemmed glasses whose curving bowls were said to have been inspired by the breast of the Empress Josephine.

Claude looked from the glasses to the breast of the woman who sank with a rustle of silk into the chair beside him, mentally folding back the swathe of lace that framed her shoulders, wondering how that smooth skin would feel beneath his hand. With an effort, he looked away. A gentleman did not allow himself to be ruled by his passions.

"Is your mine producing well?" Corquisa asked.

What did she see as she looked at him? A slim, fair-haired gentleman who carried himself with the assurance of a citizen of the most cultured city in the world? Or a man at the end of his resources, clinging to a façade of gentility?

"Not according to Monsieur Braga's reports—" Claude forced his gaze back to the champagne coupe Carneiro was offering him. "I will have to ride there, see for myself what is wrong."

"If the surface deposits have been exhausted, it may take a considerable investment to find and develop the veins that will make it productive again," Carneiro said easily.

The observation was reasonable. Why, Claude wondered, did he feel that sudden frisson along his spine? The man was too sleek, waving dun hair plastered to his skull, his skin almost the same shade of tan. But the shoulders inside the black coat were burly, and Carneiro moved like a man who could handle himself in the salle d'armes.

Claude's glance flicked back to Braga, who was watching them warily. Why had the little man invited Carneiro to join them? More to the point, why had the owner of the Tres Rosas and her companion agreed?

"It is a pity that such a gentleman should leave us before he has had a chance to know the city," Corquisa said softly.

"Perhaps when you have learned more, you will find that you can spare yourself a journey," Carneiro added smoothly. "You might be wiser to sell."

"To you?" Claude asked baldly.

Carneiro shrugged. "My business is entertainment, not emeralds, but I know people who have such interests. Think of me as an *arranger* . . . ."

For whom? wondered Claude.

Corquisa shivered and her eyes closed. When she opened them once more, he could not look away. She had been beautiful before, but suddenly her radiance compelled the eye.

"You must call on me," she said softly, "whether you stay or go. You will find my lodgings on the Rua Boa Sorte, near the Passeo Publico, by the lovely gardens."

The Street of Good Luck was a good address, he thought with appreciation. Whether it would it be good luck or the opposite for him, he could not tell, but he knew that he would accept her invitation, and soon.

છ૮ર૬ળ૯૦

Claude stood on the brick pavement outside the Tres Rosas, jingling the coins in his pocket and breathing deeply to clear his head. It was late. The musicians were coming out of a side entrance in a chattering mob and piling their instrument cases into a wagon, which presently rumbled away. In his mind, he still heard their music. Later in the evening, Corquisa had joined them. Braga had translated some of her song:

> *Who comes to me must take his chances,*
> *In lust or luck, so that he dances,*
> *Come to me and roll the dice,*
> *Win my love and pay the price!*

It was a song about Pomba Gira, queen of courtesans and wife of the trickster Exu who ruled the crossroads, though some said that they were different sides of the same being; whether the *orixas* were gods or spirits was not quite clear.

After that, it might have been rash to move to the casino room for a game or two of piquet. But even the Baron Claude DeLorme could not always be ruled by reason. Was it something in the air of Brazil, warmly scented even at this hour, that made him so resentful of the code by which he had been taught to live? In any case, tonight's winnings would cover another week at the hotel.

Perhaps he should not have accepted that last glass of rum. In Paris he never drank enough to cloud his faculties. It was this country, so full of dangers and opportunities, tempting a man to forget the old rules.

A ragged fellow in the road gabbled something about a carriage, but Claude shook his head. If he met a footpad, he had a sword in his silverheaded cane. He needed to think, to distinguish between difference and danger, between safety and seduction. There were no streetlights here, but a waxing moon lit the sky. A beautiful moon—he blinked to bring it into focus. The moon would show him his way.

If the mine required an infusion of capital to make it productive, perhaps he might do better to sell. For certain, he had no funds to invest, unless he mortgaged the property to the hilt and stayed here to manage it. The prospect did not attract him. He knew nothing about the frontier. His life was in Paris, with Manon. But when he tried to bring her face to mind, what filled his vision was Corquisa's brilliant gaze.

For that reason alone, Claude thought unhappily, he ought to flee anything proposed by an associate of hers. It had all been too neat, Braga's choice of a place for their conference, the offer, and the lovely woman to distract him, although indeed, she was a woman for whom one might count the world well lost. Despite their reputation, the French were a practical people. No doubt that was why he had not killed first Manon and then himself when she announced the end of their liaison. As she had told him, it was a matter of business. One must consider one's future, after all.

Claude felt a change in the footing and saw that the brick paving had been replaced by cobbles. As he paused to confirm his direction, he heard footsteps that were not his own. They stopped a moment after he did, and when he resumed his progress, listening carefully now, that soft echo picked up once more.

Claude, mon ami, he asked himself, *what kind of fix have you gotten yourself into now?* Frowning, he turned down a side-street, hearing tuned to the whisper of footfalls. Many footfalls, he thought as he quickened his own pace down the road.

The way forked, and he turned and turned again. The road was hard earth now, the cabarets and taverns of the *brega* giving way to a huddle of ramshackle dwellings. A door opened as he passed, releasing a breath of something hot and spicy, and was swiftly shut once more. The European part of the city seemed far away. Anything could happen here. But the distinctive humped shapes of the surrounding hills still rose beyond the rooftops. If he could work his way down to the avenue that followed the shore he could find his way back to his hotel. Surely he could not get lost, between the mountains and the sea.

Ahead lay a crossroads. Claude's pace slowed as he realized that the road led through the wrought iron gates of a cemetery. Over the gate was a sign, "Cemitério San Pedro" and the saint's crossed keys.

Should he turn left or right?

He stopped short in the intersection as a dark-skinned man stepped out from the shadows of the gate. His shirt, even leached of color by the moonlight, showed red. It was the drummer from the Tres Rosas.

"Monsieur le Baron, bonsoir."

Claude stiffened. How did the man come to speak French, to know who Claude was, *to know he would be here?* As if the thought had summoned them, his pursuers came clattering down the road.

"Are those your friends, following me?"

"*I* don't have any enemies. Do you?"

Until this evening, Claude would not have thought so, but he was suddenly acutely aware of being a stranger, and alone.

"If you are not with them, tell me how to get out of here!"

"Depends on where you want to go . . . ."

Good question. He had come here to restore his fortune,

so he could live like a civilized man. But at what price civilization now? The sound of pursuit grew abruptly louder as a dozen figures burst into the crossroads. Claude recoiled, a sudden sweat that owed nothing to the temperature moistening his skin. The training in swordplay usual for his class had not included practice in holding off a mob. By reflex, he pressed the release and the swordstick's mahogany casing spun through the air to strike the first man's face with a meaty *thwap*. Gulping, Claude whipped the blade up to guard.

"Choose, man—choose!"

The second man yelped as Claude's lunge sent the tip of the blade ripping up the length of his arm. Appalled, he jerked the blade free.

"You got reach, but they got numbers," the lazy voice continued. "Quality or quantity, which gonna win?"

Moonlight glinted on steel as the others closed in. Seven left, Claude thought frantically, his blade wavering among targets.

"He's only one—" mocked the drummer. "You afraid to fight man-to-man?"

Oh, that's a great help! thought Claude as his assailants gathered for another rush. *Why don't you go for the gendarmes or—*

He gritted his teeth and settled to guard once more as one of the toughs stepped out to meet him, knife weaving in glittering arcs. He slashed upward as the knife-man leaped, connecting more by chance than design.

"Merda!" came the exclamation as his attacker fell back, clutching his arm, and that was close enough to French to need no translation. A thrown blade flicked past Claude's ear and clattered across the road.

His assailants were spreading out now, regrettably

showing sense at last. He might hit one or two before they reached him, but the long blade would hamper him when the rest closed in.

"Time to cast again an' change the odds," said the drummer, stepping forward himself as the rush began, his drumsticks in his hands.

Then the attackers were on them. A fist split the skin above Claude's cheekbone, and something harder, a club perhaps, struck his left shoulder, numbing his arm. As he tried to retreat, he glimpsed a pale flicker. The drummer's sticks beat out a new rhythm on arms and legs. In the next moment, all of the attackers were sprawling in a chorus of oaths and a great tangle of limbs.

"Come, if you want to live, " said the dry voice at his ear. A strong hand jerked him through the iron gateway.

They ran, careering through the cemetery, leaping gravestones and dodging around tombs. As they passed the great central cross, Claude saw lit candles, a black chicken, a red rose. Were they offerings to the *orixas*? The strong hand hauled him past before he could ask, and once more they hurtled through a wilderness of tombs. The shadow of another gate barred the path. A hard push propelled him through. When he caught his balance and turned, the drummer was gone.

Claude stood blinking at the white road that ran beside the bay, waiting for the wild drumbeat of his heart to slow. He still felt the pressure of that muscular hand. But there was no movement. No sound of running feet, no sound at all but the sigh of the sea, silver-spangled by the moonlight beyond the deserted shore.

అ౪౩౭౬

"They say you fought well," said Corquisa, pouring tea from a silver pot.

Claude stilled. Was she mocking him? The white suit covered most of his bruises, but the skin around the gash on his cheek was purple, and stressed muscles made him move like an old man. "And who would *they* be, Madame?" With an effort, he kept his voice cool. He had reached his hotel well after midnight and slept past noon. When he at last forced himself to rise, the invitation from Corquisa lay before his door.

Carefully, he eased back against the cushions of the wrought iron couch. They sat on a shaded balcony overlooking a small garden at the back of the building, where the broad, shiny leaves of the banana trees stirred gently in the wind from the sea and magenta bougainvillea blazed against the wall. Nearby, someone played a guitar, but thank the good God, he could hear no drums.

"I may live like the ladies of Europe, but do not delude yourself that I am one of them." Corquisa offered him a porcelain cup. "I have . . . sisters . . . in every part of town. What is known to one is known to all."

Today she was dressed in white lawn with insets of lace against which her skin glowed like gold. Her lush curves seemed even more sensual, veiled by the garment's purity, and the lithe grace with which she moved made him abruptly certain she was not corseted. He swallowed, blood stirring as he imagined what that thin cloth concealed.

"Do you know your enemies?"

With an effort he focused on her face once more. "They were street toughs, robbers who thought a gentleman lost in the wrong part of town would be easy prey."

"They were sent," she corrected him, "by Carneiro."

Carefully Claude set down the tea-cup. "They were?

Why are you telling me? I thought—"

"You thought he owned me?" The courtesan shook her head. "Unfortunately, *he* thinks so too. *Senhor*, no one owns Corquisa, but if nothing is done, Carneiro will soon own the Tres Rosas," she added bitterly. "I became his mistress and he gave me the money to buy the building, told me to spare no expense in furnishing. I signed a note—he said it was only a legal formality, a matter of business. I paid his price, and he paid mine, and I thought we were done. Now he shows me papers that say there is interest due. I cannot pay it, and next week he will take the cabaret."

"If you are looking for a new protector," Claude's lips twisted, "you are speaking to the wrong man. The emerald mine was all I had left, and it is worthless, if *Senhor* Braga is to be believed."

"But *do* you believe him?" she asked. "I think that if someone were to gain a look at Carneiro's papers, they might find evidence of what happened with your mine, along, perhaps, with the original of the agreement he signed with me. I know such a someone, but he would have to be paid. 'Dom Julio' guards his secrets well. . . . They are thieves!" she added viciously. "I do not pay money to men, they give it to me! But even if you prove they have robbed you, it will take time to restore your profits."

She leaned forward. Several buttons at the neck of her gown were open, offering a tantalizing glimpse of smooth skin, and a string of red and black beads. He wondered if she was a devotee of Pomba Gira, whose colors those were.

"But you have other resources, my friend. I am told you have great skill at cards."

Claude stared, and then began to laugh. "My dear lady, if you think I can play for a fortune with no stake but my father's stickpin, I do not wonder at the state of your affairs."

Corquisa's eyes flashed and she rose from her chair.

"Do you think so? I have not the price of the cabaret, but my jewels would bring enough for you to begin a game. Once you are playing, you can challenge him to gamble his claim on the cabaret!"

Claude began to shake his head. "Madame, I am honored by your confidence, but—"

He saw a shudder pass through her body and wondered if she were going to weep. Then she straightened and turned, seeming suddenly not larger, but more *real,* as she had for that moment in the cabaret. Words failed as she moved around the little table, sinking down onto the cushions beside him. He breathed in musk and roses. His head spun.

"You can defeat him! I know! When you have won, you will set me free! In return, my friend will find the evidence to make the thieves return what they stole from you."

She ran her fingers through his hair and drew him closer, guiding his lips to hers. His control shattered. Beneath his groping fingers the fine cloth tore. Her flesh was fire. With a fury that Manon had never kindled, he plunged into that flame.

ೞ❀ೞ❀ೞ❀

*C*ourage, mon ami. . . . Claude forced his breathing to slow. The flutter of cards through his fingers was familiar and comforting. The scent of cigar smoke, the aftertaste of brandy, all belonged on a battlefield where he was thoroughly at home. The luck was with him so far, for the first cut had made him dealer. The cards flicked from his fingers in neat fans. If Carneiro had sent the thugs who attacked him, he would find Claude a much more formidable opponent here.

It was only a game of piquet, Claude thought smiling,

and the stakes not even his own. With swift, efficient movements, he squared the remaining cards and set the stack in the center of the little table, then gathered up his hand. The backs of the cards were shiny black with a design of red roses. Corquisa was wearing black this evening as well, a silk taffeta with crimson roses tucked into her decolletage. Claude suppressed his body's response to her perfume. This evening, he thought wryly, he must not think with his balls, but with his brain.

He considered his hand. There were the Queen of Hearts—a good sign, considering—and the eight and a ten. He looked up, waiting for his opponent to discard. His face impassive, Carneiro slapped five cards down on the green baize table and took five more from the central pile. Claude nodded, discarded the Seven of Spades and the Eight of Diamonds and took two more. His heart leaped as he saw Hearts—a seven and a nine. He looked up, waiting for his opponent to declare his hand.

"A point of five," said Carneiro.

"Not good," answered Claude, glancing down at the sheaf of Hearts in his hand. "A point of six." The familiar patter of the declarations alternated between the two players.

"Six points to the *Senhor Barão*," a new voice said when they were done. Claude glanced up and felt a jolt of recognition as the drummer in red and black lounged in an armchair with the score card in his hand. Why was he not with the orchestra whose beat Claude felt, rather than heard, through the boards of the floor? Or perhaps the beat was in his head and not coming from the other room at all.

Carneiro, holding the elder hand, led with a Ten of Clubs for the first trick. Claude smiled and took it with the Jack. Turn and turn about, the play continued, and at the end of the hand he found himself the winner with seven tricks to Carneiro's four. A promising start, he thought, as Carneiro took up the deck to deal the next. So far he was ahead, but his opponent had no reason to give up yet. With six deals in each partie, there was plenty of room for things to change.

"No need to worry . . . no way you gonna lose."

The thought was welcome, but odd, as if it were not his own.

Claude led his cards carefully, using the first deals to learn the shape of his opponent's mind. They had agreed to play for 500 reis per point, and by the end of the game, Claude was ahead. Since both men had scored over a hundred points, Carneiro had to pay him only the difference between their scores.

"Another partie?" Carneiro asked as Claude tucked the banknotes into an inner pocket. "It is only polite to give me a chance at revenge . . ."

Claude nodded. He had been hoping for this; the margin of the first defeat had been small enough to encourage his opponent. Perhaps the older man had reason, for he scored much better in the first exchange. Claude allowed himself to appear shaken, but he was playing carefully, aware by now that his memory for the cards was better than the other man's.

"Win, or lose? Which stings the man so he gotta accept when you challenge?" Again, a thought that did not quite seem his own.

If Claude won again, Carneiro might decide to cut his losses and end the play. What would tempt him to stake Corquisa's note? *Not mere money,* he realized, *not even the stake Corquisa gave me. But he does want the mine. . . .* She held court now on the other side of the room, the sequins scattered across the black silk glinting as she moved. Even one look sent fire through his flesh, but was that worth risking the only security he had?

"She is the end of all desire . . ." came the voice in his head. In her arms, he had been free. . . .

The roulette tables were deserted as the other gamblers gathered to watch the play. Claude was dimly aware of the drummer's sardonic voice calling out the mounting scores, and once, the heady rush of Corquisa's perfume. He sipped from the glass of brandy she brought him without looking up. The only real things in the world were the cards in the two men's hands.

As the play progressed, Claude allowed himself to appear more reckless, discarding his maximum of five cards with each exchange, confident that Carneiro would not realize when he had sunk a declaration to make his hand appear worse than it was. And when the game was over, he was the one who counted out the wad of notes into Carneiro's broad hand.

"Now I suppose you want *your* revenge?" Carneiro leaned back in his chair with a predatory grin.

"I'm afraid that my cash is gone—" Claude patted his pocket sadly. "But I do retain one thing you value, my deed to the Santo Pedro mine. If you will stake Madame Corquisa's debt on the outcome, I will play a third game, winner take all. . . ."

In the sudden silence, Carneiro looked from Claude to Corquisa and back again. His face grew dark.

"He smells a trick," the voice in his head spoke again. *"But he can't see one . . . an' he did win the second game. . . ."*

With an effort, Claude maintained an expression of bland innocence, even when Corquisa draped herself over the back of his chair, fixing her former protector with a challenging stare. Everybody in the place was watching them.

"He loses face if he backs down. Can't say no. . . ."

"Very well," Carneiro said with a grin, but there were

beads of sweat on the broad brow. "I've always wanted to own a mine."

The atmosphere had changed. There was now no pretense of a friendly game of cards. Carneiro was already in his shirtsleeves. Claude eased off his coat and rolled up his own.

"Since you playin' for the Tres Rosas," said the drummer with a soft laugh, "why not let the lady shuffle the cards?"

Startled, Claude recognized the accent he had been hearing in his head throughout the game.

Frowning, Carneiro handed the deck to Corquisa. They fluttered through her fingers as if spun from the silk and roses of her gown. It seemed to Claude that light shimmered around them when she set the stack upon the baize of the table once more.

Carneiro won the cut, and began to deal. Corquisa stayed by Claude, her scent, far from distracting, now an intoxication that set his mind racing. He held the images of his opponent's cards in his mind as he held his own in his hand, calculating with joyful speed.

"I am your luck. . . ." Her warm breath tickled his ear. "Win for me. . . ."

Whether Claude's hand was the elder or younger, the cards loved him, giving him long sequences of any suit, and sets of face cards to inflate his scores even before they began the play. As they played hand after hand, the tension mounted along with his score.

Unless he can repique *me in the next deal, and win that, and the one that follows, he cannot catch me now,* thought Claude as they finished the fourth hand. Grimly, Carneiro shuffled the cards and began to deal.

Claude took up his cards and considered the hand. The deal had given him a useful selection of Court cards. He thought a moment, and exchanged three lesser cards for the Jack of

Clubs, the Queen of Hearts and the Ace of Spades. Smiling slightly, he waited for the declarations. Carneiro took another drink from the glass of *cachaça* by his hand.

"Watch out . . . he's got no judgement now. . . ."

Points danced in his head, the sixteen that those clubs would win him. Play began, and Carneiro's tricks began to fall. Claude's grin broadened. At this rate, he could not fail to win the hand.

"Monsieur the Baron, twenty-seven—" said the drummer, waiting for Carneiro to lead again.

Claude watched the man with some sympathy, reminded of a bull in the ring with himself as the tormenting picador.

"The luck of the *Barão* is good," someone observed.

The burly shoulders tensed, and Carneiro surged to his feet, casting down his cards.

"*Too* good!" he exclaimed. "You know the backs of the cards as well as their fronts!"

"These are the cards we have been playing with since the beginning," Claude protested in disbelief. He had heard of quarrels over cards, but he had only played with civilized men.

"No—your whore has changed them! I see a nick in the edge there, and there!"

Claude could see nothing, but the murmur of the crowd was changing, even Corquisa had drawn away. The heat in his body dissipated as he realized what they were expecting. Even in Paris, to propose the rational solution of replacing the deck and replaying the game would have dishonored him. How sudden a reversal, from imminent victory to mortal danger.

He looked from his furious enemy to meet the drummer's amused glance. *Why did you help me, only to betray me now?* They were in it together . . . he thought with sick certainty. The drummer, and Carneiro, and Corquisa. His stomach churned as he remembered the intoxication of her embrace. Lies. It had all been a lie.

I can walk out of here, and I might even make it back to my hotel alive, he realized, *but there would be no life here for a man who has all but admitted to cheating at cards. And if I returned to France the story would follow me. . . .* Slowly he got to his feet. Suddenly everything had become very simple. He could die with honor or give up all that made life worthwhile.

"Are you challenging me?" With an effort he kept his voice from wavering.

"Name your seconds!" Carneiro growled.

A man came forward—*Senhor* Teixeira—Claude had played cards with him two evenings before. What weapons did he choose? And where?

"The sword." At least, he had studied fencing. He had never learned to shoot a gun. His gaze fell upon the drummer, who still watched him with that ambiguous smile. *A nightmare for a nightmare,* he thought grimly.

"At the crossroads before the cemetery of Santo Pedro," he said clearly. "At midnight, tomorrow. . . ."

ೞೞೞ

The crossroads was a place of glimmering light and shifting shadow, the full moon that Claude had thought would light his way half-hidden by cloud. *What possessed me to say I would fight at midnight?* he wondered. Yet this murky scene was no darker than the confusion that surrounded him. Tonight, the rational clarity of France seemed very far away.

A light wind stirred his hair, bringing the rank scent of decay to mingle with the perfume of flowers he could not name. *Like this land,* he thought unhappily, *whose beauty has trapped me.* When tomorrow's sun rose, what would remain of his life?

A paragraph for the papers with nothing to add to the bare fact of its ending, except that he was the last of his line.

The men in the other party became featureless shapes as the night grew darker, but now a face glowed suddenly in the light of a candle. More points of light pricked into life along the streets that met at the crossroads. A crowd was gathering. The flicker of candleflame revealed people of the upper class in dark coats and gowns, and others in pale trousers or full white skirts with headwraps hiding their hair.

Like the people who used to attend a hanging, thought Claude. *They have come to see me die. . . .* But the murmur had none of the expectant glee of a crowd who had come to be entertained.

"Ssh, shu," they whispered, "Eh-shu . . ." as if they were gathering for some ceremony.

Both men stripped off their coats. Claude's skin chilled beneath the light cloth despite the warmth of the air, as Senhor Teixeira beckoned him to the middle of the crossroads.

"I am required to ask if this quarrel can be reconciled," said a small dark man with a baton under his arm, who must be the referee.

What, and disappoint all these people? Claude shook his head. A derisive snort from Carneiro expressed his opinion. The referee gestured, and another man brought out a long rosewood box. Candlelight glinted on the sleek deadly length of the matched swords within.

Claude settled his fist inside the sabre's bell-shaped guard and lifted the weapon. *I hold death in my hand . . . but is it mine, or his?* He extended his arm, feeling the stretch in his arm muscles as they took the weight. Carneiro's sword whistled as he slashed at the air.

"You will fight until one party is wounded or disabled.

Take your places, and salute your foe. . . ."

Beyond the upright bar of his blade, Claude saw a blaze of crimson. Corquisa stood at the edge of the circle, resplendent in red. Beside her stood the drummer. Red and black, the colors linked them, flowing together to complete an unsuspected design.

Carneiro had not seen them. For a moment, Claude hovered on the edge of understanding. *Whoever wins, he is as much a victim as I. . . .* The referee extended his baton beneath the crossing blades.

"En garde!" The baton struck upward.

Even as Claude lowered his sword to guard, Carneiro came after him, sabre flashing. Instinct got Claude's weapon up; the other blade scraped along it in an ear-rending screech of steel. Saints, the man was strong! Claude disengaged and skipped backward, ducking another slash. Each blow shocked through his arm as he caught it on his uplifted blade.

Carneiro rushed again and the crowd gave way. Claude dodged, got his feet under him, and settled into position at last, presenting his side to his foe, his sword guarding his torso in prime. As his opponent paused, breathing hoarsely, the light changed. Between the parting clouds, Claude saw a blackened moon in which only a rim of silver still showed. An eclipse! In that moment, it seemed quite natural that the moon should be beleaguered too.

There was no time to wonder. Carneiro lurched into motion once more. *He is a bull,* Claude thought then. *Can I make my sword a red rag?*

Experimentally, he twirled the blade, saw the glitter of the other man's eye as he followed the motion. He danced forward, wrist flexing to shift his guard from *quarte* to *sixte* and back again, enveloping his enemy's blade. Steel rang and flashed as the swords kissed, bootheels beat out a rhythm, or was it drumming that he heard? Claude feinted high, disengaged and lunged. The tip of the sabre tore through his enemy's sleeve. With an oath, Carneiro twisted away, but Claude saw blood seeping through the white cloth. The crowd saw it too, and cheered.

First blood! he thought. *We can stop*—He tried to pull back, but Carneiro, pushed by rage beyond caring, attacked once more.

Claude might have better form, but he was not in condition, and the strain of beating back that blade began to tell. His opponent looked as if he could keep fighting until dawn. Why not end it now? Claude had no heir to dispute whatever Carneiro and Braga might do with the mine, and if he were dead, why should he care?

It would be over in moments if he lowered his guard.

"Choose. . . ." That was the voice he had heard at the card game, the voice in which the drummer had mocked him during his first fight on this ground.

Life, or death? That was not the question, not whether a man lived, but *how*—always fearing to break the rules, or dancing though them?

Over the rasp of breath and the clang of steel came the song that he had heard at the cabaret. He understood the lyrics now.

> *I am the queen of hearts and fires,*
> *I am the Lady of dark desires. . . .*

Once more, fire flared through him. Was he Corquisa's knight, or Pomba Gira's sacrifice? It no longer mattered, for suddenly the inhibitions that had imprisoned him lifelong shattered, and he fought with the same raging power he had felt in her arms.

The singing continued, the female voice growing deeper.

> *I watch the crossing of the ways,*
> *Where everyone gambles, everyone pays,*
> *While the Blood Moon shines above,*
> *I deal out life and death and love. . . .*

Claude laughed and whirled, blade sweeping behind his back in the ninth parry to deflect Carneiro's slash. He was the sword, he was the dance, he was the drum. If he had won that third card game, he would only have freed Corquisa. By fighting the duel, he achieved something more.

He stood at the crossroads. He could go anywhere, do anything now—return to Paris or find a new life in Brazil, win a fortune at cards or wrest riches from the mine. He could love Corquisa or leave her. She had only been the means by which a far greater and more dangerous Lady transformed him.

Perceiving the pattern, he saw how his opponent would move and sank down with arm extended in a stop-thrust. His enemy's lunge passed so close it stung his scalp as Carneiro spitted himself on the blade.

The sword was jerked from his hand as the other man fell. Gagging on the stink of blood and bowels, Claude thrust the convulsing body aside and staggered to his feet. Above, the moon was a bloody coin.

His wavering gaze sought Corquisa and her companion, but there was only one figure there, one moment with skin pale and in the next, black; first the seductive form of the courtesan and then a shape that was aggressively male.

"Lady!" he cried, "I have paid your price!"

And Exu replied, "You have paid, and you are free. . . ."

TOUCH OF MOONLIGHT

By Robin Wayne Bailey

Robin Wayne Bailey is the author of numerous novels, including the *Dragonkin* series, the *Brothers of the Dragon* trilogy, and the *Frost* saga, among others. His science fiction stories were recently collected in *Turn Left to Tomorrow*, and his work has appeared in many anthologies and magazines. He lives in Kansas City, Missouri. Visit him at his website: http://www.robinwaynebailey.net/

"Touch of Moonlight" is the first of two Spanish highwayman stories in this anthology, each with its own blend of romance and magic . . . and surprising heroines. Here, Robin weaves in a delicious thread of mystery, not only concerning the true nature of the characters, but the alchemy of the human heart.

Racing nightfall, the old black coach rattled through the Galician countryside in northwest Spain along the road from Lugo to Pontevedra. Its springs and joints creaked, and the wooden wheels wobbled treacherously as if they might fly off their hubs at the next rut or bump. Occasionally, when the road narrowed, low-hanging branches scraped the sides, and the driver cursed and snapped the reins.

Inside the coach, Lady Elena Sanchez y Vega braced

herself as best she could in one leather-padded corner. With one gloved hand, she clutched her small purse in the lap of her black satin dress. With the other, she grasped the back of the seat and tried to maintain a semblance of aristocratic composure. Her neck and shoulders ached from the long, jolting ride, a journey made longer by the unexpected washout of a bridge near the village of Vigo that had caused them to detour from the main route to this backcountry highway. She felt sweaty and grimy and impatient, yet there was nothing she could do, so she listened to the rhythmic fall of the horses' hooves and watched the rise of the golden moon, almost full in an indigo twilit sky, through the coach's narrow window.

A foot brushed against her ankle as the gentleman directly across from her shifted on his seat. His name was Diego Franco, an *hidalgo* from Madrid. "My apologies, *señorita,*" he murmured, but the grin on his thin lips told Elena it had been no accident. It wasn't the first time he had taken such liberty. She glanced at him with annoyance and said nothing, having long wearied of his open stares and vulgar approaches.

The shame was, Franco wasn't a bad-looking man. However, his manners betrayed him. Like so many Spanish nobles, he viewed women as entitlements and possessions or as objects of conquest. His initial banter had been charming and flirtatious, and it had passed the time, but when his conversation became too bold, she retreated into herself and fell silent.

A loud snore came suddenly from the small man on the seat beside Franco, and his bald head bounced backward against the rear of the coach. The impact didn't wake him. Franco sneered at his manservant. "Garcia will sleep through the apocalypse," he said, making yet another effort to engage her.

Elena turned away and, with the tips of her gloved fingers, raised the stiff curtain over the coach's window to its

highest. They would not make Pontevedra before nightfall.
Twilight was already yielding to night, and the first stars of
evening twinkled in the gloomy Galician sky. The forest, at
least, was behind them, and the open land shimmered with a
darkly mysterious beauty.

The breeze took on a refreshing tang of salt. Elena leaned
closer to the window to let the wind play upon her face and
throat. Ignoring Franco's leer, she loosened the clasp of her
traveling cloak and pushed it back from her shoulders. As she
did so, she brushed her fingers furtively over the ruby necklace
hidden beneath her bodice. It was her dearest treasure, not for
the eyes of strangers.

"This is your country, is it not, *bonita*?" Franco leaned
toward the window and peered out. "Do you know where we
are?"

"The province of Galicia," she answered without looking
at him. "I can smell the sea, so we must be near the *Costa de la
Muerte*—the Coast of Death."

The road veered suddenly, pitching Garcia against the far
side of the coach. He snorted, but didn't wake. Elena eyed him
suspiciously for a moment, wondering if he were truly asleep.

"*Costa de la Muerte*," Franco repeated in a tone too
sardonic to be sincere. "The sound of it drips with romance."

They were traveling now at a good pace. The road veered
again, and just as Elena had guessed, they were racing along
coastal cliffs. The brightening moonlight glimmered on a
tempestuous sea that stretched toward the black horizon, a
tossing oceanscape dotted with jagged rocks and tiny islands.
Over the creak and groan of the coach, Elena heard the boom of
the surf.

"It's an appropriate name," she answered. "More ships
and lives have been lost on those rocks than you can imagine."

Franco leaned closer, bringing his face next to hers. "Imagination is overrated," he whispered into her ear. "I'm a practical man with practical goals. And practical needs."

A tart reply froze on Elena's lips. Everything Franco said carried a hint of a sneer or an insinuation. Before she could frame a response, however, a streak of light, deep blue in color and trailing smoke, shot across the darkness. The air vibrated, and her ears tingled with its strange rush. A shooting star like none she'd ever seen! She followed it with a rapt gaze as it plunged toward the horizon and winked out.

Forgetting her annoyance, Elena glanced at Franco, wondering if he'd seen it, too. His open-jawed expression proved he had.

Then, without warning, the driver gave a shout and jerked on the reins. The coach lurched to a stop. Elena flew out of her seat and into Franco's arms. Even Garcia shot awake, and for a moment, the interior became a confusing fluster of arms and legs. When Elena finally recovered her balance and righted herself, she blushed to find herself on Franco's lap with one of his hands on her breast while his other hand worked its way beneath the hem of her dress and up her calf.

"Pardon me, *señorita*," he said with a devilish grin. "It appears that fate has thrown us together."

"Pardon me, *señor!*" She pushed his hands away and adjusted her bodice. Then she dealt him a stinging slap. "Fate is overrated, and so are practical men."

Franco rubbed his cheek as Elena repositioned herself on her side of the coach. The *hidalgo's* eyes smoldered with controlled anger as he glared at Garcia. His manservant lay awkwardly crumpled on the coach's floor with one foot up on the seat and a hand pinned beneath him. His face bore an expression of dumbfounded confusion.

"Don't just lie there, you fool," Franco ordered. "Find out what happened! Why have we stopped?"

Garcia struggled to right himself. One fumbling hand found the latch of the coach's door, and instead of rising, he tumbled head over heels out into the road. Without a word, as if such things happened every day, Garcia got to his feet, mustered his dignity and brushed himself off. Then he looked up at the driver. "My master demands. . . ."

The driver interrupted in a breathless, trembling voice. "Ramon Estrada!" he said, loud enough for all to hear. "The ghost of Ramon Estrada!"

Franco shot a look at Elena and then at his manservant. "What nonsense is this?" He launched himself from the coach. "Look here, driver, we're late enough as it is!"

Elena followed Franco. Accepting Garcia's offered hand, she stepped down from the coach, welcoming any excuse to stretch her legs. "It's a local legend," she answered. "Ramon Estrada was a famous highwayman. The people believe his ghost has haunted the back roads of Galicia for more than a hundred years."

"*Sí!* She knows!" the driver exclaimed as he clutched the reins nervously. "*Es verdad!* It's true! A shooting star always heralds the appearance of Ramon Estrada's ghost!"

"*Madre mia!*" Franco cursed. "You would delay us for this old wives' tale? Get this coach moving before I pull you down and beat you!"

Elena tilted her head, amused at the spectacle of the sputtering nobleman. "If you beat him, who would drive the coach? Surely one of your breeding wouldn't sully his hands."

Franco's eyes narrowed with anger, but before he could answer, another sound caught everyone's attention, a sound that came from up the road. They turned their heads to listen to the soft clip-clop of a horse's hooves in the dark, but it was difficult to judge if it was close or far. Along this coastal road, the smallest sound could be heard over a great distance.

"It's nothing!" Franco scoffed, but his hand slipped inside his jacket pocket, and he drew out a small gentleman's pistol.

"No!" the driver insisted. "A gun will not avail you!"

Elena couldn't hide her amusement at Franco's posturing. "Can you shoot an old wives' tale? It could be any rider even at this hour. We don't own the road." She shivered with anticipation.

Stealing a nervous glance at the moon, Elena stepped out of the coach's shadow, away from the men and into its light. She felt the blaze of it on her face. The breeze from the sea blew a long lock of her hair free as it rustled the folds of her dress.

The stiffness of the coach ride melted away. She felt suddenly wild and alive. Her senses sharpened as she sniffed the air—Franco's cologne, the salt tang, the driver's fear, and something more, something strange that she couldn't quite identify.

The sound of hooves grew louder, steady and unhurried. The shape of a rider took form, emerging into moonlight as if the darkness had parted to let him through.

"My sword!" Franco hissed to the driver.

The frightened man turned on his bench, reached behind and handed down the weapon. "If it is Ramon Estrada, neither your sword or your pistol will save you!"

"If it's not Ramon Estrada, then I will use them on you for causing us this delay!" Franco moved closer to Elena and struck a pose. "Don't worry, *bonita.* If there is any real danger, I will protect you."

Elena said nothing. She smelled the *hidalgo's* sweat and

heard his quickening breath, but for all that, she smelled no fear on him. She had to give him that, at least. She focused her attention on the approaching rider, watching as he drew closer with measured pace. She couldn't see his face, yet somehow she felt his eyes upon her, and her own breathing quickened, too.

"See!" The driver rose to his feet and pointed. The horses gave a start, and he clutched the seat again to avoid falling off. "It is Estrada's ghost! We are lost!"

Elena's heart pounded. The rider was all in white, and his horse was white as well. The moon glowed upon them so that his form and outline wavered even as he drew closer and closer. She could see the shape of a head upon broad shoulders, but no face. It was a ghost! It had to be! The pale specter of Ramon Estrada!

Franco raised his pistol and fired. The blast of flame from the barrel of the weapon lit up the ground and the side of the coach, and belched a cloud of black powder. The wind blew the cloud into Elena's eyes, and it stung. She blinked and silently cursed Franco as she wiped away tears with a gloved hand.

"*Madre de dios!*" Franco lowered his pistol as he stared. "I couldn't have missed at this range! I know I didn't miss!" Swallowing hard, he dropped his pistol, drew his sword, and cast the scabbard aside.

The rider sat calmly in his saddle with a thin rapier balanced over the bow of his saddle. He wasn't in white, after all, but gray, a strange gray silk that played tricks with the light and shimmered with every movement. A broad cloak of the same fabric draped his form, and a cowled mask concealed his features. Dark, intense eyes burned through the slitted holes.

His voice was deep, masculine and sure. "Do you call yourself a marksman, *señor*?" Reaching into his belt, he drew out a full-sized pistol and smiled. "It seems that mine is bigger than yours."

Wide-eyed, Elena studied the rider. His waist was narrow, but his chest swelled against his shirt. He sat upon his mount with a good seat that emphasized casual strength, and his thighs bulged above well-made boots of the best Spanish leather. She looked higher, noting the mouth, the lips and the strong chin, all that she could see beneath the cowl. "What kind of ghost carries a gun?"

The rider inclined his head toward her and made a cavalier gesture with the barrel. "The kind that is about to relieve you of your purse and baubles and anything else of value you might have upon your lovely person." He waved the pistol at Franco, Garcia and the driver. "You, too, *señores*, though you are not so lovely."

"Do you think we'll fall for your fakery?" Franco answered with indignation. "I'll relieve you of your life before I give you a *peso*!" Leading with the point of his sword, he ran at the rider, but the pale figure moved like subtle lightning to parry the thrust. At the same time, his booted foot brushed Franco's shoulder, sending him sprawling in the road.

The *hidalgo* sprang up, sputtering. "You costumed swine! Get down and settle this like a man!"

The gray highwayman tucked his pistol into his belt, then slipped gracefully to the ground. "Such a challenge assumes that we are both men," he answered in a mocking tone. "In your case, I'm not so sure."

Franco growled a curse and lunged. Swords clanged, and steel flashed. The rider turned Franco's blade aside with a neat twist of the wrist. Franco yelped and danced back, staring at the rip in the lapel of his jacket. "You swine!"

"You repeat yourself," the rider answered with a grin. "Allow me to do the same." Before Franco could move, the rider struck again, moonlight flickering along his blade as it made an

identical slice in Franco's other lapel. Yelling, the *hidalgo*
launched a clumsy attack. The rider parried with ease.

"Stop, *señor*," he said at last, "before you hurt yourself or
your companions fall asleep from boredom." With a subtle flick,
he knocked Franco's blade from his grip and sent it into the dust.
He placed the tip of his sword against Franco's chest and backed
him into line with Elena and Garcia. "Enough entertainment.
Your valuables, if you please. I have a living to make."

Elena dared to take a step forward. "You would rob a
woman?" In truth, part of her had cheered for Franco, hoping he
might save her. She saw now that was not to be. Without
thinking, she put a hand to her throat, fearing the loss of her
most precious possession. Her fingers clutched her bodice, then
her eyes snapped wide, and she gave a cry of dismay. "My
necklace! It's gone!"

The rider chuckled as he drew out his pistol again. "Not
to worry, *señorita*," he said, covering Franco with one weapon
and Garcia with the other. "I'll wager you'll find it on one of
these gentlemen."

Franco feigned a look of outrage, but when the rider
tapped the point of his sword against his jacket, he sighed and
reached into an inner pocket. A moment later, he withdrew the
jeweled pendant. Elena gave an enraged scream and swung her
hand at the *hidalgo*. He caught her wrist. "Please," he said,
rubbing his cheek with his free hand. "I've already sampled your
charms once tonight."

"You are no gentleman!" she shouted.

"Nor a nobleman, either," Garcia said, speaking for the
first time, as he reached beneath his own jacket and held out her
purse. "Just a pick-pocket like myself who found it wise to
abandon Madrid quickly." He bowed to Elena. "If you would
care to take your anger out on me, I'm partial to such peculiar

pleasures."

The rider cleared his throat noisily. "Forgive my haste, but the night is passing, and even the ghost of Ramon Estrada has other places to be." He waved the point of his rapier toward the driver. "*Amigo*, if you would unload and open the luggage, please." Then, sheathing his sword, but keeping the pistol ready, he tossed a saddlebag at Franco's feet. "The rest of you will please empty your pockets into this."

Elena stamped her foot. "You will pay for this, Ramon Estrada, or whoever you are!"

The rider bowed again. "To be sure. There is always a price to pay." He waved at the driver, who was climbing down. "*Rapido, por favor!* It is best if you hurry."

While Franco and Garcia placed wallets and watches and rings, along with Elena's necklace and purse, in the saddlebag, the driver wasted no time in breaking open the luggage. Jackets and shirts, underclothes and nightgowns soon littered the ground. The wind picked up a pair of silk stockings and swept them toward the moon. Franco grinned and whistled.

Elena paid no attention. Her gaze fastened on an old leather valise, and she held her breath as the driver opened it and turned it upside down. A pair of lace-trimmed petticoats fell into the road, but nothing else.

"By hell!" Forgetting the rider, she pushed the driver aside and snatched up the empty case, shook it, and turned it upside down herself. "I am thrice-robbed!" In a fiery temper, she grabbed Franco's sword from the dust and pressed the point to his throat.

"Give it back!" Elena drew a thin scratch of blood. "My brother's life depends on the gold that was in that valise!" She dropped the sword's point to his groin. "I swear my next cut will draw dearer blood!"

Ramon Estrada cleared his throat with some annoyance. "Despite my reputation, I feel that I have lost control here." He gestured to the driver. "If you would be so kind as to hand me the saddlebag, it is enough for me, and I will leave you to settle these squabbles. So many thieves in one place cannot be a good thing."

"Wait, you pretty popinjay!" Elena shouted as the rider mounted. "You can't take my necklace. You don't. . . !"

Accepting the saddlebag from the driver's hands, Ramon Estrada tugged on the reins and turned his horse in a tight circle. "Such language!" he said, feigning shock. "A beautiful necklace and much gold!" He grinned as he turned again to ride away. "You are my kind of woman, and perhaps we will meet again." He glanced toward the pair of pickpockets. "As for you two, *buena suerte!*"

With that, the ghost of Ramon Estrada rode away and vanished into the night. Elena watched him from the corner of her eye, and then turned back to Franco and waved the sword beneath his nose. "I mean to have my gold," she said in a dangerous voice. "Strip!"

❧

Elena paced her small hotel room in the darkness, avoiding the moonbeams that strayed through her window. She might have closed the curtains, but the night was warm and the breeze welcome as it brushed her hair and rustled her nightgown. Her hand kept wandering to her throat, searching for the necklace that wasn't there.

She had bigger worries, though. She thought of her brother, only twelve years old, somewhere in the hills outside of Pontevedra, a prisoner of the sorcerer, Joaquin Cortez. She cursed his name, cursed his entire clan of *hungaros*. She cursed the one who had stolen the necklace. Most of all, she cursed whoever had stolen her gold, the ransom with which she would have freed her brother.

Nervously, she went to the window and peered out. The moon floated over Pontevedra like a leering face, waiting for her with a hunger.

After a time, weary of pacing, she pulled back the covers on her bed and crawled under the threadbare sheet. She was accustomed to better accommodations. If not for the single gold coin secreted in her slipper, she wouldn't have had even this poor room. Tomorrow, she would find a way to contact Cortez. For her brother's sake and for her own, she must come to terms quickly with that gypsy monster.

She barked a short, almost hysterical, laugh, then clapped her hands to her mouth to stifle the sound. *Monster* was not a word she was entitled to use. She threw back the sheet. The room felt too close, and she doubted she could sleep; yet finally, fatigue and worry took their toll.

Elena did not sleep long. A weight settled on the side of her bed, and a hand closed over her mouth. She woke with a start, her eyes snapping wide as she stared at the masked face of Ramon Estrada. In his other hand, he held up her ruby pendant. The pale light danced upon it, casting crimson reflections upon the walls as it spun on its chain. He placed it on her bedside table. Then he drew his pistol from his belt and put it beside the necklace.

"Do not scream, *señorita*," he whispered as he removed his hand from her mouth.

Elena licked her lips delicately before she answered. He had a scent upon him, and she recognized it. Her gaze darted toward the necklace, then back to her unexpected visitor. "I have no intention of screaming."

His fingers went to the lacings of her nightgown as he leaned closer and gently kissed her. "Do not resist."

Her eyes locked with his. At first sight, she had found him attractive. Now that he had returned her necklace, she still found him so. "I have no intention of resisting."

His hands roamed over her body as he kissed her again, and Elena was true to her word. Forgetting her worries, she surrendered to his touch, welcomed his lips as he planted little fires on her flesh. She inhaled the fine sweat of his desire. "You are no ghost," she whispered.

Ramon Estrada swept away his cowl to reveal a handsome face with glittering black eyes and strong features. Not a youth, but not yet in sight of middle age. Her heart raced, and her breath became shallow as he unfastened his sword and quickly undressed. His shirt, then his boots, followed the cowl to the floor. Elena reached up to stroke the fine hair on his chest, and she pulled him down again. She didn't know why he had returned her necklace, and at the moment, she didn't care.

ଓ୪ଉ୫ଉୀ

Elena woke in Ramon Estrada's arms. Her first drowsy thought was that she had never before experienced such delicious passion. Her second, sharper thought was that some sound or some instinct had awakened her. She glanced toward the window. Blackness filled the alley beyond. The moon had moved on, so the hour was late. The sound came again, a scratching as of claws on wood. Ramon's eyes snapped open; he heard it, too, and sat up.

Before either Elena or Ramon could make another move, a man-like shape appeared at the sill and stared through the window. Elena couldn't see the face in the darkness, but a low snarl sent a shiver through her. "Cortez!"

The figure sprang through the window and shook a fist. The snarling intensified as cloth ripped.

"Whore!" the intruder shouted, but the word turned into a guttural rasp, and then a howl. Darkness and shadow shifted, swirled and deepened unnaturally in the small room.

The hair on Elena's neck rose as she sat up. The figure grew taller, thicker, shedding all semblance of humanity. She glimpsed shaggy fur, teeth, a lupine snout and claws like scimitars, and she screamed. Clutching the coverlet to her breasts, she scrambled out of bed.

With a half-uttered curse, Ramon grabbed his pistol from the bedside table and fired. Elena cried a warning as she threw up a hand to shield her eyes from the dazzling flash. A bullet would do no good! Unharmed, the beast glared at her highwayman lover and crouched to spring.

Elena's heart pounded, and her face flushed hot. Her head churned with fear and anger.

"Over here, monster!" she shouted. "It's me you've come for!"

The beast hesitated, then turned away from Ramon. In one smooth motion, she tossed the coverlet, hoping to blind it. At the same time, Ramon flung away his empty pistol and sprang naked to the floor. Rolling on one shoulder, he snatched up his sword and whipped it from its sheath.

"Get away, Ramon!" Elena warned. "You can't hurt him!" Whirling, she seized a pitcher of water from the night table and flung it with all her might. It shattered on the monster's furry skull, drenching head and shoulders. Without a pause, she hurled the porcelain washbowl. Ramon ducked as he pushed the point of his blade into the intruder's side.

"Sorry!" she apologized.

"Your apology is accepted," he shouted in response, "but

your aim is lacking!'"

The beast turned on Ramon again, slashing with its razor claws, backing him into the wall as the highwayman drove his sword home twice more to no effect. Ramon kicked the monster in the stomach. It howled as it tumbled backward. Claws scored four deep cuts on Ramon's thigh before it fell, and blood welled.

"What in all the hells?" Ramon clutched his wounds. "I thought it was a man!

Elena didn't pause to explain. Picking up the chair, she brought it down on the monster's head. Splinters of wood flew. The beast shrugged off the impact and rose up on powerful legs, teeth flashing and eyes blazing with red fire.

No longer afraid, Elena faced the monster. "Get out, Joaquin! Your jealousy doesn't impress me!"

The beast swung a shaggy fist and bashed her to the floor. Her head exploded with stars and lights, yet she managed to look up as Ramon lunged and drove his blade through the heart of the thing that was Joaquin Cortez. Again and again, he struck, attacking with a masterful fury. Finally, he sank his blade into the monster's neck so deeply that the point emerged from the other side.

Joaquin Cortez howled, and the sound turned into a gurgle. Still, he didn't fall. Instead, he shoved Ramon through the hotel room door with such force the entire room shook.

Elena screamed again and shook her head to clear her vision. The monster rose up to its full, imposing height. Still impaled by Ramon's blade, it spread its arms and swelled its chest.

"You bastard!" Elena's words were a hiss, almost a challenge. "This is what you want, isn't it?"

Steeling herself, she ripped away the shreds of her nightgown. Naked, she faced Cortez and clenched her fists.

Scarlet flame flared in her eyes. The monster hesitated, then fell back a step.

When Elena opened her mouth again, the sound that came out was utterly inhuman.

Shadows closed around Elena as they had Cortez. As if jolted by lightning, her spine arched. She threw back her head. A strange agony shot through her body, but also a strange pleasure. Her senses tingled with ice and fire, with unnameable sensations. She stepped out of the corner with claws of her own to match the monster's.

Her gaze fell briefly on Ramon Estrada, who leaned in the broken doorway, one hand on the shattered frame. His body shimmered with heat and sweat and blood, and he smelled like food. He stared back at her and muttered, *" Dios!"*

Cortez snarled, and she snarled back. Forgetting Ramon, she leaped. Cortez was larger and more powerful, but she was faster. They rolled over the bed, crashed into the night table and against a wardrobe. Elena's clothing, spilling out, entangled them in silks and satins. His claws locked into her shoulders; she buried her teeth in his throat, dislodging Ramon's sword as she tasted blood.

The bed crashed as they fell upon it again. Pillow feathers and mattress stuffing swirled through the air like snow. In a dim corner of her awareness, Elena watched her ruby necklace slide across the floor to rest at Ramon's feet.

Joaquin Cortez howled in pain. With his greater strength, he flung Elena off and backed against the wall on shaky legs. Breathing hard, he regarded Elena with cold wolf eyes, glanced toward Ramon, then dived through the window and disappeared.

Elena lunged toward the window and stared outward after Cortez, barely aware of her own ragged breathing or the saliva dripping from her furred and bloody lips. With no sign of

Cortez, she noticed Ramon's smell again. He still stood in the doorway. She advanced a step toward him. Another step, and she stopped again. Her breathing softened, and the fire that filled her senses diminished ever so subtly. Fighting dangerous instincts, she extended a clawed but vaguely human hand.

Without taking his eyes away, Ramon picked up the necklace. Elena snarled, but with less menace. She opened her mouth, lashed a tongue over rough teeth as she tried to remember words.

"Ramon! Give it . . . to me!"

Nodding, he complied. With the ruby in her clumsy grasp, she shambled to the far side of the room and crouched down. Again she felt the pain and pleasure of the change. It was like waking from a dream, she thought as her senses cleared. Or falling into one. She wasn't sure any longer which state was real.

With human hands, she fastened the necklace around her neck and sagged against the wall. Her eyes closed briefly. When she opened them, she looked upon Ramon's worried face. He was kneeling beside her. She closed her hand around his and forced a half-hearted smile.

Ramon kissed the palm of her hand as he leaned closer. "I knew from the moment we met that you were not what you seemed. But this?" He hesitated, drawing a deep breath before saying the word. "A werewolf?"

Elena gave a soft laugh as she touched the wounds on her shoulder and licked the blood from her fingers. She shivered at the taste, as thrilled by it as she was frightened.

"You think I'll eat you, and not in a nice way?" She fought a creeping hysteria. In a shadowy part of her mind, Ramon still smelled like food. Her head spun at the thought, and she clutched the ruby necklace in a tight fist.

Ramon left her side long enough to dress. Then,

wrapping her in a sheet, he picked her up in his arms. A wave of sickness hit her, and Elena Sanchez y Vega slipped into unconsciousness.

❦❧☙❧❦

The bright sunshine of midmorning woke her. Elena turned her face from the pillow, blinked and rubbed her eyes. She didn't recognize the room; she didn't even know where she was, but the furnishings were lavish. The half-open curtains hinted of blue sky and the green hills, and a gentle, fresh breeze played through the open window.

Slowly, the details of the night came back to her. She touched her shoulder. Her wounds were already healed. She felt for the ruby necklace around her neck to make sure it was there.

Unseen until now, Ramon Estrada rose from a high-backed chair near the window and closed the book he'd been reading. He wore only a dressing gown, but he had bathed, and his face and hair were groomed.

"Awake at last," he said cheerfully. "Sunlight becomes you!"

Elena turned her head, ashamed to meet his gaze. "You brought me to your home. You should be afraid of me, and of Joaquin Cortez, too. He'll come for me again."

Ramon laughed as he sat down on the bed and took her hand. "So that really was Cortez." He put a finger to her lips before she could answer. "I'll make breakfast, and you will tell me everything."

"You will—?" Her eyes widened. "Are you alone here?" She gazed around the room again. The furniture was mahogany, baroque and expensive, and there were other signs of wealth around the room. Surely there were servants! Her host was not a poor man.

He looked down at her with a quiet expression. "I've been alone for a long time, Elena. There are worse things in the world than being alone."

His mood brightened as he pointed to a door in the corner. "You can bathe in the next room. The water is cool, but the towels are fresh. I'm afraid I have only men's clothing to offer you."

When Ramon returned with coffee, cheese, and toast with apricot jam, she was clean and her hair combed. She faced him in black trousers and a white silk shirt with lace cuffs, which she thought became her, and she turned for his approval. Even the small leather boots fit her well.

"Joaquin Cortez was my lover," she explained as they sat down to eat at a table near the window. "That was before I knew what he was and the cruelties he was capable of. I grew to hate him. He's a sorcerer, skilled in the gypsy ways."

She hesitated and looked out the window. "To keep me at his side, he made me what I am. What he is. A monster—a werewolf." She touched the jewel on her throat, and her voice became stronger, angry. "Even so, I found a way to escape. But now he has my brother, Alexandro, and he will make him the same unless I pay a ransom in gold!!"

"He doesn't want your gold," Ramon said with quiet certainty. "He wants you back. He still loves you."

Elena sneered. "Loves me and hates me. To Cortez, it's all the same. He tried to kill us last night when he found us together. Perhaps he *does* want me back—he's jealous of his possessions." Her expression turned bitter as she picked up her coffee cup. "And he can have me if that's what it takes to buy Alexandro's freedom!"

Ramon looked thoughtful. "Your necklace, what part does it play?"

Elena set the cup down. "We can change to our wolven forms whenever we wish. But the urge—the *need*—to do so is strongest during the full moon. Under its influence, we lose control of ourselves. The wolf instinct, the hunger and the blood-thirst, take over."

She grimaced, forcing herself to go on. "We become killers, Ramon. We even . . . feed on our kill."

Elena tapped the ruby necklace. "This allows me to resist the moon's power and keep control." Her head throbbed from the unwanted memories. "Cortez made it for me with his sorcery, a gift at first, but he locked it away when I threatened to leave him. He thought I'd have to stay if I couldn't control the changes."

She paused, then slammed her fist down suddenly, splashing the coffee and making the plates jump. "But I found his charm and stole it, and then I made my escape. I hate him, Ramon!"

"And he tried to steal it back."

Embarrassed by her outburst, Elena dabbed at the spill with her napkin. Then, her hand froze. She stared. "What did you say?"

"He tried to steal it back," Ramon repeated. "I'll wager an afternoon of love-making that your friends on the stagecoach, Franco and Garcia, were hired by Cortez. They were after your necklace."

Elena touched the ruby again. "It was hidden under my bodice all the time," she said thoughtfully. "How could Franco have known?" Her face darkened with realization.

"Franco doesn't matter now. You know where Cortez is and together, we can free your brother."

Elena looked out the window again. The daylight shone on a beautiful land, but her thoughts were of the night and the full moon it would bring. She could already feel its allure. "Cortez is a dangerous man. He will expect us."

"He will expect a werewolf," Ramon answered, leaning back in his chair. But not . . ." He sipped his coffee with a brooding look, and Elena saw him once again as the highwayman she had met on the road to Pontevedra. She couldn't help but wonder what was in his mind.

"I think this *hungaro*—this gypsy—was a fool to make an enemy of you." Ramon Estrada leaned forward once more.

Elena studied her host, trying to reconcile her impressions of him. *And a bigger fool to make an enemy of* you, she thought.

"Cortez has a collar," she said aloud. "Not a necklace, but a leather band. If he manages to put it around my neck he will control me completely, and it will never come off." She bit her lip and squeezed his hand. "We must plan well, Ramon."

She gave a soft sigh, fearing what failure would mean, but saying no more. Instead, she glanced toward the bed. "For now, I think you are right about Franco, and if you care to collect, you've won your wager."

ဆလ၇ၐ

The moon had not yet risen when they halted their horses atop a low hill. Pontevedra lay fifteen miles behind them. On the next hill stood an old stone keep. Its ancient walls dripped with gray moss and ivy, and two broken towers stood at angles, as if collapsed under the weight of the sky. A long crack ran down the side of one structure. The other tower had no roof. Once, it had been a fort to guard the coast. Now Joaquin Cortez claimed it.

The wind blew through Elena's hair as she leaned on the pommel of her saddle. She drew a breath and stared into the deepening twilight, feeling the coming of the moon with all her senses, knowing where to look before it even appeared. It intoxicated her, made her *want* to change. She craved the thrill, even as she resisted it.

"Are you all right?" Ramon sat straight in his saddle. Clad once again in the gray silks, the cloak and the mask of the ghostly highwayman, he cut a handsome profile. She looked at his sword and the pistol in his belt. They wouldn't be enough. But his courage, that might make the difference. She realized that she still didn't know his real name.

"I am Ramon Estrada," he answered without looking at her as if he'd read her thoughts. "In case you're wondering, it took no magic to intercept your coach, only a question to the stationmaster to learn that the Vigo bridge was out and the coach was late. After that, I watched and waited."

"But the shooting star!" she insisted, surprising herself. "The stories say you always appear under a shooting star, and there was such a beautiful one!"

Ramon looked toward the first winking stars. "A lucky coincidence," he answered with a hint of amusement. "In the dark countryside there are always shooting stars, and legends grow from the smallest seeds if you nurture them."

It seemed such a commonplace explanation, and part of Elena felt disappointment. Still, another part of her marveled at the trick he had pulled on the townspeople and locals of Galicia. A thief he might be, but Ramon Estrada was a man of imagination!

"Let's tie your hands," Ramon said, holding out a thin strip of leather.

"Masked men and bondage." Elena gave an exaggerated sigh as he wrapped the cord around her wrists. "Why didn't you think of these things this afternoon?"

Side by side, they rode down the hill and up the next to the gate of the keep, making no effort to hide their approach. Elena listened to the distant rush of the sea and the boom of the surf, savored the salt-tinged air, and tried not to be afraid.

The gates to the keep were as broken as the towers. Rust colored the old iron hinges, and earth had mounded up against the bottoms so that they would never shut without excavation. The wood looked rotted and worm-eaten, and there was nothing inviting about them. However, on the wall to one side of the gates, a pair of gypsy men stared down with watchful eyes.

"We'll leave the horses here," Ramon said, dismounting. Elena didn't wait for assistance, but threw a leg over her horse's head and slid to the ground on her own. Ramon seized her arm, and gave her a rough shake.

"Tell your master I have something he wants!" he called to the gypsies. With a flourish, he produced the ruby necklace from his waistband and held it high. "Be quick, before I lose an arm or a leg to the bitch! The moon's coming on!"

"Bitch?" Elena whispered indignantly.

Ramon gave a subtle shrug and uncorked a flask of brandy hanging on a cord over his shoulder. "Female canine," he replied as he prepared to sip. "Figure of speech."

Elena inhaled the aroma of the liquor, wishing for a drink to steady her nerves, but Ramon didn't offer. "I think I'll piss on your leg," she said.

One of the gypsy guards disappeared, only to return a moment later. He beckoned them to follow. Inside the gate, Elena surveyed the grounds, noting the stables and abandoned barracks, the now-empty munitions storage sheds and the numerous other buildings. She ran her gaze up the sides of the towers. On the outside, at least, nothing had changed.

The gypsy guard led them toward the officers' quarters,

the only part of the keep to which Cortez had made improvements. The outer doors were of stout, polished wood with good locks. A pair of torches in sconces illumined the threshold and beyond. Inside, the walls of the smaller quarters had been torn out to make a larger common area and a dining hall.

"Take your hand off me!" Elena cried, wrenching free of Ramon's grip. "I hate you for bringing me back here!"

Ramon grabbed her by the back of her neck and forced her to her knees. "Play nice!" he hissed, tightening his grip and bending her head back until she whimpered. "Even with a few bruises, I'll wager you're worth something!"

The gypsy guard pushed back another pair of doors. The room inside shone with lamps and candles in tall iron candelabras, many backed with plates of burnished copper to intensity their light. Rich carpets covered the stone floor, and tapestries adorned the walls. Artfully crafted divans, chairs and tables were scattered about.

"It fortifies me," Ramon announced as he rubbed the toe of his boot over the carpet, "to see that the owner of this ruin has some taste for the fineries, after all. Truly, you hide your light under a bushel."

At the far side of the room, Joaquin Cortez looked up from behind a table where he was eating a meal and reading at the same time. Several bottles of wine stood near his elbow, and he set aside a crystal goblet of amber beverage as he looked up. A man of dark good looks, straight hair tied back, and hungry eyes that pierced like knives, he rose slowly and leaned forward. Elena loathed the sight of him. Worse, she felt the moon burning in her brain and remembered the taste of his blood.

No doubt, he remembered the same. Cortez, though, didn't need a necklace to control his changes. The strength of his will was enough.

"You have something that belongs to me," he said to Ramon.

"And you have something I want," Ramon answered, equally direct. "The boy, Alexandro."

Cortez came around the table, and his gaze fell on Elena's bound hands as he spoke to her. "I told you to bring gold if you wanted your brother!"

Elena tried to shake free of Ramon's grip. "I know you too well, Joaquin," she sneered. "I had it on the coach, but you stole it. I smelled something out of place that night. It was you."

Ramon cuffed her lightly, then gave his attention back to Cortez. "She has such a mouth," he said, wrinkling his nose beneath his mask. "Still, she has a point. You might consider that a bath is in order."

Cortez glared at the insult. "What do you want with the boy?"

Ramon shrugged. "I like boys."

"You don't care about gold!" Elena shouted. "It's me you want! Give him Alexandro, and I'll stay!!"

"Enough!" Without warning, Cortez swung a fist and sent Ramon sprawling. "Did you think I wouldn't recognize *your* scent?" He turned to Elena, grabbed her arm and slapped her hard. "Whore! You were together last night! I can still smell your lust!"

"And today, too! Twice!" Elena shot back. "Jealous fool! I can't stand your touch!"

Cortez produced a leather collar from his pocket. She guessed he'd been carrying it all day, waiting for this opportunity. It looked like no more than a simple band, but it had no buckle or snap, only a silver lock without a keyhole, upon which was engraved a gypsy symbol. If he got that collar around her throat, she was lost.

"It's not a pretty necklace for you this time, Elena! This time, there will be no leaving me! I own you, your wealth, and your brother!"

Ramon sprang up from the floor, pistol in hand. Before he could fire, the gypsy guard at his back snarled and began to change. With a swipe, it knocked the gun from the highwayman's hand, but the weapon discharged with a bright flash and a pungent smoke. Ramon sprang back and drew his sword.

A howl sounded from the doorway—the second guard already fully transformed. It filled the doorway, man-like but hideously misshapen, black-furred and frightening in its power. It flashed its teeth at Ramon and howled.

"The moon is up!" Cortez laughed as he, too, began to transform. "Give in to it, Elena! Your foolish friend will make our wedding meal!"

Elena screamed. In her planning with Ramon, she had not counted on two acolyte werewolves. She watched with sudden fear as Ramon swiftly reloaded his pistol and fired at the second guard. It howled, but the bullet had no effect. He drew his sword and dodged as the first one attacked him again.

"He is nothing but meat!" Cortez muttered.

Elena said nothing. Spinning suddenly, she smashed her elbow into Cortez's face and kicked him between the legs. Even a wolf knew that kind of pain. Caught off-guard, he fell forward. She kicked him again in the face, knocking the collar from his hand.

She shrugged out of the bonds on her wrists. "I got free of you, once, Cortez, and free I will remain!"

Ripping open her blouse, she exposed the ruby necklace. Ramon had returned it to her under the pretense of roughness.

Protected from her animal instincts, Elena allowed herself to change.

A howl of pain and a flash of heat distracted her. The first of the acolyte werewolves lunged at Ramon. Grim-faced, he stood his ground, waving a torch at the monster as he sprayed brandy from his flask. Fur exploded in flame. The stench of singing hair filled the room. Blinded and burning, it ran from the room and out into the night.

The distraction proved a mistake for Elena. Fully transformed, Cortez sprang up and howled with rage. Razor-sharp claws raked her, tearing away the rest of her blouse. Barely in time, she flung herself away and rolled.

Cortez tore away his clothing. Elena did the same. No words were possible now. Two monsters faced off in a test of domination.

Elena circled warily, mindful of Cortez's strength. He leaped at her, and she avoided a swipe of his claws as she raked his shoulder with her own. With a snarl, he attacked again, and they collided in a savage embrace.

"Elena!" Ramon cried.

Snapping her jaws, she pushed Cortez back and shot a glance toward Ramon. His shirt hung about his waist in ribbons, and blood stained his arms. The remaining acolyte leaped at him. He swung a blazing candelabrum at its eyes to drive it back.

But she had her own fight to worry about. Cortez tackled her, but Elena's teeth found *hungaro's* shoulder. She bit deep. The salty, coppery taste of blood filled her head like wine. She sank her fangs deeper, savoring Cortez's howls of pain until he knocked her away. He hit her again, slamming her into a wall with enough force to stun her.

Stars exploded in her head, but over Cortez's shoulder, she watched the second acolyte run howling, stinking of brandy, burning like the first.

Fire! As she had told Ramon, it was the one sure weapon against werewolves.

Snarling, Cortez bent closer and showed his teeth. One clawed hand held her down. The other dug at her neck. Elena kicked and thrashed as she tried to get away. She ripped at his arms, at his chest and face. She tore one of his eyes, but still he held her down.

Suddenly, a bottle crashed down on Cortez's furry skull. Brandy splashed over his face. It spilled on Elena, too. Behind Cortez, Ramon stood with sword in one hand and torch in the other. His mask had been ripped away, and his eyes blazed with a fire as fierce and feral as any animal's.

"Cortez!" he screamed. "Get your damned, stinking paws off her!"

It was challenge enough for the beast in Cortez. He attacked Ramon with wild slashes. Ramon thrust once with his sword, impaling Cortez through the chest. At the same time, he swung the torch at the gypsy's brandy-soaked snout.

Cortez sidestepped the torch and knocked it out of Ramon's hand. His claws closed on the highwayman's neck. Effortlessly, he lifted Ramon and held him at arms' length as he pulled out the sword with his other hand.

Ramon ceased to struggle, as if knowing what was to come. Cortez gave a low growl of satisfaction. In the next instant, he plunged the blade through Ramon Estrada's heart.

Elena cried out in horror and despair. Without willing the change, she felt herself transforming, becoming human again. Cortez dropped Ramon's lifeless body and turned back to her. His shaggy form seemed to swell even larger as he savored his triumph. Looking down on Elena, he also allowed himself to shift back.

He knelt beside her without speaking. His hand closed about the ruby necklace and tore it away. "It's over, Elena," he said with an air of finality. "Now you are mine forever."

"You are over-confident," said a voice behind Cortez.

Two hands closed around the gypsy's neck. A lock snapped closed, and a leather band tightened to make a perfect fit. *The collar! Gypsy magic!*

Cortez uttered a half-strangled cry. His eyes snapped wide with surprise and terror as his fingers dug frantically at the band. Then his expression glazed over. Slowly he sank to his knees, and his hands hung limp at his sides. Completely docile, he sat as if awaiting an order.

"What happens to him now?" Ramon knelt and gathered Elena in his arms.

Tears sprang into Elena's eyes. She touched his chest, ran her hand along his arms. He had no wounds, not a scratch or cut. "I saw the blade! How can you live?"

He shrugged. "I just do."

"You are the legend!" She wrapped her arms around his neck, weeping as he pulled her up. "The highwayman for a hundred years and more!"

"I told you," he said, "I am Ramon Estrada. Now stop crying. We have to find your brother in this ruin, and I'll wager there will be gold around here. I have an appetite for gold."

"I'm sure," she said, recovering some measure of strength. "But put me down. The collar was made for me, not for Cortez. His own magic has backfired in some horrible way. In his human form, he'll be vulnerable when the sun comes up."

Ramon looked down on the blank-eyed, collared man. "No matter," he answered. "I can't kill a helpless foe."

Elena looked at her highwayman for a long moment, meeting his even gaze, feeling emotions she couldn't understand. Biting her lip, her heart churning, she considered her responsibilities and her options. Finally, she bent down beside Cortez and whispered in his ear.

Cortez just sat there.

"What did you tell him?" Ramon asked with a quizzical tilt of his head.

Elena pursed her lips as she shook her head. "It doesn't matter, Ramon," she said, turning away. "It really doesn't matter."

⅏

On a sun-drenched, beautiful day with blue skies like she had never seen, Elena Sanchez y Vega looked out the window over her breakfast and smiled. Her brother, Alexandro, a handsome blond-haired child approaching his teen years, sat astride Ramon's white horse, learning to handle the reins under the highwayman's watchful eye. The boy had never had anyone to teach him before.

With a sigh, she looked down at the white tablecloth. Pale splinters of red light danced over it as the sun reflected on her ruby necklace. Ramon had fixed the clasp.

Her curse was not over, for she remained a werewolf. She thought briefly of Cortez, too, still sitting where she'd left him. Sitting there unmoving, forever.

And Ramon? He remained Ramon. Whatever he was, he had yet to tell her. He could be close-mouthed when he wished. She didn't know how long she would stay with him, but this she knew. For a time, at least, when he rode the back roads, in darkness or in moonlight, he would not ride alone.

LACE-MAKER, BLADE-TAKER, GRAVE-BREAKER, PRIEST

by Tanith Lee

Tanith Lee is not the child of actor Bernard Lee, and she did not spend three years posing as a flamingo in order to research a few pages for one of her Venus novels. She is, however, a prolific and versatile writer whose work includes adult and children's fantasy, science fiction, horror, gothic romance, and historical novels, as well as poetry and screenplays.

Tanith calls this story a "passionate and crazy tale." In a 1998 interview, she said, "I have to write longhand, and no one can read my writing, I have to type my own manuscripts, because I'm going almost in a zigzag, across and then down. (I don't write backwards, I've never been able to do that!) I used to throw away my holograph manuscripts after I'd typed them, but I'm keeping a lot of them now, because I'm starting to think, if anyone ever is interested in me after I'm dead, they can look and see, 'My god, this woman was a maniac!'"

"It is," says her character Ymil, cautious and quite gentle, "a *kind* of madness." A madness as delicious and inexorable as the sea. A madness we all yearn for.

Her blog is at: http://www.tanithlee.com/

The sea! The sea!

Xenophon: *Anabasis. IV vii.*

෨ଊ **1.** ๛๏

It seemed as if only one second after the double blow was struck, the storm came up in answer out of the ocean. Of course, it did not happen quite in that way. Ymil, who had briefly turned his back on the argument and was staring out to starboard, said and believed that, directly following the sound of the leather glove slapping the fine blond cheeks, a bubble of sable cloud rose on the horizon's curve. The first kick of the sea unbalanced the ship.

Until then, the voyage had been tranquil and pleasant. They were bound for the Levant. Blue skies canopied blue water with emerald margins and frills of lacy foam. Suns were born and died in splendor. Scents of oleanders and olive trees drifted from the edges of the land. The nights dripped heavily with stars.

But from the very first, those two had formed a dislike for each other.

Surely, any intelligent man realized it was unsensible to take offense, let alone so overtly, against a fellow passenger on a voyage of more than two or three days. Apparently, neither could help it. And both, one saw, were arrogant.

Vendrei was the worst, however, and he seemed to be the one to start the feud openly. It was he, in those last moments before the tempest, who offered the duelist's invitation. He had been idly slapping one of his elegant gloves against his boot. Rising suddenly, he slapped the glove once, twice, against Zephyrin's face. "Do you know what that means, you damned gutter-rat?"

Pale, fair Zephyrin, now with two cheeks pink as a Paris fondant, smiled thinly and replied, "Oh yes. Do *you?* "

After which, Ymil insisted, the ship rumbled and arched her spine, and storm-breath coughed vulgarly in the sails. What had been carelessly noted before—that no land was then visible—now seemed of consequence.

In less than five minutes, the sky turned black, the vessel raced sidelong, masts and yards leaning and cracking and screeching, things crashing below-decks, the groans, bellows, and shouts of crew and passengers already lost in tumult.

Less than *twenty* minutes more and the ship, partly dismasted and having struck some unseen obstacle, reeled headlong into the maelstrom and began to go down.

All on deck had been swept into the water. Here they whirled among the terrible, smothering sheets of the waves.

Ymil lost consciousness, expecting to awaken dead. When he regained his senses, he found that he, with a small group of others, had fetched up alive on an unidentified shore. Whether this was the hem of mainland or isle, none of them knew.

They huddled on the sand as the storm dissolved in distance, its mission fulfilled. There was no sign of the foundered ship, not even a broken spar, barrel, or shred of canvas. Only the repaired lace of the foam followed them to the beach.

Sunset had gone by in a mask of weather. Night was constructing itself, brick by brick.

ೞ ಢ **2.** ೞ ಢ

Prince Mhikal Vendrei had come aboard at the Mediterranean port with the seamless modesty of a flamboyant man. His luggage was meager and soon stowed in the better part of the passengers' quarters. He was a very beautiful picture, tall and slim, with a sunburst of dark gold hair, augmented by silk, leather, and clean linen. At his side, in a satin-cased sheath, rested the final accessory of the true gentleman, a sword of damascened steel, with a lynx engraved under the hilt. He spoke like a gentleman, too, and in many languages. French he had, and several of the coiled tongues of the Eastern Steppes; from his few immaculate books, he could read Latin and Greek. The local patois he had no trouble with, even the slangy argot of the sailors. He did not keep to himself, graciously appearing at meal-times or walking the upper deck to gaze at sea and stars with the others. He flirted with the rich elderly lady from Tint, as with the younger, less wealthy ladies from Athens. He played cards, prayed on the three saints' days that fell during the voyage, and was virtually faultless. He even consented to being sketched by the motherless son of the merchant from Chabbit.

They learned a little about the prince. He was a landowner's son from the north-east, schooled in Paris and at the great University in Petragrava. He had lived a dissolute life until deciding to change his ways and to become, as he put it with a flippant, rueful smile, *"Virtuous"* for his father's sake.

No one ever learned *where* precisely he had been born or raised, where he had carried on his dissolution, nor what made him give it up, assuming he had, for he still gambled and drank quite an amount before, during, and after supper.

The general consensus was that he was likeable and liked. A pleasure to the eye, the ear, and—for he often good-naturedly lost at cards—the pockets of many aboard.

Five days into the voyage, the ship called at the port of Ghuzel. Here a handful of additional passengers joined her. Only one was notable, for this figure too was a glamorous creation quite out of the ordinary.

Zephyrin—if Zephyrin owned another name, nobody

discovered it during the trip—looked a very young man, at least ten years the junior of Prince Vendrei, sixteen perhaps or at most, eighteen. Unusual in one so immature, however, was Zephyrin's knowledge, poise, and ability to charm and to contend with everyone and everything—saving, of course, the prince himself. It was evident by the end of Zephyrin's first day onboard that the young one and the elder one had fallen into an immediate hatred of each other.

Could they be jealous? Unlikely as it seemed, some of the passengers suggested it. Two men, they said, of such wonderful looks and such otherwise incompatible aspects could well find cause for resentment. Vendrei *was* the elder and might not approve of so much youth to spare. Formerly, after all, Vendrei had been the voyage's sole magician, particularly among the women passengers. It seemed they liked the newcomer just as much. Or more . . .

As for Zephyrin: clearly not well-off, occupying quarters in the ship's belly, airless below-decks, private but dark, dank and rat-nipped. Zephyrin wore an old black cavalry uniform from an unrecognizable European battalion. Some said this might even be a mercenary band. The sword, for Zephyrin claimed to be an army officer, was plain steel in a drab sheath and showed no crest.

There was another odd thing.

Zephyrin's thick, almost white hair was a wig. That was not uncommon among the gentry, but for an impoverished army captain, it could have seemed an odd affectation, if Zephyrin had not made allusion to it in an off-hand way.

"In infancy, I fell deathly ill and almost died. Although a clever physician saved my life, my hair dropped out and never fully regrew, except for my brows and lashes, as you see." For this reason, Zephyrin wore the realistic wig, a moon-blond mane, on which was clapped a protective hat when anything more than a faint breeze blew. The captain was beardless for the same cause; not even the long, strong fingers showed any evidence of hair. These facts neither embarrassed nor inconvenienced Zephyrin. Yet the shade of the wig, chosen presumably to complement the soldier's pale coloring, might it not hint of vanity? The brows, too—were they perhaps a little darkened? The eyes needed no help at all. They were large and of a somber green, more malachite than jade.

Eyes not withstanding, did this interloper loathe the luxuriantly-locked Vendrei? Covet his good birth, education, and money? Zephyrin had revealed nothing of parentage or natal country, and spoke, albeit in a musical tenor, only the language of the ship, and that with an army accent. Such a life as his must have been perilous and disgraceful. All of which might be a cause for discontent.

Whatever touched the spark to the powder, each of the drama's actors quickly became a foe to the other.

Ymil had seen their quarrel begin. He himself was nothing, a writer. He had neither excess cash nor fame, no property, no clout, had been born in a back alley of Petragrava itself but to a street-girl who knew less of Ymil's father than Ymil knew of the kingdom of God. Dragged up as through a thorn-hedge, as he himself sometimes said, Ymil traveled about on the business of others and wrote when he had a moment, on paper, with a series of leaky ink-pencils. But *always* he was writing in his mind.

Frankly, he thought, he might have devised and written the first umbridgement between Ven and Zeph himself. If unacknowledged, Ymil was more arrogant then either of these slender, be-sworded, masculined beauties, and had a brain like a thirsty sponge.

That first day, starting off from the port of Ghuzel with the sea skillfully hooking and knotting together its delicate foam of lace. . .

"And so, sir. I seem to interest you?" This from golden-maned Vendrei to the soldier they did not yet know as Zephyrin.

"Your pardon. *You?* And . . . *I?*"

"Just so. Ever since you came aboard this vessel. Not a great while, I admit. But sufficient time, it appears, to learn to stare."

"You must excuse me," said the shabby, beautiful, *young,* flaxen captain. "I failed to see you at all. How remiss, as you seem to require to be looked at. And I, so rudely, did not notice you and looked—directly, er—*through* you."

Ymil, at the scene's perimeter, raised mental ears as high as a hare's.

"Truly? Through me. How quaint. But I suppose you're not accustomed to mixing with my sort."

"Your . . . sort?" questioned the captain.

"Oh, an aristocrat, an educated man who travels—"

"I see. In the traveling way of a merchant, do you mean? One who sells things?" asked the captain, raising an eyebrow.

"Not in that way at all, *sir.* In the way of a man of leisure, who may *please himself.*"

"Ah," said the fair captain. Then paused as if admiringly impressed. Adding, with mildest interest, "And do you, sir? I mean, please *yourself?* Or . . . anyone?"

For a heartbeat, Gold-hair looked as if he might laugh. Then he coldly said, "Your impertinence is evidently due to your lack both of breeding and grasp of any language you are attempting to converse in. I'll leave you to compose yourself. Good morning. Perchance, a word of advice from one a little older than yourself. Don't *stare.*"

The captain bowed curtly. "I shall attempt to benefit from your estimable warning. *Perchance*, I can return the favor by exhorting *you,* sir, to avoid giving such cause."

Thus, their first exchange.

જીભ્જ્ઞ

Certainly, a very childish way of going on. Fascinated nevertheless, Ymil thought so. Being as he was, and doing what he did, human beings intrigued and captivated him, and to a greater extent by their displays of extremis.

He already watched all and everyone, constant to his normal formula. When the boyish captain came aboard, Ymil prepared to watch especially hard. Anyone might think Zephyrin a curiosity.

Unlike Zephyrin, Ymil's close but cunning scrutiny had not been noted. Indeed, as Ymil had seen, Zephyrin *had* stared on and on at Vendrei. Spoiling for a fight from the start, seemingly.

Their duel stayed verbal, however, for eight further days and nights.

They would not keep a minute in each other's vicinity without some quip or carp. Zephyrin, passing Vendrei, who was strolling with the two Athenians, whistled a snatch of song, a ballad from a popular play, concerning a fop who fancied he was a king among women while at his back, all females scorned him. Leaving the ladies, Vendrei walked over to Zephyrin.

"It's unlucky to whistle at sea."

"Oh, is it? Why?"

"Because, captain, you may summon something to you that may prove unwelcome."

At this, Zephyrin shrugged and smilingly asked,

"Yourself?"

They could not even hand each other the salt at table in the saloon, or blow their noses, or look at the stars, without one making unfavorable comment in the hearing of the other.

On the eighth day, as the ship bore north-easterly under peerless skies, Zephyrin came on deck, apparently *searching* for Vendrei. Instead, the searcher found a seat the older man had occupied, where lay one of Vendrei's Latin books, the writings of Catullus. To Ymil's surprise—could Zeph decipher Latin?— the slender captain began to read, or pretend to read, the book.

Back came Vendrei.

"What do you think you're at, sir? Put that down. It is my property. It was my father's—I won't have your unclean paws on it—*down,* I say!" he shouted, as if to some unruly hound.

Never before had Ymil witnessed Vendrei quite so out of his coolth.

Zephyrin looked up calmly and recited from the book, in excellent Latin: *"Miser Vendre, desinas ineptire et quot vides perisse perditum ducas."*

Ymil's not unlessoned brain bounded after the words. They came, he thought, from the lyric poems, but Zephyrin had replaced the name of Catullus with a version of *Vendrei.* The meaning? Approximately, "Pitiable Vendrei, leave off your clowning and relinquish as lost what you can see is lost."

The prince had gone white.

"What do you suppose, you *dog,* I have lost? What can *you* know of loss, *dog,* that never possessed a single thing of worth, nor would know one now if ever it should lie before you?"

"Ah," said Zephyrin, getting up and replacing the book neatly on the seat. "But I *do* know a thing of worth when it is before me. Even if it lies there dead on its back."

So saying, the younger antagonist walked off, leaving the elder one in a definite state of ire and discomfort.

Dead on its back? What could *that* mean?

The Athenian ladies (with both of whom, Ymil believed, Vendrei had a romantic nocturnal understanding) were whispering nervously. Prince Vendrei went to them, flirting and soothing, apologizing for his annoyance, saying the other fellow was scum and not to be thought of any more.

Gradually, Vendrei's color returned to normal. The "other fellow," Ymil thought, had flushed in equal amounts to Vendrei's pallor, as if they were a balance of heat and cold.

This must be more than jealous antipathy, must it not? Ymil was already quite informed that madness motivated Zephyrin. But in this matter, the cause remained unsure.

Zephyrin did not ornament the saloon with his presence that evening. The following afternoon, the ninth of the voyage, not even a hint of an island appeared on the horizon. A card game was started up.

The gaming table had been set on the deck, under the sail aft, for the light was mellow and the weather slow and honey-sweet. Vendrei was losing, as so often he did, and with his usual good manners, to the old merchant from Chabbit and the wily widow from Tint, plus two or three others that Ymil later could not quite remember, for which, in the wake of the shipwreck and their vanishment, he chided himself.

About three o'clock by the sun, Zephyrin appeared like an early moon. What a beautiful creature, all that ivory blondness, and such a face—nearly, Ymil judged, as fine-carved as a woman's—and those black-green eyes, level as two silver spoons full-drawn from the deeps of the sea.

Never before had this rogue officer deigned to join the gambling. Now a chair was selected and the figure sat, facing

Vendrei across the painted oblongs of the cards.

"The stakes are high," said Vendrei flatly.

Zephyrin did something that chilled Ymil through; drawing the dull, notched blade of cavalry sword, that pale hand laid it along the table's edge. "The sword's all I possess of any value. Will it do?"

The table was silent as the inside of a lead box.

Much later, Ymil believed that this, in actuality, was the moment when the temper of sea and sky changed.

"Young sir," the Tintian widow said in hesitant Greek, "are thee so desperate thee does risk the weapon of thy trade?"

"I've risked it in battle, madam. Now I do so again. For here's *another* battle."

"Come, lad," said the Chabbit merchant. "You're hardly older than my boy, my last-born by my dear wife, now in Heaven's garden. Put up the sword. I'll lend you coins—"

"No, sir, with my thanks. My fight, not yours."

"What fight is this, then?" asked another man. But they all knew it was the eternal feud between the captain and the prince.

Zephyrin stretched out long legs. Despite that slender frame, Zephyrin was strong, and only three or four inches less in height than tall Vendrei himself.

"*He* cheats," Zephyrin said casually, and nodding at Vendrei almost companionably. "I wish to prove it."

Few jaws did not drop. A buzz of astonishment next. Then the Chabbitese, not illogically, exclaimed, "*Cheats*, boy? You're cracked. His honor *loses* nine times out of ten!"

"Yes, such is his cleverness, gentlemen and lady. For he lulls you all. During the last days, when we near the wine-red shore of Taurus, he'll win the hoard back by his tricks and fleece you of the rest down to the very skin, like shorn goats. I've met his sort before. A prince? You only have his word for that. I'd not put it past the devil to search your luggage and filch your wallets, too."

All this while, a steady background syncopation, there had been the *slap-slap* of Vendrei's glove on his boot; Vendrei keeping time.

Now that ceased. Vendrei got to his feet. Ymil glanced to starboard, dazzled, his mind leaping and crying, *Of course, you idiot Ymil! It's THAT! What else can it be? All bloody lies—*

After which he heard the duelist's challenge, the blow of the glove to each of Zephyrin's cheeks. The sky filled as if from one of Ymil's leaky ink-pencils, and the storm rose from the belly of the deep.

⊰⊂⊗ **3.** ⊗⊃⊱

Above the sands of the rock-strewn beach, the land lifted into wild green woods of feathery poplar and giant freckled laurel, shadowed by pine and fir and other conifers. Beyond, nothing else was visible. The Chabbitese merchant's son had said at dawn he had seen something vague and far away that might be a mountain or a cloud. An hour after, this had disappeared.

Conversely, to either side of the landfall, the shore tapered gradually into high, grainy cliffs, perhaps impassable.

Their party was small, a pair of sailors named Dakos and Crazt, the merchant and his son (said son having helped his father ashore, since the merchant could not swim), the old Tintian widow, who claimed God and her skirts had borne her up, and Ymil. There were just two others. Vendrei. Zephyrin.

It transpired they both could swim very well. Even Zephyrin's precious wig had been spared by the sea, for it had somehow been kept clamped on under the hat.

Everything else of moment or use was lost, drunk by the greedy water.

Not a single gun had been saved. The flintlocks from Ymil's, Vendrei's, and the widow's baggage lay in the ocean basement. Not even the ancient matchlock Dakos had prided himself on remained. The sailors and the widow, commendably well-armed, had retained a variety of small knives. But they would be effective for no more, as the merchant remarked, than picking one's teeth or nails. The merchant's son had his pocket catapult, but the string had snapped.

As for Vendrei and Zephyrin's blades, they were gone.

The latter's sword, as everyone well recalled, had been placed on the card table as surety minutes before the storm. Vendrei's sword-belt, blade included, had been ripped from his waist by the violence of the waves. Gone too were his coat and waistcoat. Most of the survivors were tattered and bereft also of certain items of clothing. The widow had suffered the least, having lost only hairpins, allowing her magnificent silver and ebony tresses to tumble free. Ymil, even in this extremity, noticed the merchant taking her in. Though not young, she was comely and had shown herself a woman of character.

Despite losses, the new day was warm once the sun rose. The previous night, they had lit a fire from driftwood and fallen branches in the wood. They had no problem with fresh water, either. A small freshet ran from the wood into a pool adjacent to the beach. They must therefore get their bearings, organize a look-out for shipping and for helpful or harmful visitors—persons, animals. A search must be made for edible food.

Vendrei stood in the morning light and scowled at them all. "Be damned to that. The lying filth there owes me his life. We are sworn to a duel. For me, nothing else shall count until I have settled it in his blood."

Zephyrin, who had been sitting on a rock, inspecting the salt damage to his boots, glanced up. "For once, he and I are in agreement. I can give my mind to nothing until the matter's seen to, in blood certainly, but his, of course, not mine."

Vendrei swore inventively and at some length. The widow and the merchant's son looked on in envy. The others, Ymil included, were slightly shocked by the words in several languages.

"But where in the name of God—" rounded off Vendrei in a roar, "are we to find two swords?"

ೞೞೞೞ

A writer's life, unless he be not only talented but also blessed by fortune, can turn out a scrabbly affair. So it had for Ymil. An educated untypical patron of his mother the street-girl had taken pity on the disheveled child and taught him to read and write, and enough figures so he could add two and two and not make seven. Otherwise, Ymil's existence was uncouth, and by the age of twelve, he was runner for a gambling den and occasional thief. By inevitable stages, he equally ascended and failed in these unchosen careers. The ascent was due to his literacy as well as his nimbleness and gift of observation. The failure came from his total dislike of brutality. He had seen enough of that in the hovel with his mother. Meanwhile, by the cliché of a solitary candle, he often wrote down stories, political reflections, and now and then, a song. Intermittently, he would enjoy the tiny success of selling them, seeing them in print in popular pamphlets, or on the sort of rough paper sheets that circulated among the poor but readerly, and were subsequently often put to use for less erudite functions.

By his majority, Ymil could count thirty-one bits and

pieces published, most long since destroyed, and none having paid more than the price of a meal that would excite only a mouse.

He kept body and soul in tandem another way.

On the day he boarded the ill-fated ship, Ymil had earned his bread for almost ten years as a blood-hound. He had discovered, watched and followed, persuaded, tricked and delivered up countless strays, runaways, villains and madmen, to those who wished to have them back, did not know where and how to search, but could pay well one who did. It was on just such an errand that Ymil had taken ship.

He had been in eastern Europe the winter before, on other business. A rich aristocrat summoned him to his palace. It was a grand one, with marble, silk drapes, gold candlesticks. Ymil was respectfully unimpressed. By that time, he had seen such stuff frequently.

"I hear you can find anyone on earth, providing he lives." The aristocrat was a big man in his middle years who, they said, possessed three houses here, another in Petragrava, and a clutch of estates in the country. His demeanor was an odd combination of expansive and guarded, but when Ymil modestly suggested tales of his wisdom were exaggerated, the aristocrat ignored that like a hiccough and told Ymil straight out what he required.

It seemed this man had a son, a very handsome, unusually sensitive and charming son who, four years ago, had been shamelessly jilted by his intended marriage partner. "Less than a day after this shock, my son fell deathly ill with a fever, such as once struck him in childhood. His hair dropped out as it had then. We believed he would die. Yet he turned the corner that very night, and hopes were high that he would recover. Then—horror! The next day, he vanished from the house. Of course, I instantly attempted to have him found. His mind had obviously become disturbed by sickness. One whole year they took to find him. And then—though by now we knew where he must have gone, and the insane mode of life he had adopted—even achieving unlikely success in it—once again, he gave my men the slip. Since that time, anyone I hire to find him has detected his whereabouts, only to lose him again. Yet he lives, this I know. I heard only yesterday that he is somewhere in the Mediterranean area, having given up at last, it seems, his totally unsuitable and unseemly post in the army."

The father then described his son in detail. He was slender, white-blond, green-eyed, and nearly feminine in appearance, the father added with some embarrassment. "Though doubtless less so now," bitterly, "dressed as a soldier and hardened by God knows what adventures. And with a sword at his side with which," now in distaste, "he has done, I am told, a great deal of damage."

The name this absconding youth had assumed—which was not his true one—was Zephyrin.

Ymil accepted the assignment. Among the cypress, orange and lemon trees of the Mediterranean sink, he uncovered Zephyrin's track. Hence the ship, which Ymil learned Zeph meant to board at Ghuzel. Prepared for the assorted results other such cases had presented, Ymil had not anticipated the instantaneous hatred that sprang to life between Zeph and Mhikal Vendrei.

And not until those last pre-tempest minutes did Ymil figure out that, on *this* occasion, two and two *indeed* added up to seven.

෩෬෮෩

In the end, Ymil, with Dakos and Jacenth, the merchant's son, went into the woods to cast about for provender.

Crazt meanwhile had rigged a line from the various debris, boot laces, one of the widow's two remaining hairpins, and baited it with a small dead sea beast found further along the beach. The old widow and the elderly merchant, now on the first name terms of Maressa and Frokash, stayed as sentries of fire and sea.

Ven and Zeph, however, stuck to their prior plan. Ignoring everyone else, seeming careless at the lack of breakfast, they swore a pact, watched by the rest in mixtures of admiration, irritation, contempt and disbelief. Both enemies were to walk in opposite directions along the two arms of the beach, searching for two suitable weapons, preferably long blades.

"Do they think they will find such hung up on the rocks?" pondered Frokash.

"Both are deranged," said Maressa, not without some enjoyment.

The two gallants, still splendid even after total immersion, and lacking portions or entireties of certain garments, faced each other, white and adamantine.

"Until this evening then, sir," said Zephyrin. "When, let us hope, I can curtail your future life, and thus spare the world further boredom from it."

"Till this evening, wretch. Delight in your last day upon earth. You'll find Hell much less pleasant."

Which said, each of them marched off along the sands, Vendrei to the west, a vision of ruined linen, lace, and icy rage; salt-stained Zephyrin heading east, face set like a mask, wig-saving hat crammed firmly on head.

ೞೞ **4.** ೞೞ

Vendrei discovered the fishing village with startled abruptness, as if Fate were jesting, playing games.

By then, he had gone about ten miles down the shore. The cliffs stood high on his right, and the sand was now covered by smooth, round, sea-greened boulders, as if a thousand tortoises had congregated and been heartlessly turned to stone by some passing gorgon. The precarious walkway had narrowed to only three or four feet, in places less. Then, slithering and sliding around a bulge in the cliff wall, Vendrei beheld a hitherto hidden bay, a long apron of glassy blue water, and a broad amble of sand where fisher craft were drawn up and small cranky houses had fixed themselves to the cliff like barnacles.

That the village might be very good news for his fellow survivors did not immediately cross Vendrei's mind. He took the village to be, not only the joke of Fate, but the provider of swords. Why else was it in his path at this fraught hour, unless to give him what he needed most desperately—not sustenance or rescue, but a means to murder his dearest foe?

The golden prince was not a solipsistic dunce, exactly. More that life, and other people, had made him sometimes resemble one.

He had fled his father's house in panic at the strictures of a stern parent determined to have his way. This man had treated his only son, Mhikal, as a possession merely. Very much, let it be said, as he also treated wife and daughters. Worse, he valued Mhikal more highly, thought him *worth* more. What the father ultimately wished from his son nevertheless was, for Mhikal, intolerable. It was horrible, coercive, *obscene.* It would have meant an end to all he valued at that time, or held dear.

But then Mhikal Vendrei's resultant resistant act, so he himself came to believe, was not only dishonorable and vile, but worthy of damnation. He had brooded on it. On nothing else.

Ever since, he had spent his life—truly spent, like cash or blood—in deliberate dissolution and itinerancy. He had been afraid to put down any root, to form any lasting attachment. He journeyed, he thought, with less baggage than a herder of camels, and now the sea had robbed him of all, even the books stolen from his father's library. Even his sword that here, of all times, he *wanted* as a lover wants the beloved—passionately and obsessively.

From the initial instant, he had loathed Zephyrin, not knowing why. Vendrei was neither a snob nor physically unconfident. Probably, he presently decided, it had been an instinctive forewarning. Zephyrin's stares and jibes had cut deep, long before the final calumny, the lie that he was a cheat and thief, propelled him to claim the satisfaction of a duel.

The worst irony of all was that he had taken ship for the express purpose of going home to face his demon and pay its price.

☾ↃↃↄↄↄↄↄ

The people in the hidden village spoke an oriental Greek that, for all his knowledge of languages, Vendrei could barely fathom. He struggled to grasp their words. To make them understand *him*. They gave him a glass of wine with milk curdled in it and sat him down on a stone in the narrow street that rambled round the houses up the cliff. After a while, an older man came along, garlanded with a vast gray beard.

"Is you to be look for," so Vendrei guessed the graybeard said, "the drownwards lost off ship-thing?"

"Ah—no—but—are men from the ship here?"

"Some is here to be have washed up always into us place, if ship sunken. We have two man-things since of yester here. They am drownward. We have of bury them, as is our way with the drown-made dead."

"Commendable," said Vendrei, repressing an hysterical

urge to bellow with laughter. Did these villagers think no one else buried the lifeless? This was a primitive place, but surely—

The wine had gone to Vendrei's head, straight into his brain. He felt dizzy and thought of his own near-drowning, and that he might have ended up being buried by these strangers. He *thought* that two men, now beyond his help, might well have been, each of them, equipped with a usable blade. Which now lay in the grave with them.

"I should wish—I should like," he faltered, "to visit the graves." He blushed with shame, a thing he had not done for several years, at his own appalling behavior. He meant to investigate the graves, *undo* them, *borrow*—oh, borrow of course only, he would return his theft (cheat, thief), replace their swords. Maybe two gentlemen would not grudge this, in order to settle one like Zephyrin? No, they would be seated in the best seats in Paradise, applauding.

I'm drunk.

The bearded man assisted him to his feet. "You come, and I to you show buried. But a long climb."

To Heaven?

Yes, for me, now.

Up the wandering street they went and so reached another treacherous path that teetered up the cliff. Wild blue and topaz flowers and stunted oleanders grew along the sides. Here and there, he saw a shell.

They climbed high above the village and then the path snagged down. A rough carving appeared beside the track, of a long-bearded man with the tail of a fish, who held in his left hand the three-pronged trident of the pagan marine god, Poisidon.

An idea attempted to invest the brain of Vendrei. He wrestled with it, then gave up as the graybeard drew him into a cool tunnel.

"Below," said the man. "Step careful. Tall sea come at sun-die. Then go they."

"They go, do they? Very well. Tall sea."

The tunnel ran through the inside of the cliff. It must lead to the village burial ground. That was strange enough, for at the edge of the village, there stood the usual church, a ramshackle little stone building with a saint painted above the door. Normally, the graveyard would lie handy. Not here, it seemed.

Turning to ask another unwieldy question, Vendrei saw the man had gone, slipped away slick as a shadow.

Vendrei shook his head to clear it, which did nothing but make him laugh. Then he stepped into the tunnel, stooping a little, for the rocky roof was uneven and low. The route had been, most likely, a natural one, hacked out to a greater space by men. Soon he came to a ledge where rested tapers, flint and tinder. Vendrei would need light, for as the tunnel descended, it grew darker. He struck flame and ignited a taper.

In that moment, a profound sense of the supernormal washed over him. How long had this death-road existed? It felt to him old as the cliff. How many unquiet ghosts flitted through the shade, attracted to light like moths but, being already dead, unable to burn. . . ?

"Steady, you fool," he said aloud, and the rock surged with a low, humming echo. "Bloody Zephyrin," Vendrei whispered. "I shall—" Yet here was not a spot to utter maledictions. Vendrei remembered the youth of his adversary, his paleness and handsomeness, and felt a terrible pity at what he meant to do to him. But Vendrei reckoned himself damned anyway, what did one more young life matter? What did anything matter?

Come on, fool, find the dead and rob them, take their

swords, go back and kill the wretch and have done.

ೞೞೞೞ

Ymil, Jacenth and Dakos returned to the beach in the late afternoon with three plump conies, slain quick and clean by the boy, who was apt with a stone even lacking his catapult. They had plucked red grapes from a wild vine, green figs, and mint and sage for flavoring.

Crazt meanwhile had caught a whole heap of fish, now toasting on sticks over the fire. Maressa and Frokash were playing a game with differently marked pebbles. They had seen no shipping and did not seem to mind.

Of the other pair, there was no sign.

"Fell off the land's edge into the ocean," said Crazt under his breath. "To both, our fondest farewell."

This opining was proved valueless when, as the sun reached the brink of the sea, scalding it to carmine, Zephyrin appeared, tramping along the eastern stretch of sand. Zephyrin's hat was off, there was no breeze at all, and the fine white wig hung limply. Hollows smudged beneath the green eyes. The captain seemed tired out, in the manner of an almost grown-up child. Looking at this, Ymil thought, one might know Zephyrin had been recently ill, or very ill some years ago, and was left weakened by it.

Coming near the fire, the slender figure slumped down a short distance from the others.

"I found this," Zephyrin said, and rolled a small barrel towards them, "up the beach."

"French brandy!" Dakos and the merchant exclaimed as one.

"Just so," said Zephyrin. "There was flotsam from the ship, or from some other casualty. I expect you'll like to go and look tomorrow."

Obviously, this one had no interest in food or brandy, nor in any of *them,* only in the missing Vendrei. Also obviously, Zeph had *not* discovered the one—or two—items searched for. No swords.

The sun went down. Lavender flooded the sky, swiftly chased in turn by the indigo of night. Stars spangled. The company feasted on grilled fish and roast meat, herbs and fruit, and passed the little brandy barrel, and were glad. Zephyrin did not join in, ate only a morsel of fish, one grape, went off again and drank sips of water from the freshet pool. Then stayed by the pool, silhouetted against the deep blue and silver of the sky.

"How he misses the prince. You'd think he was in love with him," said Crazt.

"He longs for Mhikal Vendrei's death," said Dakos. "Hate is always worse than love, whatever the wise men say."

"Oh, *love* is strong," said the merchant Frokash. "And sometimes begins unexpectedly." He glanced at the widow.

Ymil was pleased to see that two people might be made happy from this muddle, perhaps even three, for Jacenth appeared to like the widow as a future addition to his father's life.

Mostly though, with a sort of curious dread, Ymil kept one of his observant eyes peeled for Vendrei, walking out of the west like Death himself in the old pictures. Ymil had no doubts the prince would return. None at all.

౪౧ఎౚ౸

He arrived about an hour before midnight. Most of them were asleep. These he woke, for Vendrei was incandescent with fury, nearly insane, as he lurched into the firelight.

"God's stars!" he shouted. "Damnable black foulness!"

His hair was wet and dripping, the remains of his shirt plastered to his body. Had he been for a swim?

He towered over the six seated or prone persons, then raised his wide and flaming eyes to the figure that now sprang toward him from the pool.

"Oh, can it be," Zephyrin asked in a silken voice, "the wondrously clever Prince Mhikal has *failed* to find a sword?" Where there had been no energy to Zephyrin, now there was nothing but. Zephyrin *glowed* in the darkness, galvanic, lightning made flesh.

Vendrei snarled. "There you're wrong, you stye-rat. I found a sword, by God's might—"

And here indeed was the blade, flashing fire and starlight as he flung it, point down, into the sand. Where it waited, quivering also with energy, *readiness.*

"Then, Vendrei, tomorrow we shall fight."

"Ha!" bawled Vendrei. What a splendid melodramatic the stage had lost in him, Ymil thought. But he was not amazed when Vendrei added, in a guttural hiss, "No."

ভা৫ **5.** ৪৩৪

Soon after he lit the taper, the tunnel had plunged unnervingly into a series of steep and sloping steps. This scoured the last tipsiness out of Vendrei. With extreme care he descended, and after about five minutes, the tunnel floor leveled somewhat and he heard, instead of his own hurried pulse, the slow heartbeat of the sea.

A vague luminous quality began. The taper became obsolete. He blew it out to save it for going back.

The rock curved and opened out into a wide low cave, where Vendrei stooped and then got down on his knees and crawled.

Full afternoon light came from the cave mouth. It displayed for him a jumble of rocks and slabs, mossed due to moisture, some clung with pallid ocean weeds. Shells were littered about, and the tiny delicate bones of fish. There was a matured fishy smell, but no note of human decay. For a burial vault it was an odorless place. Empty also. No grave or tomb of any sort that Vendrei could see. All there was—

All there was were two heaps of broken twigs and branches, small stones, sand strewn with wildflowers. The heaps lay side by side against the opening in the cliff that showed the sea. They were each the size and length of a man's body, lying flat.

Vendrei, despite his former superstitious unease, swore colorfully. He had heard of such customs among the primal fisher communities of the region. Although devoutly orthodox in religion, antique rites of conception, birth, marriage or death were celebrated, going back to the sunrise of time and the ancient gods who then supposedly ruled the world. Just as a newborn babe might be baptized by such people in the sea, before ever it felt holy water, those the sea had drowned but cast up on land were blessed in the names of the saints before being returned to the waters. They were the sea-god's, Neptune's, Poisidon's. He sent them home to say goodbye; thereafter, they must be restored to him.

It was true luck for Vendrei. *Meant* for him. Now he would not have to unearth some deep-dug grave, but need only lift the branches and flowers to find the pair of swords of his destiny.

Carefully, being as respectful as he could, he removed the covering of the first man.

Yes, he recalled the poor fellow from the voyage.

Wealthy and young, his sad face battered, bloated by the water. And yes, *yes*—here in the spoiled scabbard, the blade of good steel, nearly the right weight, just a touch light, but that would not matter. Cursed thin Zephyrin should have this one.

With less respect, for he was in haste now, Vendrei pulled the piecemeal carapace from the second man.

And froze. Froze there, and let his arms fall loose, leaning, staring, not crediting what he saw.

For the second dead man, one Vendrei did not even recollect, was a sailor, handsome and oddly unmarked, but most of his clothes and accouterments had been taken by the waves. He bore no blade of any type, not even a knife to whittle sea-ivory.

Two men, two swords. But it was two men and one sword. Only one.

Vendrei kneeled there like the fool he had called himself, almost blind and half-dead with leaden disappointment.

One. Only one.

Fate's joke.

The graybeard had tried to explain the method of burial, the giving back to the god. Vendrei had forgotten the "tall sea."

In the Mediterranean sink, tides were mild and sluggish. Here and there, due to some eccentricity of rock or sea-floor, a rogue tide might arise, such as the one that flushed the survivors of the wrecked ship on to this coast and brought in some of her dead.

At sunfall, here in the hidden bay, an even more sprightly element of the rogue tide would, at certain seasons, leap upward to the cliff, missing the village but bursting into the cave. Swirling like a giant spoon, it would set down fish and weeds and shells, and gather up in payment any unfastened thing left for it. Such as two dead men in easily broken "graves" of twigs.

The sun went, carmine red, and Vendrei lingered in the cave, nursing the single sword, stunned as a child promised a horse and given only saddle and bridle.

As the sun went, the sea came.

It crashed up and washed the cave from end to end, poured out and came plowing back, smashing off the remains of the burial covers, picking up the two dead without difficulty, trying to pick up as well a third, living man.

He resisted, having woken to himself at the last instant. By dint of youth, strength and fright, Vendrei expelled himself from Poisidon's hungry sea, which pursued him, growling like green dogs, back along the tunnel to the awful steps. Even *up* the first steps the sea chased him. Perhaps it was simply chasing him off.

Stars saw him drag himself out of the tunnel above the village. He was soaked through, demented, clutching the useless uniqueness of the sword. Below, lamps were lighting in the little houses. Vendrei did not go there. He turned from the village as from a cruel mocker, and getting down the cliff by another track, to the interest of five or six goats stationed there, he regained the shore and staggered towards the camp of the survivors. And his enemy.

෬ⓒⱤ **6.** ꙮ

"Heaven pardon me," Vendrei would murmur, much later. "I should have begged their forgiveness, too. Should have prayed for them, those drowned men in the cave. Have I lost my human heart? What have I become through all this?"

But *much later* was not yet, certainly not that night.

Having heard of the village and that some form of civilization was near—food, shelter, a small boat that might ferry them to larger settlements—Frokash and Jacenth, with the help of Dakos and Crazt, created a smaller second fire in the lea of the cliffs, and settled there for the night with the widow Maressa.

Vendrei and Zephyrin were left at the larger fire, to their own devices, they and the single sword. Ymil also remained. "Someone should stay," Ymil answered the merchant quietly, when invited to the second, calmer fireside.

"Not to leave them to their madness, eh?"

"Merely to watch," Ymil replied, with abnormal truth. Nevertheless, he sat some feet away from them.

No one spoke. From the other fire drifted faint talk, silences, presently the low snores of Crazt. The moon had come and gone long before.

When the big fire sank, Vendrei or Ymil replenished it from the store of driftwood and branches. Once Vendrei went up to the pool, then came back and sat down again. He had eaten nothing and refused the brandy. Although he was quiet, the smolder of his rage was upon him. His hair had dried, shone like guineas in the firelight. The sword shone, too, planted there, presiding, deriding the two unarmed men and their mortal dream of a duel.

Ymil, watching, saw how Zeph watched only Ven. Those dark green eyes scarcely blinked, so fixed they were. But Ven watched nothing, or else only the angry blank his thoughts had become.

Well past midnight, Ymil began quietly but audibly to talk, as if to himself.

"How bizarre it is, that just the few of us were saved. Is our rescue for a purpose? I mean, some purpose we have yet to fulfill? What can it be? Maybe, in my own life . . . I once did a cruel and stupid thing. There was a young lady I was set to marry. But I changed my mind. I abandoned her."

Under his watchful eyelids, for Ymil sometimes watched with his eyes shut, he studied Zeph's finely chiseled profile. True to the aristocratic father's embarrassed words, this young captain did look delicate enough to be taken for a woman if one ignored the clothes. But that would be most unwise, for the core of Zephyrin was made of purest steel.

Did the invented story touch a nerve? (Admittedly, it was in the father's account, the genders were reversed, it was the son who had been abandoned by a girl.) No reaction? It was impossible to be sure.

"I regretted my actions afterwards. I heard she had fallen very ill. My fault, I must assume. I wonder if I can atone for my crime against her. Or am I too late?"

Vendrei said nothing, did not even look up. Had he heard? Why should he besides have any response to the tale, either the father of Zephyrin's tale, or Ymil's altered one?

Now Zephyrin turned that pale, wonderfully-wigged head and stared full at Ymil, so for an instant Ymil reckoned his role as tracker and spy had been sussed. Zephyrin said, however, "She sounds like a spineless simpleton, your *lady*. Some dolt deserts her. She falls into a sickness. You're better, sir, well shot of the ninny."

And that was that. At least, upon the subject of desertion.

For in another hour, as the stars wheeled into the west, Zephyrin announced, "Well, Vendrei, it appears you're content to sulk and do nothing else to conclude our quarrel. Why am I not astonished?" Vendrei offered no word. "As I said, quantities of stuff from the doomed ship are scattered over the beaches further east. Where the cliffs close down upon the sea, I saw some wreckage far out on the water. There could be weapons in with it, if only the weapons of dead men that you, Vendrei, naturally, would never mind thieving and employing."

Vendrei spoke. "Tomorrow I shall go and see."

"Such a hero. I gasp at you."

"Go to Hell, Zephyrin. Once I find a second sword, whatever its caliber, I'll send you there with it. You may as well familiarize yourself with the country."

ೞೞೞೞ

Of all things, Ymil did not expect to do more than doze. Sleep accordingly took him by surprise.

As also it must have done Vendrei who, exhausted by water, shocks, walking, but mostly by the hundred conflicting emotions in his mind, had slumped over like a boy, with his cheek pillowed on his hand.

The sun blew out of the sea, the color of Vendrei's golden-guinea hair. The people at the two fires woke, or were woken by the wakening of others. They were in number seven, and should have been counted eight. Zephyrin had left them.

ೞೞೞೞ

They went down the shore, striding eastward, Mhikal Vendrei and Ymil. On Ymil's personal involvement in searching for and locating Zephyrin, Vendrei made no comment. No doubt he was so obsessed with the captain, Ymil's dissimilar yet total obsession seemed only inevitable.

"He's swum out to that wreckage he claimed to see," Vendrei had shouted, rather illogically, for if the wreckage were not real, why swim out to it? "The currents here, the tides, are crazed. He'll drown himself, the devil—anything to deny me the satisfaction of killing him myself."

Not long after, unbreakfasted, their toilette consisting of hand-rubbed faces, finger-combed hair, and brandy-moistened mouths, the two men set off.

Both barely kept themselves from running.

The day, however, ran. Forward, upward.

Eventually, in the solar light that was like smashed crystal, they reached a stretch of sand where, gleaming and sparkled by sun, lay the spars and barrels of the shipwreck, a torn sail spread like dirty washing, a handful of iron bits, bolts and nails, the dreadful inefficacious irony of a holy medallion.

Here and there along the route, the booted footfalls of Zephyrin had been discernible. Now, these narrow markers led, infallible clues, to the water's edge.

The sea had drawn out some way from the beach. This in itself showed a variant tide, since from what Zephyrin had said, yesterday the margin had been consistently far more slender here.

"Look! There they are, his bloody boots thrown off—and the uniform jacket, too, the better to swim."

They scanned the sunlit splinters of ocean. Nothing obvious was to be made out, neither the wreckage nor any mortal form.

"If anything was here, the sea's moved it. And the fool's gone after it."

They stood between earth and water, under air and fire, dumbfounded.

"Oh God," Vendrei said then, softly, "why do I hate him so? Why? What did he ever to do me but gaze and jeer, and what's that to a grown man? What have I done to myself these past years of my escape, to bring me down to this baseness and idiocy? I was never happy in all that time. I was never free. I drank and gamed and made love and played at living, and look where it's carried me. And carried this young man who so enraged me. Have I gone mad, Ymil, do you think?"

"It is," said Ymil, cautious and quite gentle, "a *kind* of madness."

"Yes, mad. The mad-house is the vile hell in which I must leave myself next." He gazed blindly across the bright water. "You talked last night, Ymil, of something you called a crime—that you'd deserted a young woman to whom you had promised marriage. You seemed to want to go back to her, to make it right. You said, I think, she fell ill. . . . Oh, Ymil, we have almost the same story, if not exactly. My father sought to force me into an arranged marriage with the daughter of a princely neighbor. I was already reluctant, yet took care I caught a glimpse of her before any formalities. Base as I was, and am, I think if I had been struck in admiration, I might have gone on with the fiasco. But no such thing occurred. Oh, she was not unpleasant, a little gawky, brown-haired, busying herself with some silly woman's pretense of gardening. Seventeen years of age. An uneducated, ignorant, skinny child. With a whole ten yards, and most of a thick hedge between us, I grew incensed. I rebelled. I thought myself in love with another woman, the clever, elegant wife of an acquaintance, and I planned to seduce this person and steal her from her husband. I tell you straight, when I proposed it to her, she laughed in my face. She said she was *"greatly tempted,"* but liked her house too well to desert it and go *"adventuring."* So I went off alone, and wasted four years of my life. And what became of the little thin girl of seventeen with the brown hair? She too fell sick, Ymil. I heard later that she died. I had this from a man who knew the family. I beat him at cards and he took it out on me by telling me this. He said it was well known, she died of shame, and her own father called me her murderer. I might as well have cut her in half with a sword. And now. Now I'll kill a man for laughing at me. Am I so friendly with death that I yearn to *feed* him?"

Vendrei breathed a moment.

"Heaven pardon me, I should have begged their forgiveness, too. Should have prayed for them, those drowned men in the cave. Have I lost my human heart? What have I become through all this? Mind lost, heart lost, a monster—"

That said, Vendrei sat down and with some labor, pulled off his own well-made boots. "I'll swim out, too. Try to find that boy, save him—"

Ymil had no words to give. He was aware Vendrei would no more hear them now than he would have listened to his own contrition, earlier. As the prince launched himself into the water, graceful and muscular, assured in this even in his sudden lack of all other assurances, Ymil squinted at the beach, attempting to gauge the sea.

They were difficult to divine, the moods, the schemes of the sea.

Once Vendrei vanished into the distance, Ymil moved on along the beach. There was for some way still a trail of objects tossed on the sand. Then the heavy masonry of the cliff put its foot down and ended the beach entire. Here one jagged rock stuck up in the water. Draped artistically across the rock was what Ymil took to be a perfectly white garment. Until he saw that it had long green hair.

Ymil had met nothing in his life that conclusively established that things supernatural did not exist. Ghosts, vampires, feys, all sorts were conceivable. So might this be. A white-skinned, naked, lovely woman lay over the arm of the rock, emerald-haired, her flat smooth belly finalizing in a coiled black tail.

He was staring at the mermaid when he heard Vendrei call from behind him, and the prince trudged up from the ocean, his own arms as empty as his distraught face. All his shirt was gone now. How much of his soul?

They stared at her, the lady from the sea.

Ymil said at last, "She's human after all. It's weed caught in her hair, that greenness. And see, the tail's just some dark torn material wrapped around her legs."

Vendrei, who had been more still than the rock, started violently and said, "She isn't dead. I thought she was. But she's breathing."

At that second, the woman who was not a mermaid stirred, coughed, and leaning sidelong, voided her lungs of water. After which she sat up, glanced at them in angry dismay, and put one slim arm across her very beautiful breasts.

Ymil identified her. Or, recognized her. For he had secretly known her from those minutes before the tempest struck.

"Is she from the ship?" asked Vendrei, as if in a stupor. "Madam," he added, "allow me to assist you."

"Keep your damned hands off me, you cur," the woman replied in the tenor voice of Captain Zephyrin.

⊰⊱⊰⊱

Those years before, Zophyra, at seventeen, had been ill-at-ease, and it was true she had been poorly educated. She could read and write, sing and sew. Aside from that, she was continually instructed in a single lesson, that she must be feminine, obedient, and ready to marry whichever suitor her father chose for her.

One day, her father did choose. Zophyra was consumed by utter terror. She had heard and read tales of young maidens wedded to evil and frequently elderly men. Not uninventive, she found a means, at a time when the proposed bridegroom was visiting the estate, to see him, herself unseen. If he were foul, she would slay herself or, perhaps, run away.

What she saw, on that amber harvest morning, when the scent of wheat and hay, apples and white alcohol was buzzing in the air, was Mhikal Vendrei, then just twenty-two years of age, marvelous as a young god.

She fell in love with him at once.

A favor, alas, he did not return on the subsequent occasion that, unbeknownst to Zophyra, *he* had spied on *her*. A trio of months following, he jilted her, unmet, and was gone into the wild world.

Her father and his vied with each other to make recompense. She meanwhile felt fragments of her shattered heart rattling in her breast, piercing her, and she succumbed to a recurrence of the dangerous fever that still lay dormant in her blood. In infancy, this malady had almost finished her. Now it made a worse assault. Unknowing in delirium, she had been given the last rites when that very midnight the febrility cracked like a burning-glass and spilled her forth.

As before, all her hair had fallen out. In childhood, the first attack of fever had turned it nearly white on its return, and ever since, her father had seen to it that this albino tendency was corrected with brown dye. He had not wanted to scare off possible swains with her almost-uncanny pallor. In adulthood, the hair grew back whiter than before, only her brows and lashes retaining their darker shade. Her father never saw this. As soon as she was able, still unhinged from heartbreak and sickness, Zophyra fled the parental home.

She rushed into the unknown and extraordinary world, which she had the sense, having read a few rather ridiculous stories of such things, to approach in male attire and the assertive pretense of masculinity as she perceived it: arrogant, overbearing, unkind, elusive. All this worked because, despite her naivety, she had the cunning instincts of a genius.

She passed herself off as fourteen. As a lad, she appeared much younger than her actual span. She joined one of the roving armies of the Steppes, more because it presented itself before her than for any concrete reason. She had been so scorched by passion and its rejection—someone had told her Vendrei had seen her and been unimpressed—she was by then fearless, reckless. The vagaries of Fate had aided her, too, for her feminine monthly courses, traumatized by the fever, ceased for the time being. By the time they resumed, she was well able to protect herself from scrutiny.

She learned early on to fight. She was skillful and daring. She took proper lessons whenever she could, from such scholars as she encountered, on many subjects, including the Latin and early Greek languages, literature and philosophy. The one she hated was, she had been told, a paragon in this area. She paid for tuition with her army pay and was otherwise abstemious. When advised to visit the brothels, she replied that she had a sweetheart at home she would not betray. As in much else, the men found her, or the youth she acted, weird but not unlikeable. And she was, they also knew, a demon with the drawn blade.

When she was nineteen, had grown taller, beautiful if she had known it, and must bind her breasts to prevent discovery, she shaved her head and told those who commented on her lack of facial hair that a fever had depilated her almost entirely. Later, leaving the battalion, she *grew* her hair, told the same tale, and claimed the real hair to be a wig. It was unusually thick and lustrous enough, added to its paleness, that she was believed.

Her goal, needless to say, remained constant.

She heard rumors of her own 'death' at home on the old estate. It seemed to her Zophyra *had* died, had indeed been murdered by the callous suitor who had not wanted her.

She intended now to find this man. Firstly, she would demonstrate to him that she was his equal or superior. Next, she would make a mock of him, present him to others as shoddily as she could. Lastly, so well able to fight, not to mention tutored in the symmetry of poetic revenge, she would run him through the heartless heart with a steel blade. For had he not, metaphysically, spiritually, *carnally,* done as much to her?

Like Ymil, Zophyra—for a time known as Zephyrin— tracked Vendrei. Just as presently, Ymil, hired and misled in embarrassment by her father, tracked *her.* Him.

Learning the passenger list on the ship, Zophyra-Zephyrin took passage. As Ymil, knowing she-he would, had likewise done.

Ymil alone had seen to the bottom of her relentless vendetta, and that not until almost the last moment.

The rest was uproar. As detailed here.

ଔ୯ **7.** ଛ୨ଡ଼

Even the most diligent observer will sometimes deliberately turn away. Ymil did so on the beach below the cliffs. He took himself off along the shore, and began to examine the flotsam broadcast there, quite studiously.

Half naked the pair of them, Vendrei and Zeph-Zophyra glared at each other. After a second, however, the young woman pulled herself to her feet and took a couple of baleful strides towards him. Her gait was not steady, needless to say, and gave way abruptly. The instant she staggered, Vendrei leapt to her like a lion at a gazelle and seized her in both arms. His grip was fierce, yet gentled. Zophyra, while her head spun, could make no proper resistance.

The weed was still tangled in her hair. Vendrei therefore

found himself kissing both her pale hair and the pale weed. Each tasted of ocean, but her hair also of her youngness and female flavor. Her skin more so.

"When I am better," she whispered, "I shall kill you for this."

"Already you kill me. One look from your eyes—Who— what—who *are* you?"

"You know me."

"Do I?" Vendrei paused, his mouth against her cheek, that his duelist's glove had slapped, this skin like silk. "I seem to have seen you. But that was in your male disguise. I should have guessed. Nothing so delicious, so rare, could be anything but a woman. . . ."

"Oh, but it can, sir. Even dead on your back, with my sword so nicely planted in your heart, you would be worth all this world to me."

Both of them sighed then. They were worn out, and leaned on each other, in a while sitting down on the sand. The sun warmed them. Their hair was drying, mingled in long strands of gold and cream.

Eventually he said, in a low penitent voice, "Are you the girl from the other estate? *That* girl? But you can read Latin—"

Then she laughed. "What shall I do?" she asked the sky and the water. "It's no use, Mhikal Vendrei."

"No use at all. You've won the duel," he said. "You won it when I saw you and thought you dead on the rock. I knew you then, somehow, and *that* was the cause of my hatred perhaps— that I'd refused something so fine. Worth ten of me. A thousand. You have won the duel."

"No. *You* won it. From the moment I first saw you, four years ago, on the harvest morning. Then."

The watcher Ymil did glance, just once, back over the

sand. A precaution perhaps. But they were embraced by then, mouth on mouth, their hands in the other's hair, yearning and almost crying aloud. Like two shipwrecked survivors who, after years of tempest, crashing waves and tumult, reach the kind arms of the land alive.

ৰৱ২৪৫

It is the sea, Ymil thinks, weeks later, when he is safe in the port of Pharos. The sea is so versatile, has so many trades. It makes itself adornments of lacy foam, disarms aggressive humans of their swords, rises to undo the graves of mankind and claim back the dead it has already destroyed, in its priestly role of sacrificer. But also the sea is the benign priest, joining in the marriage of love old widows and aging wifeless merchants, and young men and women who have lost what they can never see they have lost, which is simply their way. Brief dusk lies on Pharos, and the stars come out in crowds to gape at the nightlife below. The waters of the Mediterranean uncurl against this Egyptian strand. The sea, the priest, Ymil thinks, is also singing orisons above the depths to honor them, those that never reach the land, those forever lost; the drowned, the lonely. The watchers far from shore.

THE BEHEADED QUEEN

by Dave Smeds

Dave Smeds is one of today's most versatile writers; his repertoire spans science fiction, contemporary fantasy, horror, erotica, superhero stories, and more. His novels include *The Sorcery Within, Piper in the Night,* and *X-Men: Law of the Jungle,* and his short fiction has appeared in *Asimov's SF, F&SF, and Realms of Fantasy,* as well as many anthologies. He particularly enjoys writing imaginary-world fantasy, and often includes romantic elements and female viewpoint characters. Dave lives with his family in Northern California, where he has practiced goju-ryu karate-do for many years. Find out more about him at http://www.sff.net/people/davesmeds/

With such a wide-ranging talent, it came as no surprise when Dave sent me a story whose viewpoint character is a disembodied head—and what a protagonist she is! To make an inexcusable pun, the story is far from "talking heads," but a deeply moving tale about truth, loyalty, passion, and love.

Ten months had passed since my lord king had deigned to liberate me from my niche. Over the years, as his fury had dimmed, I had become little more to him than an ornament—akin perhaps to the portrait of his great-grandfather, the Reaver, that hung in his council chamber. In some ways the indifference was not unlike his treatment of me during our marriage.

The yeoman set me down on the pedestal beside the throne, where once my lesser chair had stood. He and a palace maid plucked the cobwebs from my eyebrows, brushed my hair, and dabbed oil of rose behind my ears.

"Regal Lady. By your leave, I will lift you from your tray," the yeoman said.

"Do as you will," I replied. My voice sounded peculiar to my ears. The enchantment did not permit me to speak when consigned to my niche. These were the first words I had uttered in three seasons.

He grasped me around the jaw and raised me. The maid removed the cloth that had lain beneath me. It was stained with a few drops of the blood that still brimmed at the end of my neck, fresh as the day the axeman had parted my head from my shoulders. The poor girl shuddered as she slipped the new linen into place.

They arranged me so that I faced the throne, not the gallery. This was the first clear sign that I was to be addressed by the king himself.

Pathren kept me in suspense nearly an hour—intentionally, I am sure. He entered alone, his men-at-arms left behind at their sentry stations at the great doors. Soon he loomed in front of me.

"Traitress," he greeted me.

"Murderer," I responded.

The last time I had called him anything other than "Father of My Sons," he had ordered me back to my niche and caused the drape to be closed, denying me the privilege of witnessing the doings of the court—the one diversion I had left to keep me from dwelling on my wretchedness. This time he did not react.

"It seems we are speaking," I said. "Why?"

"The crown prince is betrothed."

Had I still possessed a heart, it would have skipped a beat. "Bredden is to marry? When? To whom?"

"To Imileya, eldest daughter of the King of Fenmarch."

I had expected a different answer. Some unpleasant prospect, revealed to torment me. I had not smiled in years, but I was ready to now. "That is a superb match."

"It has advantages," admitted Pathren.

Then I saw the problem. "What does her father ask of you in return?"

"My watchtower at Goblin Pass."

"Are these terms you can bide by?"

He held his hand low, palm up in a curl, as he had in bygone times cupped my womanhood. A possessive pose. "The Reaver built that watchtower. It has been part of the realm for over a century." He sighed. "You are right. I cannot simply let Alvos have it."

"Yet the betrothal is a fact? You have agreed?"

"I have," he admitted. "We are committed to the courtship year."

"How can this be?"

"I have made peace with it in this way: I will give the watchtower to Bredden. He will pass it to Imileya as a wedding gift. For a number of years it will be manned by a garrison of her choosing—one from Fenmarch, if she likes. Upon her eventual death, title passes to her heir. Who will also be Bredden's heir. So the tower will ultimately be part of Sorregal again, and in the meantime, it will never actually belong to Alvos."

"I take it you will not put your seal upon the transfer until near the end of the courtship year?"

"Naturally."

So he had until next summer to reconsider. But if realized,

these were unprecedented concessions on his part. He could not
be the instigator of this scheme. "You are doing all this at
Bredden's request," I said. It was not a question.

"I am."

"That was bold of him," I said. "How is it you did not tell
him no?"

He shrugged. A simple gesture, and one more honest and
unguarded than I had seen from him since we had been
newlyweds.

"Bredden has always done as I have asked. Perhaps it is
time to do as he asks, simply because he asks. He is the future of
Sorregal. It is his right to lay the foundation of his reign. I would
rather see him do so now, while I am here to catch him if he
stumbles. And if he should enjoy success, let it be while I am
here to witness it."

Pathren was feeling his age. He had not been young when
he took me to wife. He now had no trace of auburn left in his
hair. It was all grey, as his beard had been for years.

"Nature will soon have its way with me. With Alvos as
well. Our sons have less reason to hate one another. Diplomacy
may succeed. If in the process Bredden wins himself a bride of
quality, so much the better."

"Does she accept this marriage?"

"Now we come to the issue," said Pathren. "She has said
yes, but she had little choice. Does she grasp what it should
mean to be Bredden's wife? I would not care to see him played
falsely."

As he gazed at me, a glimmer of the old rage flickered.

I said nothing. Any comment would only have sent him
into a litany of my crimes. That was a speech I had heard too
many times.

"I have made a pact with Bredden," he went on. "Father to

son. King to crown prince. During this coming year, while Imileya dwells among us here in Sorregal, things must go well. If they do, the wedding will be held. If they do not, the betrothal shall be dissolved. And I keep my watchtower."

"How would you determine if it has 'gone well?'"

"In sundry ways, but only one that need involve you. I must be satisfied of Imileya's nature. Will she be loyal to Bredden, or an agent of Fenmarch? Will she be a source of harmony in my castle, or a seed of dissension? You are to judge."

I could barely credit what I had heard. "I?"

"You. It cannot be left to Bredden. If the sight and scent of Imileya makes him keen to get between her legs, he will be blinded to any flaws she has. I need a woman's perspective. I would not trust the assessments of the ladies of my court. They all have their own schemes in play. You are the mother of the Heir. You will want what is genuinely best for him."

"That could not be more true."

"Then we have an accord. You will leave in the morning with the entourage I am sending to fetch Imileya from Fenmarch. You will observe the princess closely from the moment you meet her. She may reveal herself in her homeland and on the journey in ways that she will not once she is ensconced within these walls, among folk entirely alien to her."

"A boon," I asked. "Fetch Bredden here. Let me see him before I go."

He chuckled. "He is already waiting."

He yanked the pull-cord. The bell of summoning resounded beyond the great doors.

Pathren rotated my tray so that I faced the supplicant's dais. Through the archway strode a young, strapping man I barely recognized. I had not seen Bredden since he had left for the wars in the south, to learn first-hand the leading of the kingdom's warriors, and to prove himself in their eyes.

Slight scars ran across his chin and right cheek—not enough to mar his handsomeness, but enough to show he had not shirked from danger on the battlefield. His armor rode smartly on his broad frame. His eyes were alert and evaluating. Yet I sensed all was not well. He was changed. Hardened. He stopped before me and gave a short bow, not deep, but precisely proper for a crown prince addressing his mother. Too proper for my liking.

"Madam, it is good to see you."

"You are a boy no longer," I murmured. Tears welled in the corners of my eyes. They did not drip down my cheeks, but it was not for lack of emotion on my part. In my current state I neither drank nor ate. The potions the demon swabbed into my mouth each month sustained me, but they did not grant me the moistness needed to weep.

"No. I am not. Not for some time."

"Are you of a mind to marry?"

"I am."

"Then we will speak of it."

I paused.

He understood at once. "Sir?" he said, turning to Pathren. "Might I hear my mother's counsel in private?"

Pathren canted an eyebrow at us, but he made no protest. Soon Bredden and I had the throne room to ourselves.

"I have heard the reports of your doings," I told my son. "You have accounted well for yourself. No one questions your fitness to lead the realm when your time comes. Even your father sees it."

"I found the strength you spoke of," he said. He did not say it triumphantly. Now that we were alone the anguish in him was vivid.

"What is it?" I asked gently.

"Such things I have seen. Such actions I have had to take. With a word I change the course of men's lives, or end those lives. I scarce know myself any longer."

"My precious boy," I murmured. "You must not despair. You have come far."

"But in what direction?" he asked.

I had never seen him so troubled. I could not know all that fueled it. When he had been young, nothing that went on inside him was opaque to me. Now he was encased within the armor of a king-to-be, and I could not know all he was. The one thing I could know with certainty is that it was no whim that had caused him to pursue a marriage at this time.

"You look to a wife to serve as your gauge." I smiled. "I gave birth to no fool."

He leaned close, undaunted by the eldritch aroma that my flesh gave off. "She must be the right one, Mother. I do not fear the battlefield. I fear only what I may be, with the wrong voice in my ear at night."

"What do you know of Imileya, to make your overture to her?"

"I have heard tales enough to give me hope. But in the end, I know no more than anyone in Sorregal. Is she right for me? If anyone can judge this, it is you, Mother."

"I will do all I can," I said. "And Bredden?"

"Yes, Mother?"

"Blessings upon you, to give me this task."

"Blessing are already upon me," he answered, "or you would not be here to give the task to." He kissed my forehead.

Ten years I had suffered. Now I knew there was meaning to my survival.

ఇరాశ్రీఅ

In the morning the cortege gathered in the main courtyard. A miniature palanquin had been created for me. It required only two bearers given the slight weight I represented, even taking into account the thick brass accouterments and the heft of the canopy. The bearers were robust plainsmen; they would easily be able to keep up. The knights were riding their battle mounts, and while those beasts might handle the burden of a man in chain mail with admirable fortitude, they could not cover long distances day after day faster than men could walk those same leagues.

Aside from me and my bearers, the party consisted of ten noblemen and twice that number of men-at-arms, along with a number of squires and grooms, a cook, and a cook's boy. And one other person. She came out of the castle last, wearing a spotless riding dress of cream silk with spun-gold embroidery. The tiara in her hair sparkled when she emerged from the shadow of the building.

I had barely seen my eldest daughter since the days when I had possessed arms and a lap to nestle her within. Bredden had visited me whenever Pathren would permit it. Clessa had never come of her own accord. We had not been in each other's immediate presence since an occasion when she had disobeyed her governess, and had been brought to my niche as a lesson in what could happen to a royal female who misbehaved. She had run screaming from the chamber.

She paused at my palanquin. She eyed me coldly. A slight tremor betrayed that she yearned to flee the sight of me again.

"Daughter," I said. "You are a striking young woman."

"Lovely princesses make the best hostages," she quipped, and stalked away to her horse.

ෆෆ෬෫෮

Clessa made a point to avoid me in the early part of our travels. I did not contend with her over it. She was already being forced to spend a year in a foreign land as surety for Imileya—one king's daughter for another. I would only have her bide with me if it were her own will.

I did not lack for distraction. The countryside was a marvel to me. For years all I had seen was the audience chamber and on occasion, when Pathren wanted to display me to the populace, I had been suspended in a cage from the parapet overlooking the square. No matter how many times I had soared over the land in my dreams, the confinement had wreaked its dulling effect. I had forgotten the scratchiness of the scent of threshed hay, the lusty attitude in the twitter of birdsong. Days brightened of nature's accord, and not because palace servants lit lamps.

We reached the mountains on the fifth day. For the first time I could see for myself what was meant by the palisades. Not just mountain slopes, but cliffs and treacherous banks of talus shielded our kingdom—save for Goblin Pass, where the glaciers of the high slopes sent their meltwater down, carving into the weak spot in the range, feeding the River of Alders. Even from the valley I could see the saddle of the divide, the one place where no snow-laden peaks blocked our path.

"Were you ever as far as this, when you were alive?" The speaker's pitch was girlish, but the delivery assertively mature.

The nose of Clessa's mount advanced into my field of view—but only far enough to bring Clessa herself straight to the left of my perch. Since my ability to swivel my head was minor, I was left unable to regard her. Which she well knew.

"I am still alive," I said. "Your father's bonded demon makes sure of that."

"Do you not wish to be dead?"

"I have wished it and I have wished it," I replied. "But no one has been willing to incur His Royal Majesty's wrath and give me my release. Will *you* do it?"

"No."

"Then I will die when Pathren dies, and his demon returns to its realm. In the meantime I linger, the better to demonstrate the power of the king."

"I thought it was to demonstrate the depth of your offense."

Many felt as she did, but it hurt more to hear it from my own offspring. "I committed no wrong. Or none, that is, save that I put my trust in a lady-in-waiting who did not deserve it."

She gasped. "No wrong? You were an adultress."

"And the king was an adulterer. With a hundred women. Two hundred."

"That is different. It was of no consequence to him. What you did was hateful."

"On the contrary. I did not hate your father. Not then. Though I had come to see him for the sort of man he was."

"And what sort was that?"

"Need I tell you?"

She hesitated.

"He is the kind a demon would serve," I pointed out. "And they are not beings who serve a man whose nature is sweet."

"But he was the king. You had a duty," she said.

"Yes. I did. And I was conscious of it. Spite would never have been enough to lead me down my path. I did as I did because of my feelings for Faeyn, and of his for me. Those feelings were the opposite of hate."

"Do not speak his name. It is forbidden."

"Faeyn, Faeyn, Faeyn," I said, wishing I could shout, but to do that required lungs I did not have. "And I lay with him *many* times."

"You are the harlot everyone says you are!"

"You decided that long ago, I think. If it is guilt you want, you will not get it from me. If you had ever been in love, you might have some concept of why I acted as I did."

"I have been in love," she objected.

"Oh?"

I waited. She tightened in the saddle enough that her mount quickened its pace. Before she restored her position I glimpsed the blush in her cheeks.

"Not the kind of love to make me . . . lose my head," she admitted.

"Well put."

಄ಞ಄಄

The last morning of our ascent, the proximity to the snowline rendered the air brisk. I, who had been tucked away so long, appreciated the novelty of my skin prickling and was disappointed that I had no breath to make little clouds in front of my face. But Clessa whined, as only a princess raised in comfort can whine. For the sake of my ears, I resolved that our quarters in the watchtower would be separated by at least one thick stone wall.

At the top of the pass, we announced our arrival with a trumpet blast and a waving of the king's standard. Men of the local garrison responded in kind. To my surprise, we did not head for the redoubt at the base of the promontory on which the keep stood, though its portcullis was lifted as we drew near. Instead the retinue gathered in formation to face an encampment that lay several hundred paces down the road that led to Fenmarch.

"Fortune be with you, Your Majesty," said Lord Ullank, the

Earl of Rowanwood, the highest ranking of our escorts.

"You go no farther?" I asked.

"Terms of the truce, these past sixteen years. No warrior of Sorregal may go beyond this point. No warrior of Fenmarch may come closer than a bowshot from the northern wall." He gestured at the archers along the battlements of the watchtower.

It seemed there would be no night of peace and solitude for me, nor any big stone hearth to melt the icicle that had apparently formed in Clessa's rectum. I wondered if Pathren had told them to leave me unaware that the exchange would happen at the instant of our arrival, or if they had kept the secret out of personal disrespect.

Clessa whimpered, having grasped that the moment had come when she was to be abandoned into the keeping of strangers, to become a hostage in truth.

"Fortune be with you all," I called to the cortege. Ullank gestured to my bearers and I and my palanquin were carried into the no man's land. I heard the erratic clip-clop of horse hoofs as Clessa followed. She kept slowing down, then having to catch up.

The strangers ahead began breaking down their tents and stowing gear in panniers and in mule packs. The group was similar in size and composition to our own. From the look of the trampled ground they had been on site about two days.

Once we were twice bowshot distance from the fortifications, one of the Fenmarchers mounted his horse and advanced toward us at a rate that perfectly matched our approach, as ritual called for. The rider's helm was decorated with a single, elegant plume of rank.

"Pus and gore," Clessa muttered. "They've sent a *boy*."

"Hush," I said.

He was no boy. He was tall and well-knit. His beard was

full. As he reined up and dismounted, his movements exuded grace.

He removed his helmet and placed it under an arm. "Your Majesty, Queen Daena. Your Highness, Princess Clessa," he said, bowing to each of us in turn. "I bring you greetings from Alvos the Fourth, King of Fenmarch."

"Well met," I answered. "And you are . . . ?"

"I am Norl of Heronpool."

"You are more than that, I think."

"I am the viscount of Heronpool, if it please Your Majesty."

Clessa snorted.

"Forgive my daughter's manners," I said. "She had no mother to teach her better, these past ten years. You are Madrak's heir?"

"I am."

"Then you are one-and-twenty. It does you credit you do not flaunt a title you've so newly acquired."

"You are kind, Ma'am."

"Clessa," I said. "Your father's men cut down Madrak, Viscount of Heronpool, at the Battle of Eagles. This young man was—what, six years old at the time?"

"Not quite, ma'am."

"Five, then. I would not antagonize him, girl. He might take that axe from his saddle and trim your toenails."

He smiled.

Clessa hiccupped.

"It seems we are in your charge now," I told Heronpool. "Lead on. How many days shall we be? I am anxious to meet my future daughter-in-law."

Away went the cheeriness I had managed to engender. "Six days," he said pensively. "Six days."

ଓଔଷଓ

T he journey continued as soon as our new escorts finished
loading their gear. It was obvious the Fenmarchers had no
desire to spend another night in the vicinity of the watchtower.

Several hours later, we came to a place where the land
dropped away. Heronpool ordered everyone into a single file,
riders on foot leading their mounts. We proceeded along a path
that was often so narrow the warhorses barely squeezed along.
Here and there retaining walls and bridges of stout rope and
planks proved this was an official route, maintained by Alvos's
roadsmen, but most sections of it had been etched into the
mountainside by no method more elaborate than the action of
foot, hoof, and boot over a period of centuries.

From time to time I caught a glimpse of trailside brush, a
rock outcropping, or a wind-twisted canyon juniper, but for the
most part I saw little. The steepness of the terrain kept the
palanquin canted at an angle, and so just before heading down,
my servants had fastened padding tight around me to keep me
from rolling off. This left me in a bowl that obscured much of
my view. To make matters worse, on the second switchback I
toppled onto one ear.

I did not call out. It was difficult enough to be so dependent
on others for simple locomotion. I refused to have to beg for aid.

The person who came to my rescue was none other than
Heronpool. He had stationed himself at a widening of the trail in
order to inspect his company as it passed by. When he saw what
had become of me, he halted my palanquin and set me upright.

"Thank you," I said.

"You are welcome," he answered. From that point on,
wherever the trail's width permitted it, he walked beside the
palanquin.

In the midst of the next section of trail, the stench of horse dung wafted strongly over us. Freed of the weight of their riders, it seemed many animals had been inspired to void their bowels, doing so at the very part of the journey when we were least able to avoid the fumes. Heronpool leaned down at trailside and plucked a flower. He lay the bloom next to my cheek, where its scent predominated.

I smiled as I took in the aroma. It was musky, very much like bell lily, a favorite of mine. "What do you call this?"

"Snow lily," he replied. "It grows only in these heights."

Eventually the grade was interrupted by a broad ledge. Here the company halted so that the knights could rest, and the grooms give the horses and mules a few mouthfuls of feed and some water.

My bearers set me down. To their credit, they chose a spot as far from the brink as they could. But as usual, they gave no thought to my angle of view.

Heronpool was not so unsolicitous. "The vantage here is like nothing else in the kingdom," he said. "Do you wish to see?"

"Very much," I replied.

He cradled me and my seep-cloth in his hands and carried me to an outlook. Finally I could properly gaze at the vista. He was correct. It was magnificent. A gorge of timbered slopes, granite faces, and waterfalls gave way to a plain of pastures, tilled fields, villages, and of course, some of the wetlands for which Fenmarch was named. Mists were burning off in the lowest places, revealing dripping green foliage and gleaming lakes.

"You are kind to me, Count Heronpool. You freely do what my own subjects would not, even should I ask."

"You are treated cruelly," he replied. "Should I echo it? I

would think less of myself if I did."

I liked him. He was a confident young buck, but in him, poise had led to forthrightness rather than arrogance.

"Tell me, sir. Do you think me a criminal?"

He hesitated.

"Please, speak you mind. I take no offense. I have no tender parts left."

"Were you guilty?" he asked.

"I cuckolded the king, if that's what you mean."

"Then yes, you are a criminal."

"But not deserving of cruelty?"

"No one deserves that. A king's laws and a king's will must be obeyed, but mercy is the mark of a true sovereign. Surely, in your case, a simple execution would have sufficed."

"Would Alvos have been merciful?"

"He is a stern king, but he is just."

"It seems I married the wrong prince," I said. "Not that I could have done otherwise. A woman of my rank rarely gets to choose her bridegroom."

He was silent.

"Is aught wrong, Count Heronpool?"

"These are somber matters we speak of, Ma'am. Let us enjoy the view. We must be on our way again soon, if we are to reach the best place to camp for the night."

He was right. Enjoy the view I did, along with the lingering essence of snow lily.

めくぐもん

The following day brought us into heavy stands of timber. Here Heronpool again demonstrated his quality.

Clessa was riding just ahead of my palanquin. I do not know what signal of danger alerted Heronpool. Perhaps he heard a creak as a bowstring tightened, perhaps he caught a glimpse of an enemy rising from a place of concealment. Whatever it was, he suddenly leaped from his mount, yanked Clessa out of her saddle, and threw her to the ground, covering her with his own armored form.

Arrows sang through the air. One whisked through the space I had just occupied, missing me only because my bearers had plunged into defensive squats.

Things happened very quickly after that, so quickly I could hardly follow it all. Heronpool sprang to his feet, barking directives. I think he said, "Archers, 'ware the branches. The rest, to your tandems."

His men understood their roles well. Most, I believe, were in motion even before he spoke. His archers fired into the trees. I heard grunts of pain and heavy impacts; they had hit at least two targets. Other knights charged around nearby trees, any with boles large enough to conceal ambushers. They moved in pairs, the first man with shield set to deflect arrows or blades, the second following with a weapon out, ready to seize the offensive.

The closest exchange happened right where I could witness it all transpire. A tandem met a brigand as he charged from a camouflaged hollow.

The brigand was a large, formidable man. He kicked so hard he knocked the shield man over. His prowess was such that when the second man skewered him with a pike thrust, he still managed to swing his axe and crush the pike wielder's ribcage. Only then did he fall.

The pikeman swayed. His knees buckled as his partner reached him and helped him to the ground.

With that, the battle ended, save for one fleeing man being noisily cut down in a patch of bracken well away from the trail.

There had been no more than half a dozen ambushers. They had come to achieve their goal with stealth and surprise, not force of arms.

A few paces from me Clessa sat up, eyes narrowing as she surveyed the dirt on her dress. Muttering, she rubbed the hip she had landed upon when Heronpool had tugged her from the saddle.

Heronpool returned, having established that the threat was dealt with, and having ordered further scouting of the vicinity.

"You read the situation well," I told him. "If I am not mistaken those first arrows were aimed at Clessa."

My daughter's sputters ceased. Her eyes widened. As I had suspected, she had not grasped the nature of what had just happened, and how fortunate she was to be alive.

"We were too strong a party for robbers to trifle with," Heronpool confirmed. "So they had to be assassins, sent to kill the royal hostage and spoil the peacemaking."

"Thank the viscount, Clessa."

Her hands were trembling. She pressed her bosom, as if needing to quiet her heart before she could utter a word. "Th-thank you, Count Heronpool."

"I am charged with your safety. I simply did my duty. You can thank me by agreeing to wear armor until we clear the forest."

"As you wish," she said. I was pleased to hear what I accepted as genuine humility in her tone.

"I see you are anxious to go to your man over there," I said. "Please do not tarry on our account. I fear he is not long for this world."

I had not even finished my statement before Heronpool knelt where his fallen comrade lay at the base of a piedmont cedar. The loam beneath the latter's torso was dark. Crimson froth leaked from his mouth as he labored to draw breath.

Heronpool clasped the pikeman's hand, providing something to squeeze during the spasms of pain. "I will tell all of your valor."

The dying man looked at Heronpool imploringly, but his attempt to speak only produced a gurgling cough. Heronpool understood despite the lack of words.

"Your widow and son need not fear. If need be I will take them into my own castle until their situation is resolved. Her name is Mantha. The boy is Vristin. I swear I will look after their welfare."

The deep creases in the pikeman's brow eased. He closed his eyes. His chest still rose and fell, but weakly. It would be not long now. Heronpool remained, keeping the vigil.

"Clessa," I said.

"M-mother?"

"Our destination is too far off to take the body with us. The rites must be held here. Begin gathering deadfall branches for the pyre. Carry the wood personally. Pile it where they recommend. Do you understand?"

"I do, Mother."

She did as I asked. It seemed that even with this child, I might still do some good.

C3C38O8O

When we reached the capital of Fenmarch, the townsfolk gawked and exclaimed during our procession through the streets. Surely they had been told the visiting queen would consist of a head on a cushioned platform, but apparently it had not struck them as something they might confirm for themselves.

Twice, rotten fruit was flung at me and at Clessa. Then excrement. The barrages came from deep within the crowds and

did not strike, save for specks of dung on the livery of my
forward bearer. Each time, the city constables quickly clubbed
anyone who might have been the offenders, before the
misbehavior was imitated at a mob level. Heronpool and all his
men rode with weapons bared.

I feared their precautions would not be enough. These
people had long thought of Sorregal as Fenmarch's greatest
enemy. Some, like the assassins in the forest, would never accept
the prospect of an alliance. But we passed over the drawbridge
of Alvos's castle before any lasting harm was done.

The palace staff was waiting in the courtyard. The
chamberlain approached me and bowed. "Your chambers have
been made ready, Your Majesty. When you and the princess
have refreshed yourselves, the royal family beckons you to the
queen's parlor."

It suited me that we were to be met intimately and out of
public view, in the traditional manner. In the same spirit of
courtesy, I made sure we did not keep our hosts waiting
overlong, though this required haranguing Clessa to finish her
bath and primping with what must, to her, have been
unprecedented alacrity.

"Your hair is fine just like that," I told her as she checked
her reflection yet again.

She frowned as she approached me. "I really have to carry
you myself?"

"It is the only proper way," I said firmly. "And do have a
care not to trip. I should not wish to meet Queen Vamia by
rolling across her parlor carpet and ending up under her skirts."

Clessa was a robust girl and managed the weight quite
easily once she put her mind to it. The chamberlain announced
us and we issued smoothly into a sumptuously appointed room. I
immediately knew Vamia to be one of those women who

compensates for personal lack of beauty by surrounding herself with loveliness. The tapestries and furnishings were of the highest order, and the attire of everyone in the room, even the servants, was resplendent.

The whole ruling clan was there, from Alvos and Vamia to all three princes and their wives to Imileya and her sisters to the white-haired, blind, and quite toothless queen mother. Outnumbered so dramatically, Clessa's hands shook as she set me down, and I briefly wobbled on the pedestal that had been provided for me in the center of the room.

Imileya, fortune be praised, had inherited none of the prunish features of her mother—luck of which her sisters could not boast. I suspected Bredden would have preferred a wife with more bosom, but all in all it did not appear he would have cause to rue what he would find in his bed come the wedding night.

I was struck, however, by what an unanimated expression she wore. She might have been made of wax. I cannot say that everyone in the group smiled as we came into the room, but all seemed to be making the attempt, save her.

Clessa curtsied. The others responded, and greetings and introductions went all round.

"I am told of bloodshed in the mountains," Alvos said. "And a lack of manners from some of the common folk in the streets today. I offer you my apologies."

"No need. Thanks to your protective measures, we are here and unruffled. May I commend in particular your choice of Count Heronpool as chief escort?"

"He is the most loyal man I have," the king said. "A pity he is so low-ranking a peer."

I had thought the compliment a fine way to brighten the conversation, but in its wake the king seemed if anything more taciturn. I would recall this later, though at that moment I credited his subsequent silence to his intrinsic nature.

The crown prince, he who was in line to become Alvos the Fifth, was more demonstrative. When he said it was the privilege of Fenmarch to keep Clessa as their guest for the year, he sounded so sincere Clessa actually smiled.

More pleasantries ensued. Whether we had an audience or not, I knew this would be the way of it, for to speak of anything controversial or unresolved at this point would be an unforgivable breach of protocol. Finally the time came for Clessa and me to return to our guest quarters, and the family to their suites, in order to prepare for supper.

"Imileya," said her mother, "you have not given Queen Daena your kisses."

Imileya blanched. It was the first real reaction I had seen from her.

Vamia frowned. Alvos opened his mouth for what I am sure would be a command for Imileya to obey her mother's directive.

"I am less kissable than I once was," I interjected. "If it please you, Clessa will be my proxy."

Vamia and Alvos looked at one another, and shrugged.

Imileya rose from her divan, jittery with relief. She kissed my daughter on each cheek, and Clessa responded in kind.

Everyone present appeared satisfied that etiquette had been observed. Once Imileya was certain no further ordeal was involved, she allowed herself to look straight at me. She blushed.

"Do not fret," I said. "We have plenty of time to get to know one another."

At this, she went pale again.

೫೫ఔ෨෨

The next evening a great banquet was held in celebration of the betrothal. Though I of course could not partake of the food, I was given the seat of honor at the foot of the high table, directly opposite Alvos and Vamia. Imileya was seated at the king's right. The arrangement gave me a fine opportunity to observe my daughter-in-law to be; moreover, I could do so from a distance where she would not overly conscious of the scrutiny.

Her role for the next few hours was to graciously accept the best wishes of the peers of the realm who had gathered for this last formal opportunity to convey their respects before she was trundled off to Sorregal. She handled the obligation with aplomb. I was encouraged to see it, for it showed she might do equally well in years to come at state functions as Bredden's queen.

But in between the speeches and the presentation of gifts, when allowed to sit and partake of her repast, she was overly quiet. Almost absent. She was only at ease when she could slip into responses of the sort any princess rehearses throughout her upbringing.

And then I caught a glimpse of the true Imileya.

She tried to be furtive, but I saw her attention drift to her right, across the table and slightly toward my end. Her glance paused on a young noble seated there.

It was Norl, Viscount of Heronpool.

Aside from Clessa, he was the one person present with whom I was acquainted to any degree, and so I had watched him, growing ever more curious why he stared so much at his plate. It certainly would not have been his interest in the food, for he ate half-heartedly and in small quantity. Now he tilted his head up and it happened that his and Imileya's gazes met.

For a moment—no more the time it took the king to lift his goblet from table to mouth—Imileya looked at Heronpool, and he looked at her.

Suddenly, I was twelve years in the past. Suddenly, I was no bodiless head. I had a heart to feel, hands with which to caress, a womanhood ready to be filled. I was gazing into the eyes of Faeyn, back in those heady days when we had recently become lovers. My nostrils widened. Air flowed into my chest. My heart began to thump. A warmth and a dampness claimed me down low, abrupt and intense—a reaction so beyond my ability to contain that it embarrassed me.

That was how it had been with me. Now, here, at this moment, that was how it was with Imileya. She shone with it. Here was a person wholly unlike the numbed, affectless princess I had seen until now.

I knew then what I had to do.

⊗⊙⅋⊘⅋⊙⊗

Four days after my arrival, the return cortege assembled in the courtyard below the main keep. Alvos stood on a balcony, observing the leavetaking where he could pretend to be stoic. Heronpool had been right to call his king stern, but I did not believe Alvos found it easy to let his child go. I suspected tears had been shed earlier, in private.

Clessa hovered near, chewing her lower lip while the saddles were cinched and final tallies of supplies counted off.

"Have you come to say good-by, child?" I asked.

She jumped at the sound of my voice. "What if all goes awry?" She was trembling. "What if I am left a prisoner here forever?"

"Attend to the things you can influence," I advised. "Make friends here, and no matter what happens in Sorregal, you may thrive."

She pondered this. "Mother?"

"Yes?"

"If I do return, I would like to talk with you more often."

"I would like that," I said.

Across the courtyard the leader of the cortege put in his first appearance. It was none other than Heronpool. All at once, Imileya's attention shifted from the balcony to the level of our company. She tried her best not to stare straight at the viscount, but I was not fooled.

ം8രു8ഠ8ഠ

W e set out across the lowlands of Fenmarch. Day by day, the mountains rose higher across our horizon. I found Heronpool difficult to engage in conversation. He had been given to serious moods the whole time I had known him, but now he was downright solemn.

Imileya contrived at least once a day to ride beside him. He did not, as far as I could tell, attempt to seek her out in kind. They were always too far to allow me to eavesdrop, but I noted that they did not smile. They did not gesture at this and that, as would two people talking about the view or recounting anecdotes meant to entertain. On the afternoon we reached the foothills, Imileya stiffened at whatever he said to her, and Heronpool parted from her with abruptness, ostensibly to tell a man to fasten a pack mule's load better.

Imileya's posture changed. She was a capable horsewoman, and typically rode with spine straight and hands easy on the reins. But from that point on she sagged, and her mare took its cues from the animal ahead of it.

ം8രു8ഠ8ഠ

Wdropcap[W]e passed through the forest where the assassins had attacked our party, and in due course we reached the steep grade. The sun had only just hidden itself behind a peak to the west, but Heronpool declared we would set up camp at the base of the incline, to leave us fresh for the climb. I judged we would negotiate the highest switchback by noon the next day. After that the final leg to the watchtower would be only a matter of hours.

The men occupied themselves setting up cookfires, stowing gear, and seeing to the horses and mules. Imileya kept stealing glances at Heronpool. The viscount pretended to be preoccupied with his responsibilities.

As usual, the tent I shared with the princess was the first to be set up. I told my bearers to place me inside at once. "Come, girl," I told Imileya. "We must talk."

When we were settled, I on my high cushioned stool and Imileya on one of normal height, so that we faced one another at the same eye level, I told my bearers to leave, and to be sure no one was lurking within hearing range.

Imileya fidgeted. "What is it, ma'am? Is aught wrong?"

"Tonight is your last night in the territory of Fenmarch. We will reach the watchtower tomorrow well before sunset."

"I have been told as much," she said.

"Then tonight is your last chance to lie with Heronpool."

Her stool rocked back, and she nearly tumbled before she restored her balance. "What are you on about? Do you seek to trap me?"

"It is no trap. If you wish it, I would allow you to stow me in that chest over there, tucked among your scarves and belts, whilst you and Heronpool seize your moment. If I am ever asked, I will swear I attended you throughout the night, and no man visited you."

"You are a madwoman."

"Granted," I said. "My head was chopped off. My lover was tortured and killed in front of my eyes. For ten years I have been loathed, even by some of my children. Would your priorities not change, had you gone through all that? I tell you the offer is real. Do you not wish to lie with Heronpool? Are you not in love with him? Have you not already consummated your affection in seasons past?"

She quailed. "Am I so transparent?"

"To me? Yes. You must learn to be more circumspect. Heronpool has the knack well enough. I will coach you. A queen must excel in hiding secrets."

"You speak as if you would let me become queen, given what you know."

"I will," I said. "I believe you are right for my son."

"How can that be?" she said, her tone growing miserable. "For I would take your offer. I would lie with Heronpool. I would ravish him all this night. But he will not be part of it. Not now I am betrothed to another man."

"Oh, my dear girl," I said. "I am so sorry."

She hiccupped. Her voice grew hoarse. "I would have run away with him a month ago, if he had been willing."

"You need not explain," I said. "Duty. Honor."

Tears began to pour down her cheeks. "Yes."

"In him, those principles trump passion. The important thing is that in you, they do not. You would have lain with him." I gave her as tender a smile of approval as I had ever summoned for anyone other than Bredden. "You have a fire in you. You failed to suppress it even when displaying it put your very life at risk. My son needs a companion with such fire."

"But surely, he would be angry with me, if he knew."

"I do not say you should tell him. I do say that if you were a woman of ice, you would be no good to him. His spirit would dwindle with such a mate as that."

"But I do not burn for *him*."

"No. Not yet."

"How can I ever?"

"Because you must?" I asked.

She uttered a small squeak.

In the gentlest voice I could manage, I said, "Tell me what you love most about Heronpool."

When she let the question truly infiltrate her consciousness, she smiled. "His compassion. His—oh, it is many things. He is *inspiring*."

"And so he is," I said. "Tell me, do you think he is the only man in the world of such character?"

She blinked.

"Tonight, it seems, will be a lonely one," I told her in fervent sympathy. "Tomorrow will be bitter. Your heart will break when your beloved turns and rides the other way. But in a year, my daughter? In a year, there will be a wedding. I believe it will be a happy occasion for all concerned. Do you think me mad to say so?"

She stared at me full on, her cheeks and lashes wet, her hands tightly clasped in her lap. I could have been looking in a mirror, cast back to the point when I was a bride-to-be, about to meet my betrothed. But my destiny had thrust me into the arms of Pathren. She was intended for Bredden. That was an entirely different thing.

"You are indeed a madwoman," Imileya murmured. "But you are growing on me."

THE TOPAZ DESERT

by Catherine Asaro

Catherine Asaro combines her scientific background (PhD, Harvard University), her artistic achievements in ballet and a rare sensitivity to human emotions. Her paper, "Complex Speeds and Special Relativity," (*The American Journal of Physics*, April 1996) forms the basis for some of her science-fiction novels, including the Saga of the Skolian Empire.

Her many awards include a Nebula® for her novel, *The Quantum Rose*, the Homer Award for her near-future suspense novel, *The Veiled Web,* and the Analog Readers Poll Award for her novellas, "Walk in Silence," "A Roll of the Dice," and "Aurora in Four Voices." Her work has been nominated for the Hugo, and she is a three-time winner of the Romantic Times Book Club award for Best Science Fiction Novel.

Her romantic fantasy, *The Charmed Sphere*, (Lost Continent Series) helped to launch Luna Books. Recent and upcoming works include a Skolian Empire novel, *The Ruby Dice* (Baen, 2008), a science fiction thriller, *Alpha* (Baen, 2007), and a new Lost Continent fantasy, *The Night Bird* (Luna, 2008).

Catherine and her family live in Columbia, Maryland. Her website is http://www.sff.net/people/asaro/

Crystals have long been used in traditional lore as well as

fantastical fiction, for their ability to focus and enhance consciousness as well as light. Here, Catherine adds a new dimension, a metaphor for seeing into the heart of another, the light that heals and binds us together.

Tanzi's gentlest spell earned her a brutal sentence.

She was doing nothing more nefarious than mopping the parquetry floor in the parlor of Goodman Arv's house. The shapes of the tiles stirred her mage power, all those diamonds and hexagons fitted together. She suppressed the swirl of magic so no spell would betray her.

In the nursery, the baby let out a wail, crying for her mother. Both Arv and his wife, however, had gone to Arv's jewelry shop in town. Tanzi was only the maid, not a nanny, but she couldn't bear to hear the infant cry. She hurried to the nursery and found the baby lying on her back in her cradle, angrily waving her tiny fists.

"It's all right, sweetings." Tanzi picked up the little girl. She swayed back and forth, crooning, but nothing calmed the child. The girl's distress tore at her. Tanzi glanced out the doorway to the parlor. She was alone. No one would know if she formed one little spell.

With care, Tanzi laid the infant in her cradle. Then she pulled out the pendant she wore on a chain and curled her fingers around the cylinder of glazed ceramic. Mages needed geometric shapes to create spells. Two-dimensional shapes worked, the more sides the better, but three-dimensional were even stronger. The cylinder was the most powerful form Tanzi could draw on.

Spells went according to color, like a rainbow. Red brought warmth or light, orange eased pain, yellow soothed emotions, green read emotions, blue healed injuries, and indigo healed emotions. Just as she could draw power from shapes up to a maximum number of sides, she could perform spells to her maximum color, starting at red and going up to green. Blue hovered at the edge of her ability.

Tanzi focused through the cylinder and called forth a spell, combining orange and yellow. Gold light bathed the crib. She sung a lullaby, soft notes enhanced by the spell. The baby's cries eased, and within moments she had quieted. She cooed and gurgled.

"Stop, witch!" a man shouted.

Tanzi whirled, her long hair flying. Arv stood in the doorway, staring as if she were a demon. Tall and heavy, with more fat than muscle, he towered. He strode forward and shoved Tanzi away from the cradle, throwing her against the wall. She lost her hold on the spell, and the gold light faded, darkening the room. The baby immediately let out a howl of protest.

Arv grabbed his daughter and backed away from Tanzi. "Don't touch her!" The frightened child began to cry in earnest.

"I was calming her," Tanzi said. "I would never hurt that beautiful child. I swear it!"

"You're wicked." His face twisted. "A witch and a temptress."

The click of boots hurrying across a floor filled the parlor. Then Arv's wife was there, taking the baby, holding her in one arm while she made warding motions against Tanzi. The infant wailed with alarm.

"Get the guardsmen," Arv told his wife, never taking his gaze off Tanzi. He had her cornered, for the only exit was the archway he filled with his overwhelming size.

"Please," Tanzi said. "I meant no harm." His guardsmen terrified her. Arv acted as a magistrate, in addition to owning the only jewelry store in the town of Azure-Tal. The guardsmen drank at the tavern with him and shared his casual, unthinking cruelty.

"Come here," he said.

She walked forward warily and stood before him. "I promise, I'll never make the light again."

He closed his hand around her arm. "That's right. Never again, witch."

Her courage faltered. Centuries ago, people had burned witches. Surely, nothing like that happened any more. . . .

Arv pushed her out of the room. "We're going to the Holding House."

"No!" Tanzi twisted in his hold, but she was no match for the beefy jeweler. He pulled her through the parlor, to the front door. As he threw it open, a shock of cold air hit her. She lurched as he drew her along the path between the lush flowerbeds with their turtle sculptures. Stones scraped the soles of her bare feet.

"Please," she said, "at least let me get my cloak and shoes."

He put his arm around her torso, forcing her to keep up with him. "You won't need anything, Tanzi girl." Loathing saturated his voice. "It's time you found out what happens to witches with your sinful behavior." His voice hardened and his hold tightened. "Yes, it's time."

"But I haven't done anything!" She felt ill. He could do whatever he wanted at the Holding House where they imprisoned criminals. Although only a magistrate, he was the highest law officer in the small town. People were in awe of him because he was so rich. If he sentenced her for witchcraft, no one would naysay him.

Four large men strode along the lane beside Arv's home. They wore the familiar blue and green uniforms of Azure-Tal guardsmen. Arv gathered with them in front of the house, surrounding Tanzi. She felt trapped. They put their hands on her, grasping her arms or shoulders. She twisted, trying to escape. As they held her firm, the neckline of her dress ripped. Arv and his men had a darkness in their stares, and she feared what they would do before they carried out her sentence.

"She almost murdered my baby," Arv said. "She's a witch. We must crush her evil or gods only know what she'll do next."

No one questioned him, and she saw no sympathy in their faces, only a relentless determination. They set off, Arv with his arm around her bared shoulders and a guardsman gripping her elbow. She had to run to keep up with their long strides or be dragged. Shadows stretched from one crooked house to another as twilight darkened the streets. They ducked into an alley where no one would see them.

Arv spoke to the guardsman holding her arm. "You have the cat-flail?" When the man nodded, Arv said, "The original sentence for witchcraft was forty lashes."

"Forty with that whip could kill her," the man told him.

"If it doesn't," Arv said grimly, "we'll use the stake and fire. We can't let her go on like this. First she tries to murder my baby. Then who? All of us?"

"Please," Tanzi said. "I never hurt anyone!"

Her plea had the opposite effect of what she hoped. Arv slid down his hand and held her breast, his thumb pressing her nipple. As he did so, his hold on her shoulders loosened. She held her breath, ready and alert. A moment later, the guardsman clenching her arm coughed—and in that instant, his grip relaxed.

With a strength driven by fear, Tanzi wrenched free and threw herself between two of the guards. Caught by surprise, they hesitated only an instant, but it was enough. She sprinted into a narrower alley and raced through the darkened town.

ଔଔୠ୰ୠ

Tanzi scrambled up the brush-laden hill. Thistles jabbed her feet, but she kept going. At the top, she dropped down so no one could see her against the starry, moonless sky. In the distance, sparks glinted in the night. Torches. Arv and his men were searching the barrows west of Azure-Tal, rather than the hills to the northeast.

Closing her eyes, Tanzi exhaled. It seemed she wouldn't die tonight after all. She could almost hear Arv shouting, *Witch!* Others had called her that, but never to her face. She tried to hide her abilities. During her mother's long illness, the spells had been a gift, allowing Tanzi to ease her pain. But since her mother's death, she had lived with Arv's family as their maid and avoided spells.

Until tonight.

If only she hadn't done it. She had always sensed darkness within Arv, but it had never burst out this way before. How could he believe she would hurt his baby? A mage would no more do harm with her spells than a doctor would hurt people with his medicine.

She slid down the hill. When her silhouette would no longer show against the sky, she jumped up and *ran.* Her bare feet hurt and she shivered in her torn dress, but she would far rather be cold and sore than dead.

At the bottom of the hill, she limped along a dry creek bed and tried to plan. Three days walking would take her to the border of her own country, Shazire, with Aronsdale in the north. To the east, the land grew more and more inhospitable until it reached the stark country of Jazid. She decided on Aronsdale.

Tanzi took a breath and ran again, racing away from Arv, from Azure-Tal, and from everything she had ever known. She ran as stars wheeled overhead, and then she ran farther, stumbling through the night. When she could run no more, she staggered, pushing herself beyond fatigue, beyond pain, until exhaustion caught her in its iron grip, and she collapsed to the ground.

❦❦❦❦

Rocks filled Zebb's shack. Ugly and uneven, they lay piled in old, cracked chests. Mottled ores sat clumped on a rickety table in one corner. An oil lamp hanging on a nail in the wall drew a few desultory sparkles from the stones. Merchant Izad, who came through every few months, claimed the rocks polished up well and looked pretty in necklaces. Except for the turquoise, Zebb thought the rocks were ugly, but as long as the merchant kept trading for them, Zebb would keep mining.

He combed his fingers through his hair and brushed sand off his tattered shirt. He supposed he should spend more time tending to himself. But why? He had no one to do it for. He had been alone for twelve years.

Zebb tried to imagine a woman here. Maybe she would caress his arm or smile. He ached with an old longing. Some men were happy alone, but he wasn't one of them. He had asked the caravan traders who came through once a year if they could find him a wife, and he offered his rocks in payment. They hadn't bothered to look at his wares, convinced it wouldn't be worth their while, unless he wanted a woman who was sixty or missing her teeth. He had considered it, for his solitude felt heavier each year. The few women he met didn't want him; he was too big, too coarse, too rough-spoken. He didn't bathe. Why bother? He never saw anyone except his friend Benjazin or Merchant Izad, and neither of them gave a dragon's fart if he stank. Maybe he wouldn't like being married. A wife might insist he wash. Hell, he'd do even that if she would have him.

With a sigh, Zebb leaned against the door frame, gazing across the desert to the low hills in the north, where he mined his stones. He dutifully gave two parts in ten to the taxmen when they came through, and the rest lay piled in his hut.

A figure appeared over the nearest hill. Zebb squinted in the heat shimmer. The stranger wore dark clothes, had dark hair, and appeared to be a tall man. Well, that defined the majority of Jazid's population. Zebb regarded him with an ingrained distrust of strangers.

Then the man waved, and Zebb grinned. *Hah!* It was Benjazin, the only other person within fifty miles. Zebb was glad to see the old grouchy mule.

Like Zebb, Benjazin had spent his life in the Jazid desert. Zebb had lived with his parents in this same hut, with his mother after his father died of lung disease, and by himself after another miner wooed away his mother twelve years ago. Zebb had been fifteen then, an adult, so he had stayed here. Alone.

Zebb supposed if he traveled to the big cities, he could see people and sell more of his wares. He never knew how to act around strangers, though.

Benjazin stalked across the desert, his black robe rippling in the hot wind. As he came nearer, Zebb could see his face, the familiar craggy eyebrows, weathered skin, and jutting nose.

"Eh, Benjazin," he said.

"Zebb." Benjazin nodded.

"How's rocks?" Zebb asked. The greeting had started as a joke years ago and become a habit.

"The same." Benjazin leaned against the shack. "Got me a water pump from a new merchant."

"Eh." Zebb could use a pump. "Izad'll be through in a few days. If I give him ten moons, he'll trade a pump." Zebb had named the white stones "moons" after the disk in the night sky.

Benjazin smirked. "This new fellow only asked for one."

"One, ten, doesn't matter." Zebb shrugged. "I got hundreds."

"I've been thinking."

Zebb grinned at him. "Did it crack your head?"

Benjazin scowled. "Not funny."

"What're you thinking, then?"

"It's hot here."

"Well, that's brilliant, Benj. Could have cracked three heads with that one."

Benjazin didn't laugh. "No one lives here. Everyone dies. *I'm* dying. That new merchant says Aronsdale has farms. And *lakes*." He squinted at Zebb. "And women. Maybe I could find me one."

"Sounds serious."

"Yep."

"So you're leaving?" Zebb didn't want it to be true.

"I think so. Not right away. But soon."

"I won't have no one to talk to."

"You can go, too."

Zebb glowered at him. "I'm happy here."

"You ever known anything else?"

"No," Zebb admitted.

"Then how do you know you're happy?"

Zebb pondered that. "I can't say."

The thought stayed with him all morning. If Benjazin left, he would have no one to talk to except the occasional merchant. Zebb didn't know how he felt, but it didn't seem "happy." More like being trapped in a mine after a cave-in. He loved this place and didn't want to leave, but if he stayed, he had nothing to look forward to. Nothing but loneliness.

ை௸

Tanzi awoke to someone treating her wounds.

She lifted her head, disoriented. She lay on a blue carpet swirled with gold dragons. An unfamiliar man was washing the cuts on her foot.

"What. . . ?" she asked thickly.

He glanced up with a start. "Ho! You're awake."

"Who are you?" she asked. He looked Jazidian, in his dark trousers and a black shirt with red slashes. Like most everyone in the settled lands, he had dark hair and eyes. It was one reason people considered Tanzi strange; she had red-gold hair.

"Name's Izad." He set down her foot and picked up a blue-glass vial from the carpet. "I'm a merchant."

Tanzi sat up, favoring her aching muscles. The last she recalled, she had been staggering through darkness. Now here she was, in a trader's wagon. The lower walls and floor were wood, at least as much as she could see of them, with chests, bolts of silk, and goods piled up. Cloth formed the upper walls and roof, patterned with red and black triangles. Jazid's Shadow Dragon curled on them in green, and daylight filtered through the material.

"Why am I in your wagon?" Tanzi asked.

Izad opened the vial and poured blue cream on his palm. "I found you half dead in the hills last night." He rubbed the salve into her torn feet.

Tanzi groaned with relief as the ointment spread its balm over her gashes. "That feels good."

"Glad to hear it." His voice oozed.

She pushed back her hair—and froze when she realized red cloth covered her arm. Looking down, she flushed. She wore nothing except a red silk robe. Izad must have changed her clothes, which meant he had seen her naked.

The merchant gave her an oily smile. "Come now, honey, don't look that way. I did nothing untoward."

It might be true, but her unease deepened. She felt painfully vulnerable under his stare. She had no family to protect her; she knew nothing of her father, and her mother was dead. She drew the robe tighter around her body. When she glanced down to see if the pendant between her breasts showed through the silk, she realized the sheer cloth outlined her nipples. Flushing, she loosened the robe.

"You can let me off at the next town," she said.

Izad watched her with indolent fascination. "I'm going to Jazid. No towns between here and the border." He leaned back on a roll of carpet. "Tell me the truth, honey. It's not safe for you to stay here, is it?"

Too quickly, she said, "Of course it is."

"A pretty girl stranded in the middle of nowhere, wearing nothing except a torn dress, with bruises on her breasts." He shrugged languidly. "It's not hard to guess what happened."

"It never went that far. I got away from them."

"Them? How many 'them'?"

"Five." She flinched at the memory. "They meant to whip me to death. Or burn me at the stake."

"Why would they whip a delicious little thing like you?" He looked far too intrigued by the thought.

Tanzi scowled at him. "Arv says I hexed his baby." Maybe that would scare him off.

Izad sat upright. "Arv? The jeweler in Azure-Tal?"

This merchant knew him? It was possible; Arv bought raw gems and designed finished jewelry, which he sold all over the settled lands, through caravans and traveling merchants.

"Not that Arv," Tanzi said.

"Only one, as far as I know. You weren't far from Azure-

Tal, either." Satisfaction spread across his face. "This changes things. I've heard say, he's the richest man in northern Shazire." Then he allowed, "Not that northern Shazire has that many people. But still. I'll bet it'd be worth a lot to him to get you back. And I'll have the favor of a powerful man."

"No!" Panic welled in Tanzi. "He'll put me to death!"

"Now there," he murmured. "Why would he kill such a scrumptious morsel?" He rubbed his palms together. "Finding you was my luck, eh? I thought of keeping you, but this is better."

"No! Let me stay with you."

"That won't get me squat." He tilted his head. "Unless you can give me as much wealth as I could get from him."

"Yes." Tanzi grasped at hope, ready to tell him anything. "All the gems you want."

"Is that so?" He smiled beneficently. "And where would you be getting all these lovely gems?"

Her face heated. "I—well, I've, um—I have them—"

"From nowhere, hmm?" His leaned forward. "You haven't anything to your name but that pretty body. I'll bet Goodman Arv is willing to pay a lot for it."

"He's married!"

"That's never stopped him before." His smirk returned. "I have to go to Jazid for a few days, finish my rounds. You can stay with me." With satisfaction, he added, "It will be my honor to escort you safely home. Then we'll see what our rich jeweler says."

Nausea surged within Tanzi. Arv would be furious over her escape, and she would pay the price of his anger. Her race to freedom had only landed her in worse trouble.

ᬓᬓᬓᬓᬓ

*Z*ebb awoke to the rattle of a wagon. He sat up, rubbing his eyes. It had been too hot to work, so he had come into his shack to sleep away the blistering afternoon. Day had since cooled into evening, and he had mostly stopped sweating. He wore only his ragged trousers, but he didn't worry. Izad couldn't care less, and that sounded like the merchant's wagon.

He ambled to the open door. He never closed it, except in the rare sandstorm. Yep, Izad's wagon was trundling up with its two ornery oxen. Izad himself sat on the driver's plank in a black robe. Zebb was glad for the company. He had been feeling dull and sad ever since Benjazin said he meant to leave.

The merchant pulled to a stop, jumped down, and strode to the shack. "Zebb," he said, by way of greeting.

"Izad."

The older man surveyed the dying garden around the hut. "Place looks bad. You want more seeds?"

Zebb snorted. "I'm glad to see you, too."

Izad gave a rusty laugh. "So. What do you need? I've food, carpets, household goods, mining equipment. Drinking water, of course. That chocolate you like. Bitter-tea." He squinted at Zebb's ramshackle hut. "Building materials."

"Food and water." Zebb scratched his stomach. "The sweets. A shovel." He stopped, distracted by Izad's wagon. Damned if it didn't look like someone had tweaked open a flap in the back.

"What's in your wagon?" Zebb asked.

"Nothing," Izad said quickly.

Before Zebb could answer, the flap rustled and a girl jumped out. Dragon's breath! He couldn't absorb the sight at first, only that a red robe shimmered around her body.

Her *body*.

He felt as if his pulse stopped. Such curves. A creature

that pretty couldn't be real. Then he realized the lighter color on her robe wasn't cloth, it was her hair. The colors! Underneath, it shone like finely polished copper. The sun had streaked the top layer gold, pure and shiny as a coin. It flowed to her waist in waves, with a luster that put the richest lodes of ore to shame.

And her face. Soft cheeks. Lips full and red. Little nose. She watched him with huge eyes. *Blue* eyes. How could she have the sky in her eyes? It was impossible. She was a goddess.

Izad started toward her, and for some bizarre reason he looked furious. The girl stood like a shy doe, frozen in place.

CRLSO80

Zebb was the largest man Tanzi had ever seen. Also the dirtiest. He wore nothing but ragged trousers that rested low on his hips, torn off at the knees. No trace of fat showed on his work-hardened frame. Tangled black hair fell over his forehead and ears, and down his neck. Curly hair covered his massive chest, arms, and legs, and a heavy beard hid his face. He had impossibly huge feet. It didn't surprise her that he went barefoot; she couldn't imagine where he would find shoes to fit. She had heard men in Jazid were larger and less civilized than in other places, but until this moment she hadn't really understood.

His large eyes were gentle, though, a startling contrast to his otherwise fierce appearance. What she noticed most, in her desperation, were his huge biceps. He could surely break a man in two—perhaps *Izad*, may the Shadow Dragon crisp the merchant's slimy soul!

Izad had kept her prisoner for six days, manacling her when he slept and watching her like a snake ready to strike the rest of the time. He never mistreated her; he wanted her in good shape, including her virginity, which he assumed Arv would pay extra for. Although he expressed remorse that Arv might hurt her, he either didn't believe they intended to execute her or else he didn't care. He didn't trust anyone. Zebb had pretty much been the only person he hadn't made some ominous comment about. She couldn't run off, for she would die without supplies in the bleak desert. Zebb was her last hope.

When Tanzi saw the huge man with the bristly face, however, she wondered if she had any hope at all. She folded her arms, ill-at-ease as hot wind fluttered her robe, for she wore nothing underneath. The only women's undergarments Izad carried were annoying metal bras and skirts meant to be sexy rather than comfortable. That he wanted her to wear them only firmed her resolve never to touch the wretched things.

Izad strode toward her, his face contorted with anger, which was no surprise given than he had ordered her to stay out of sight. She darted around the wagon. When Izad followed, she sprinted to Zebb. Standing in front of the miner, she looked up— and up—into his face.

"Let me stay with you," she entreated him. "Please. The merchant is going to hurt me."

Zebb seemed bewildered. "Why would Izad hurt you?"

Izad reached them and grasped her arm. "Don't mind her, she's unstable."

"No!" Tanzi jerked away. To Zebb she said, "Please help me. He's going to sell me."

Zebb looked uncomfortable. "That's what merchants do."

"No! I'll go to a monster who will kill me." Her voice caught. "I want to stay with you."

His face gentled. "I can't afford a girl like you." He spoke with longing. "Though if I could, I surely would."

"Please," she whispered.

Zebb spoke awkwardly to the merchant. "How much?"

Izad blinked at him. "You want to trade rocks for her?"

"You can have all I got," Zebb offered.

"You have *ten chests* of those rocks."

"Izad, I've been alone for so long." Zebb's voice rumbled. "And she *wants* to stay." He seemed stunned by that last.

Tanzi doubted Izad cared about Zebb's loneliness. The merchant didn't immediately turn him down, though. Instead he said, "You'd give me all ten chests?"

"All of 'em," Zebb said, hope in his voice.

"I don't have room in the wagon."

"You're going to see Benjazin, eh?" Zebb asked. When Izad nodded, the miner said, "You always unload a lot of goods with him. You'll have room when you come back."

"What the hell," Izad said. "All right. Buy yourself a pleasure girl."

Tanzi stared in disbelief. She didn't trust Izad's response. He had given in too easily, for Zebb obviously had neither wealth nor influence.

"Not a pleasure girl," Zebb said gruffly. "A wife."

"What difference does it make?" Izad said.

"She's a goddess." Zebb said it with a perfectly straight face. "She might smite me if I offend her."

Tanzi almost laughed, despite her fear. Goodness. What a thought. "I'm not a goddess."

"You look like one." Zebb's sun-weathered skin turned red.

"Oh." Flustered, she said, "Thank you." Then she added, "I promise, I won't smite you."

Rather than laughing, he looked relieved. "I won't force myself on you, neither."

"Then it's decided." Izad pulled Tanzi toward the wagon.

"We'll be back tomorrow."

Zebb took a giant step after him and almost knocked Tanzi over. As she jumped back, she lost her balance.

"Ach!" Zebb grabbed her, his fingers circling her arm and overlapping his thumb. He could have easily crushed her, yet he held her with astonishing gentleness. He dropped her arm quickly, blushing. "I didn't mean to offend."

"It's all right," Tanzi said.

"You have to leave her here," he told Izad. "Otherwise, I'll never see her again."

"I don't have room for your rocks," Izad said. "And I'm sure as hell not giving her to you until you pay me."

Zebb scowled at him. "You told me the same thing when I wanted that pick axe. Then you sold it to someone else."

To Tanzi's surprise, Izad said, "Oh, all right. I'm kind, eh? But you have to marry her now so I know you won't try to give her back instead of paying me."

Tanzi didn't believe for one moment that Izad acted out kindness. He had some sort of plot.

Zebb regarded Tanzi, his gaze softening. "Is that all right? Will y-you m-m-m—" He took a breath. "Marry me?"

Tanzi hoped she wasn't making a mistake. "If you'll have me."

He stared as if she had offered him a gift instead of saddling him with a complete stranger. Then he swung around to Izad. "You get them marriage contracts, afore she changes her mind."

છ૭૨૪૭૪

Zebb stood in the doorway watching as Izad drove away in his wagon. The girl had gone into the house, no doubt staring around his meager hut in shock. He couldn't face her dismay.

No, not "the girl." His wife. He had no idea how to deal with this ethereal apparition. Such an angel couldn't be his.

"Zebb?" Even her sweet voice sounded unreal.

Taking a breath, he around. She stood watching him with those wide, impossibly blue eyes. "I wondered if . . . if you . . ."

"Yes?" His voice cracked and he winced. Fine impression he was making.

"It's been a while, yes?" she asked. "Would you . . . I could—could help—"

He had no idea what she was talking about. "Help what?"

"With your bath."

So! He knew it. A wife would insist on soap and water. Well, he *had* told himself he would do it if he convinced a woman to marry him.

Another thought came to him. She hadn't said, *You should bathe.* She offered to help. He flushed with a heat that had nothing to do with the desert. He had never touched a woman, except hugging his mother when he was very small. He had no idea what women liked, but he knew what he wanted when faced with her beautiful face and ripe body.

"All right." He didn't believe it would happen. She would disappear. Or he would wake up.

"Where do you get water?" she asked.

"At the spring." He started out the door.

"Zebb, wait."

He turned again. She was in the same place, and behind her, his rocks sat grimly in their chests. Maybe he should clean them, too, so she didn't think he lived in a complete hovel.

"Don't you need shoes?" she asked. "A towel? Fresh clothes?"

"Why?"

"You walk barefoot in the desert?"

"Sometimes."

"Oh."

Unsure, he held out his hand. She came forward and clasped her fingers with his. It seemed he should do more, but he didn't know what. She tried to smile, but her lips shook.

A thought came to Zebb. He could smile. He did it sometimes without thinking, when Benjazin made him laugh. He tried, and his face felt as if it creaked, but it seemed to work. She blushed, then dimpled at him.

"Tazina?" he asked. "Is that your name?"

"Tanzi," she said.

"Tanzi. That's nice."

They walked outside, holding hands, Tanzi soft and small at his side.

ೞ⚬ꞥ⚬

The desert looked dead to Tanzi. In the west, the Jagged Teeth cut a serrated line on the horizon; to the east, the Fractured Mountains rose in broken spires against the sky, even larger and more foreboding. As the sun set, shadows enveloped the land. She felt as if she were in an eerie world where time had stopped before the Shadow Dragon finished making the earth.

Gradually, she realized plants did grow here, tough scrub, low to the ground. Zebb took her to a cave in a hillock that buckled out of the earth. He bent over to get through its opening, and she stooped to follow. Inside, he took a lamp from a ledge and lit it with a spark-flint.

As the glow spread, Tanzi gasped. Below them, a cavern glistened. Stalactites hung from the ceiling like gigantic stone icicles, and stalagmites jutted up from the ground in narrow pyramids. A curtain of rock rippled out from one wall, so thin the lamplight shone through it. A spring bubbled across the cavern, and its pool reflected glints of light.

"It's incredible," Tanzi said.

"You like?" Zebb indicated the pool. "We can wash there."

"All right." She blushed, feeling shy. But she couldn't back out. The bath had been her idea, after all.

As they crossed the cave, Zebb took her hand. The pool had clear water and a tumble of stones on its bottom. Sparkly rocks glinted in it, feldspar, called fool's gold, worth almost nothing. Tanzi knew about such things because Arv often brought home gemstones and talked about his work.

Zebb shed his pants with no fuss. She didn't know whether to die of embarrassment or stare in awe. He was utterly unself-conscious, as if it were perfectly natural to disrobe in front of her. Maybe he knew too few women to realize it would startle her. His beautiful body reminded her of statues in Azure-Tal that depicted ancient gods with sculpted physiques. What mesmerized her the most, though, was the evidence of how much he wanted her. Although she had a vague idea about what happened with husbands, she had never seen a man aroused.

"You going to stare at it all day?" he asked curiously.

Her face flaming, Tanzi raised her gaze. "You're beautiful."

He gave a startled snort of laughter. "I'm a warthog!"

"Definitely not," she murmured.

His look changed then, turning sensual as his thick lashes lowered, though she didn't think he realized it. He came forward and put his hands on her shoulders, then slid his palms down her arms, drawing off her robe. She stood still, her eyes downcast. What if he didn't like what he saw? The robe pooled at her feet in ripples of red silk.

"Tanzi." His voice was hoarse. "Look at me, sweetheart."

Startled by the endearment, she raised her gaze. The tenderness in his eyes melted her heart. She laid her hands against his abdomen, and his hair curled under her palms, springy and softer than she expected. It covered his chest and narrowed down to the nest of curls around his erection.

Zebb groaned and pulled her close. As good as his body felt against hers, she also wrinkled her nose. Goodness, didn't the man notice how he smelled?

"Let's get into the water," she said.

He spoke gruffly. "If I'd known you were coming, I would've made myself more presentable."

She reddened, wondering if she would always be so transparent to him. He didn't sound angry, though. In fact, he seemed a good-natured man. He let himself into the pool, and the water rose halfway up his chest. Tanzi sat on the edge and dangled her legs in the water. It slid cool and soothing over her skin, but she still felt too shy to join him.

Zebb retrieved soap from the far edge and lathered his skin and hair. She tingled as she watched, enticed by the ripple of his muscles. His biceps flexed when he lifted his arms to clean his mane of hair. Water glistened on his chest, and the evidence of his desire showed under the surface. He was at ease in her presence; her company seemed to comfort as much as arouse him.

After he finished, he ducked under the water to rinse off. When he came back up, he shook his head, splashing water everywhere. Then he put his hand on his chin. "Did you want this gone, too?"

"Only if you don't mind." She didn't want him to shave if he would rather keep his beard.

"It's just there. Doesn't matter to me." He returned to where he had left the soaps and unsheathed a knife that was lying there. A metal plate served as his mirror. It surprised her that he left his belongings in the open. Then again, if he was the only person for miles, he had no reason to keep them in the shack when he used them here.

She loved watching him shave. His muscles flexed as he soaped his beard and scraped it off with the knife. Water dripped from his hair onto his powerful shoulders and torso. She could see his strong legs under the water, his firm buttocks. She wanted to press up to his back and feel his bottom against her stomach. It took him a while to shave, given all that hair, but she enjoyed watching so much, it seemed no time at all before he finished.

Finally he turned around. "So." He seemed far more awkward about uncovering his face than his body. "Bearable, do you think?"

Bearable? His square chin, high cheekbones, and straight nose were finely made, a good match for his large eyes. The way his features went together took him from attractive to devastating. The scar that ran from his ear partway to his chin only added to his appearance. She couldn't believe such a handsome man had hidden his face behind that bristly beard.

"Very bearable," she said, her voice husky.

His look turned sultry. "Thought you were going to help me wash," he murmured. He seemed unreal, an earth god here in the desert, minding his own business until she barged into his life.

Tanzi eased into the pool and waded deeper. By the time she reached him, the water came over her breasts.

"You're so small," he said. Putting his hands on her waist, he lifted her in the water and walked to a boulder, then set her down so she was sitting on the rock. Water swirled around her waist, and her eyes were almost even with his. Standing between her thighs, he patted her shoulders, her breasts, her arms, as if he wanted to touch her in so many places, he didn't know where to start. He bent his head, but he seemed unsure what to do. Tanzi wasn't sure, either, but she had an idea. Putting her arms around his neck, she drew his head down and closed her eyes.

When their lips touched, though, he jerked back. "What are you doing?"

She opened her eyes halfway. "Kissing you."

"What is that?"

"We press our lips together."

"Why?"

"It feels good." She hesitated. "Or so I've heard."

"Oh." He sounded bewildered, but he closed his eyes as she had done and bent his head, hugging her.

His lips were full and warm. At first, he just touched his mouth on hers. Soon, though, his lips melted against hers. With a sigh, she relaxed into his embrace. Their kiss became an exploration, sensual and languorous. His tongue traced her lips, and she parted them instinctively. He stopped, then kissed her more deeply. With their bodies fitted together and the water lapping on their skin, she felt as if they were floating.

Zebb kept one arm around her waist while he caressed her breast. The more he played with her, the more she tingled. He pulled her hips forward so she was sitting on the edge of the rock with her sensitive folds pressed against his erection. When he tried to enter her, though, she panicked.

"Wait!" she said.

He drew back, his eyes glossy and unfocused. "What?"

"I never—I don't—" She stuttered to a stop.

His smile gentled his face. "Neither have I. Think we can figure it out?"

Tanzi smiled shakily. "I think so. But please don't . . ." She wasn't even sure what she didn't want him to do. Tear her apart? She didn't see how that could *not* happen.

"It's what husbands and wives do," he said. "Why they marry."

"Some marry because they love each other."

"It's the same thing." He hesitated. "Isn't it?"

He thought intimacy was the same as being in love? "I don't think so," she said softly. "But when we know each other better, we might have both."

He pulled her close, his muscles sensuous against her skin. He frightened her, for she felt his tension and contained power. But he took care with her, and it hardly hurt when he entered. At first he went slowly, controlling his force. Then he groaned and buried himself inside of her, and she cried out from a stab of pain.

"Tanzi? What's wrong?" He glanced down, his face concerned. Then his eyes widened. "There's blood!"

Startled, she looked and saw red swirls in the water around their hips, where they were joined together. "It's just me," she said. "It happens when a woman is a virgin."

"Oh." He clumsily stroked her hair back from her face. "Are you all right? Should I stop?"

She touched his cheek. "I have the most finely made man in the settled lands in my arms. I couldn't be better."

With a sigh, he drew her back into his embrace. His hips moved with hers in a steady rhythm. It felt timeless, as if her body knew what her mind had yet to understand. They rocked together and the water swirled around them.

So Tanzi and Zebb made long, sweet love, two lonely

people at risk in a harsh world, coming to each other in tenderness. Together, they found a refuge, though they were in the most inhospitable desert known. It bloomed not with flowers, but with the fertile shoots of what could become love.

ⓢⓒⓡⓢⓞⓢⓞ

Tanzi drifted in a haze. The wavelets in the pool had settled after the passion that she and Zebb shared spent itself. He stood between her legs, sheathed inside of her, his arms around her body, his cheek resting on her head. Night had fallen, leaving them in a small sphere of light from the lamp.

Zebb spoke in a voice rough and full of warmth. "Thank you."

"I'm glad we have each other," Tanzi said as he lifted his head to look at her.

For the first time he gave her a full smile. The grin lit his entire face, and she wondered that she didn't swoon right there. "You can have me like this as long as you want. All the time."

Her laugh sparkled. "We can't *every* moment."

"I suppose we have to eat," he allowed.

Tanzi kissed him. "Let's go back to your house and do that."

"It's dirty. Full of rocks."

"I'll fix it up."

He hesitated. "You don't mind? You're so highborn."

"Highborn! I'm nothing."

"You're something to me."

They clasped hands and crossed the pool. Sitting on its edge, he leaned against a stalagmite and pushed to his feet. He reached down to offer her a hand—and bent too far. Even as she inhaled to call a warning, he pitched forward. He grabbed the stalagmite, but it only caused him to swing to one side. As his feet flew out from under him, he toppled into the pool. His head hit the edge with a loud crack, and he slid under the water.

"No!" Tanzi grabbed his arm. His eyes were closed and bubbles streamed out of his mouth. Pulling him up, she braced him against the side so she could keep his nose and mouth above water. "Zebb! Wake up!"

He didn't stir. Blood ran out of a gash in his head, far too much blood. Although the water buoyed him enough so she could keep his head up, she wasn't strong enough to hoist him out of the pool, and she couldn't hold him for long. She needed to treat his wound, but if she let go, he would sink under the water and drown.

"Wake up," she entreated. "Please."

No response.

Tanzi knew what she must do, but she hoped he wouldn't hate her afterward. She used her body to hold him in place while she grasped her pendant. When he slipped into the water, she yanked on the pendant and broke the chain. Gripping it in her hand, she slid him back up, straining with his weight.

Then she reached for her mage power.

Tanzi had never created a spell beyond green. The blue spells of healing had always tantalized her, just at the edges of her ability. Now she went deep within and called on the blue.

Nothing.

Desperate, she concentrated harder.

Nothing. Zebb began to slip.

Tanzi clenched the pendant, her fingernails stabbing her palms as she funneled her power into the cylinder.

Noth—

A sphere of blue light formed around them. With a gasp, Tanzi deepened the spell, straining—and the blue poured into Zebb as if it were an elixir. She saturated his wound with healing balm.

The spell soon drained her; she would have to stop or she would pass out, and he would drown despite her efforts.

"Tanzi?" Zebb whispered. He was staring at her through the blue haze, his eyes stunned and wide.

"You have to stay awake," she said. She released the spell and the blue vanished, leaving them in an almost dark cave. Her head fell forward with her exhaustion.

Zebb slowly stood up, embracing her so her cheek rested on his broad chest. "What angel's magic was that?"

"It's nothing. Please don't hate me."

"Hate you?" He sounded bewildered. "For what?"

"My spells. Arv was going to kill me—" Finally, for the first time since her nightmare had begun, she cried. Tears rolled down her face. "I s-sang a spell to Arv's baby. That's all I did. Warmth, comfort, healing. But A-Arv was going to kill me after he—he and his men—" Her voice broke. "Please. Don't hurt me."

"But why would he kill you for that?"

"He said I was evil."

"Man's an idiot," Zebb said. "Whatever you did, it felt fine. Good. What, a spell? Hell if I know what that means."

"It's sort of magic."

He spoke pensively. "People say Jazid is magic, that it's unnatural how this desert has so many different minerals so close to the surface. Supposedly, long ago, an angry sorceress made it too hot and harsh for anyone to live here. When she tore up the ground, her magic left the rocks behind." He gave a wry laugh. "Crazy, eh? Whatever the reason, my land has some good rocks, nothing fancy, but enough for a living."

Tanzi wiped her tears. "I never heard that part of the legend. Just that she cursed our continent so it was lost from the

Earth."

"I only know what I can see and touch." Zebb touched the back of his head "This is almost healed. You did that?"

Solemn, she nodded. "Are you angry?"

He lifted her up, then set her on the edge of the pool, his face gentle. "Well, let me see. You're soft-hearted. Sweet. You can fix even my rock-hard head. I'm supposed to be bothered by this? Why the blazes would that be?"

"I don't know," she said, laughing softly with relief.

"You want to stay here tonight? Or go to the shack?" He hesitated. "It's cleaner here. But I got food at the house."

Tanzi couldn't believe his response. *She's a mage, she casts spells,* and just like that, he went on to where would they sleep and eat.

"Zebb, you're a nice man," she said.

"I'm a terrible man," he growled. "Ornery as a boar, stupid as a mud brick dried in the sun, and as smelly as an old goat."

She dimpled at him. "You're sweet. And you smell good now."

"Sweet?" He stared as if she had grown another head.

"Maybe we should go to the hut," she decided. "I'm starving."

"You're deluded." He pretended to glower, but he didn't fool her; she could tell he was pleased. She read him more easily when he didn't have his beard. Or maybe she had made a low-level green spell along with the blue. Green let her feel moods.

He climbed out, picked up their clothes, and drew her to her feet. With no more ado, they headed out of the cavern.

"Uh, Zebb. Shouldn't we dress?"

"Why? No one here but us."

It was true. She should have been mortified at the idea of

walking naked in the desert night, but unexpectedly, it appealed to her. Outside the cave, they stood below a sky ablaze with stars. The crystalline air turned the heavens into a glittering panorama.

"This is all your home, isn't it?" Tanzi said with wonder. "The cavern, house, mines. It's *all* where you live."

He tilted his head, considering the thought. "I guess so."

They walked together across the desert, hand in hand.

ങ‌Cℜℰ‌Oൠ

Zebb was leaning in the doorway, his usual place, when the sun cleared the Fractured Mountains and a wagon crested the nearest hill. It didn't surprise him to see another man sitting with Izad on the driver's plank. He grinned. Benjazin would have to investigate this development, that Zebb Miner had a wife.

He heard Tanzi puttering around the hut, making things better. She had already done it outside, setting out rocks to define a path, sweeping away dirt, tending the garden. She said the plants would grow better if she gave them more water. He helped by lifting, carrying, whatever she needed. He could listen to her melodic voice for hours, watch her smiles, see her curves under that robe. When his muscles ached, she created gold light and he felt better.

And last night. Well, last night. His shack had never been so warm, although the temperature outside had plunged.

As Izad's wagon clattered up to the hut, Benjazin jumped down. "Ho!" He strode over to Zebb. "Did she run away?" He stopped and frowned. "You scraped your chin!"

Zebb laughed. "My wife thinks I'm pretty."

"You're uglier than a rock boar!"

"No doubt," Zebb said. "But she likes the way I look."

Benjazin peered into the shack. "Where is she?"

Turning, Zebb saw Tanzi clutching a rock in her hand. She had that trapped-deer look, like yesterday, but today she came over to *him* and stared at Benjazin. He felt filled somehow, knowing she sought him for security.

She spoke softly to Benjazin. "Good morning."

He gaped at her. "By the dragon!"

"What's wrong?" Tanzi asked.

Zebb grinned amiably. "He's shocked that I'm so lucky."

Benjazin scowled at him. "You put a hex on her?"

"*She's* the magician." Zebb started to say more, when Tanzi stiffened. She had suffered because of her spells. It angered him that people had treated her so badly, but he was more grateful than he knew how to say that she had come to him. She was an angel, and they didn't even know.

"You should see your face," Benjazin told him. "You look like you've been hit by lightening and got no brain left."

Merchant Izad came up next to Benjazin and gave Zebb an appraising stare. "You got my payment?"

Zebb tilted his head toward the hut. "It's all set."

Benjazin peered at Izad. "You could bring me a wife. Then I wouldn't have to go to Aronsdale. I could stay here."

"You could build a house near us," Zebb said, hopeful. "None of us would be alone. Hell, there'd be four. Children, maybe."

"Wives aren't so easy," Izad told Benjazin. "You can't afford it, anyway."

"*He* did," Benjazin said, jerking his chin at Zebb.

"I was feeling softhearted," Izad growled.

"Is that so?" Tanzi murmured. "Tell me something, Merchant. You bring Zebb and Benjazin all these wonderful supplies, being so soft-hearted and all, and in return you only want dirty rocks?"

Benjazin laughed. "It's the truth."

Zebb blinked. Tanzi spoke with her usual gentle tones, but he heard steel in her voice, and her gaze was ice.

"I give him one of each color," Zebb said, wondering what she was about. "White, gold, blue, red, and especially yellow. I got lots of yellow. Izad gives me all the supplies I want."

"How generous of him." Tanzi continued to stare at Izad.

The merchant spoke tightly. "The rocks are common here. Their value depends on their rarity."

She opened her fist, revealing a mottled yellow rock. Anger sparked in her voice. "This is a raw *topaz.*"

Turning to Zebb, she said, "I know gems. I cleaned house for a jeweler. You have diamonds there, gold, sapphires, rubies, all those gorgeous topazes. The quality is incredible. What you trade for a few measly supplies would buy an entire farm where I live. Saints, Zebb, you've more wealth than everyone in Azure-Tal combined."

She fixed Izad with a furious gaze. "You're stealing him *blind.* You were willing to trade me because those ten chests have to be worth three times what Arv could give you."

"Tanzi, it doesn't matter," Zebb said, dismayed by her anger and Izad's red face. He thought a faint green glow surrounded her, but he wasn't sure. "I can't do nothing with the rocks. He can have them."

"He's a thief." Tanzi folded her arms and studied Izad. "Listen, Merchant. Zebb has underground springs that could irrigate this land. With the right equipment and some work, it could support a small community, maybe several families. We could build a real house and get better gear for his mines, so he doesn't risk so many cave-ins. You *know* he can afford it with just a few of his 'rocks.' We are going to renegotiate terms—or Zebb will never trade with you again."

Izad stared with his mouth open. Then he snapped it closed and spoke angrily. "Zebb and I had a deal."

"He'll give you the ten chests," Tanzi said. "But it's going to buy him more than a wife."

Their exchange fascinated Zebb. Could his rocks be worth so much? "You always said we were friends, Izad," he reminded the merchant.

"That you did," Benjazin chipped in. "You know, another merchant came through here. Didn't charge me nearly so much as you, and you wouldn't believe how happy he was to get one rock. Sounds like maybe you've been tricking both of us, hmmm?"

"Ah, flaming hell," Izad growled. He did not, however, deny it.

Zebb pulled himself up. Not only did he have a pretty wife, she was smart, too. He wasn't certain what she did with the green light, but she had certainly figured out Izad right off.

"We got bargaining to do," he told the merchant. "Got a lot to order, new things. Be a good order for you. If you don't try to trick me." He drew Tanzi against his side. "Me and my wife will pick out what we need."

"Fine," Izad muttered. "This conversation is giving me indigestion."

"One other thing," Zebb said, suddenly quiet.

Izad paled at the sound of his voice. "Yes?"

"If you ever tell this Arv how to find my wife," Zebb said, "then after I kill him, I will find you and break your neck into a hundred pieces."

Sweat beaded on Izad's forehead. "I won't say squat."

Zebb nodded. "Good."

They went to Izad's wagon then and set to their business.

⊗෮ᲠᏏᲝᏏᏏ

Tanzi sat on a large boulder behind Zebb's house and watched the red sky fading to stars. Compared to the meadows of Shazire, the air here felt parched, but its pristine, untamed quality exhilarated her.

Zebb came up behind her and put his arms around her waist. The boulder was high enough that he didn't have to bend over. He pressed his lips against the top of her head. "I like this kissing thing."

Her lips curved upward. "I do, too." They had been doing it all day. While heat scorched the harsh desert, they had lain together in the cavern pool. The land reminded her of Zebb and his rocks, stark and raw, yet with a great beauty.

"Do you think Benjazin will stay?" she asked. "If our plans work for the irrigation and all, it will be easier to live here." It still angered her that Izad would get all Zebb's stones, but at least the merchant agreed to two payments, half now and the rest when he brought their materials and equipment. Her green spells had served her well this morning, both in judging how far he had cheated Zebb and how much they could push in negotiating.

"I think Benjazin would like to live closer to me," Zebb said. "But he'd have to give up his old claims or else travel to them every day. He's never wanted to."

"If he goes to Aronsdale, he'll be giving it all up."

"Oh, he'll come back after he finds a wife." Zebb chuckled. "He figures if I can get one, anyone can."

Tanzi wondered why he denigrated himself. "You're wonderful."

He spoke quietly. "Benjazin asked me something a while

back. If I was happy. I didn't know then." He stroked her hair. "I do now."

"Are you, Zebb? I would like you to be."

He hesitated. "You say a man and a woman can't be in love after so short a time. I've no idea about these things. But if I'm wrong about loving you, if I don't really feel that yet and I just *think* I do, well, when enough time goes by for it to be true, I know I will love you, I mean really, the right way."

Tanzi didn't know whether to smile or cry. Turning, she put her arms around his waist and her head against his chest. "I feel it, too. If it's not love yet, what we feel, it will be someday. So we can say it now if we want."

He tilted up her head and kissed her. Then he sat next to her and put his arm around her shoulders while she leaned her head against him. They gazed over the desert in the glistening night.

NIGHT WIND

By Mary Rosenblum

Mary Rosenblum has been writing science fiction and fantasy since 1990, with an occasional sidetrack into mystery as Mary Freeman. The author of eight published novels and more than sixty short stories, she has been a Hugo finalist and a nominee for many major awards. Currently, her SF novel *Horizons* is available from Tor Books, and *Water Rites*, a compendium of a novel and three prequel novellas, from Fairwood Press. She will be teaching the Clarion West writers workshop in 2008 and when she's not writing, she herds sheep and attends sheep dog trials with her dogs. You can find out more about her at her website www.maryrosenblum.com

Now, she takes the classic romantic image of the highwayman and spins it into a tale of the yearning of the heart—for freedom, for belonging, for the soul mate that complements and completes the lover.

M ama sent the family coach for him. He hated riding in the coach. Alvaro raised the window-shade and peered out at the dusty-silver olive leaves drooping in the fading light of evening. The fruit looked sparse. Shriveled. His fault. He took a shallow breath of dust, old leather, and Mama's imported scents gone stale in the upholstered cushions.

Lord Salvaria will have arrived. You cannot gallop in all dusty on one of your wild horses, like some cavalier. Think of your father. Her words, penned in her precise hand.

He had not ceased to think of Father. Not since the attack that had stolen his magic. And he doubted Lord Salvaria cared what he looked like. It was the bloodline Salvaria was buying, magic in the blood. He was getting a bad bargain.

Alvaro peered to the rear, where Ciro, his servant, led Elena, Alvaro's fiery mare. She should have been a stallion, and he took some small pride in the fact that he had gentled her without horse magic. He smiled crookedly as he heard Ciro cursing under his breath. Elena did not lead well, didn't like Ciro's dun gelding, and allowed no one on her back but Alvaro. His smile faded as the apricot orchard came into view. Blight. This had been the most productive manor in the kingdom, its richness woven of the magic of Earth and Sun and Water.

The coach lurched to halt, throwing him forward. The driver shouted and Alvaro heard more shouts, stranger voices. Alvaro threw the door open, his sword in hand, and froze as he found himself staring at the muzzle of a heavy, cap-lock pistol in the grip of a broad-shouldered man wearing a coarse peasant shirt and a cloth mask. Two more masked peasants aimed pistols at the driver, the guard, and Ciro.

"Stay calm," Alvaro commanded.

"Good advice. You size up a situation well. Put the sword down. I've heard of your talent with it."

The cool tenor voice yanked Alvaro's gaze away from the pistols. He stared up at a slender rider sitting a restless chestnut. The man looked young, dressed in a nicely tailored coat with a hint of lace at the cuffs, although a mask hid his face. A sword with a basket-work hilt hung at his side and he controlled the fretting stallion with ease.

Highwaymen. Alvaro nearly spat. Bloated brigands, often the younger, ne'er-do-well sons of petty lords, preying on the main roads, wringing every last coin from the unarmed peasants as well as the nobility.

Still, it had been a pretty ambush, he thought as he laid the sword down, feeling utterly naked. The almond trees clustered around the 'friar's well' narrowed the road here and offered cover for anyone brave enough to prey this close to the walls of La Casa. Alvaro strained his ears for the sounds of the outriders Mama would have sent out to meet the coach.

The brigand smiled, revealing even, pearly teeth. One of his men stepped forward and thrust a cloth sack in front of Alvaro.

"Just let us through in one piece." Alvaro pulled out his purse and tossed it into the sack, his lips twisting. "There's enough there to pay our way. *All* of us." Too many of these bands took the servants, sold them to crew-slavers who supplied the merchant ships.

The highwayman was studying him and he caught a glimpse of green-flecked hazel eyes, sharp on his face. "You're paying for your slaves?"

"They're not slaves." Alvaro snapped out the words.

The brigand looked past him. "I'll take the horse."

"No!" Ciro's voice was rough.

Elena squealed and Alvaro spun. One of the thieves had tried to grab the mare's reins. Ciro drew his knife, long enough to behead someone. Sword in hand, Alvaro leaped forward as the robber aimed his pistol at Ciro. A hammer blow caught him between the shoulder blades and he went down in the dust, then scrambled to his knees, blade up.

"Hold!" The highwayman pushed his chestnut between

Alvaro and the man who had struck him. "All of you, hold!"

Everyone froze. Alvaro lowered his blade. "Take the horse. Ciro, stand down."

"But, sir!" Ciro looked aghast.

"She's not worth your life, man."

The silence held. The chestnut snorted and Alvaro looked up, found the brigand staring at him, those odd hazel and jade eyes narrowed. Abruptly, the brigand swung down from his stallion, handed the reins to the man who had nearly shot Ciro. Without a word, he took Elena's reins. The mare skittered away, ears flat.

"She'll dump you," Alvaro said conversationally.

The highwayman paid no attention. Tension hung thick and bitter as dust in the air. The highwayman held out a hand and Elena shied, then snorted through flared, blood-red nostrils, bent her long, arched neck and blew loudly on the highwayman's hand. Without a wasted gesture, the highwayman flowed up and onto the mare's back. Elena reared, eyes wild, then bolted.

Alvaro watched, transfixed, as the highwayman sat the mare's fury lightly, making no move to punish her with bit or spur as she bucked across the dusty ground. Finally, the mare broke into a hard, angry gallop, racing flat out for the distant, purple hills. The robbers whooped and the mare bucked once more, heels and tail flirting with the sky. The highwayman turned the mare in a sweeping arc, brought her cantering back to the coach, her tail a black flag in the fading light. Horse magic, Alvaro thought. This had to be a lesser son of one of the Old Families. Only someone with horse magic could have mastered Elena that easily.

"A fine mare." The highwayman halted her lightly in front of Alvaro, his coat flecked with the mare's lather, a smile glinting in those strange hazel eyes. "She's too good for you."

"You can't have her." Alvaro took a step forward, fists clenched. "Take the money. There's plenty."

"They get the money." He jerked his head at his band and those strange eyes gleamed. "And you already offered her to me. I accept." He wheeled the mare away. "Let's go."

The tallest of the thieves gathered up the bag and he and his two partners retreated to the horses hidden beside the spring. They mounted and the highwayman whistled. The chestnut threw his head up and bolted after the riders as they galloped away westward. Alvaro's eyes narrowed. Horse magic, for sure.

Ciro kicked his gelding and started after them.

"Wait!" Alvaro cried. "They'll shoot you."

Ciro reined up. His face was red with fury. "But—"

"It's only a horse."

Mama's outriders appeared at this moment, four of them, all armed, the family pennant flicking red and black above the leader. Ciro spurred to meet them, pointing at the highwaymen's dust still hanging in the air. The foursome wheeled their horses after the vanished highwaymen.

"They'll catch the sons of dogs." Ciro reined in beside the coach, grim satisfaction on his face. "Those brigands only had a few minutes' start."

"Don't be too sure." Alvaro stared at the summer-parched hills. The robbers hadn't been riding farm stock. Their mounts had the look of desert blood. If their leader had magic, they'd run like the wind. "That fox won't need much of a head start to escape the hounds."

Alvaro swung himself into the coach, slammed the door. *A filthy thief*, he thought. *But what a rider! What a waste of talent, even if it was a minor talent.* He threw himself against the cushions as the coach lurched into motion once more, fixed a brooding stare on La Casa's sprawling pile of stone, webbed with the wrought-iron lace of balconies. *One of the Old Families*, he thought. His lips twisted. Blood should run true. Any horse breeder would say so.

ଔଔଷ୧ଓ୫

The silvery branches of the olives held the dusty heat and the sweet scent of ripening apricots filled the evening air as the coach rumbled onto the flagstones beneath the portico.

"My lord." Sevil, the *mayordomo* who had ruled the house since Alvaro was a child, emerged from the huge, carved doors. "You are late. *La Señora* was worried." His dark eyes noticed the absence of the outriders, even as he did not comment. "And your time at the university? With the great Delarentaro?"

Alvaro looked away from the bright hope in Sevil's eyes. "I learned much," he said flatly. "I am home now."

"I see."

The fading of that hope in Sevil's eyes pierced Alvaro.

"*La Señora* is in the sitting room. Lord Salvaria has arrived and is with her." Sevil's tone betrayed nothing, but Alvaro caught the ever-so-slight narrowing of his eyes as he spoke.

"Ah, yes, His Lordship Salvaria." Alvaro let his breath out in a rush. Salvaria was the son of a horse trader who had become a very successful and very wealthy shipowner. He had money and a lordship which, rumor had it, had cost him dearly in gifts to the current King, who was not good about balancing the exchequer but knew the price of a title. The King had settled a small holding not far from La Casa on the new Lord. What Salvaria lacked was magic in the blood. That would cost him dearly in the drawing rooms of the Families.

Once upon a time, Requesato blood had not been for sale. The family had married magic to magic. What difference, ultimately, had that made?

"*La Señora* said to tell you that your rooms are ready. That after you have refreshed yourself—"

"I think Lord Salvaria will not be insulted if I wear a bit of road dust."

Alvaro realized with a jolt that, Sevil had *aged*. His skin had the translucent look of the elderly, and a fine tremor shivered his white-gloved hands, even though he kept them firmly clasped to hide it. The ending of Father's magic affected everything.

"I'm quite presentable and Mama won't blame you." He put a gentle hand on Sevil's shoulder, a bit shocked by the fragile bones. How old was he? Another stone of guilt to carry. "We were attacked by highwaymen. I gave them my purse." His father would have called on the land itself to aid them. "No one was hurt."

"Ah, the one they call the Night Wind." Sevil lowered his voice. "He has been very active in these parts."

Was that a glimmer of approval in the old man's eyes? It vanished before Alvaro could be sure. Squaring his shoulders, Alvaro strode into La Casa's tiled entry hall.

The daughter would not be here, of course. Her father would come alone to bargain, to horse trade over just how much of his vast fortune must accompany his daughter into this marriage. They would weigh the value of Old Family magic versus cash, like fish mongers haggling in the marketplace, he and Mama. Alvaro wondered if a man who had made his fortune in trade might not out-bargain his mother. He wondered if the man had heard the whispers already circulating in the Old Family drawing rooms. *No talent . . .*

For your father. He closed his eyes, his mother's acid words burning in his mind's ear. *You will do this for your father. Because it will destroy him if he loses La Casa and you are clearly not going to save it with magic.* She was right. This one time he would cede her that. The oil and apricots were not enough now, and debts mounted like drifts of summer dust. The shadow-demon had found a tear in the fabric between the worlds in the northwest orchard just as his father took his daily ride. Father had destroyed the demon. At a cost.

Alvaro drew a deep breath. What was a wife after all? An acquisition, like a bloodstock mare, a contract like any contract. It wasn't as if he already had a love in his life.

That had been a youth's dream, a soulmate. A love for eternity, not just a pretty face. Dreams did not always come true.

He smoothed the bitter smile from his face and strode into the drawing room.

"You are late." His mother pressed a wrist to her forehead as she reclined on a chaise. "I feared for you." But her eyes darted accusations at him even as her lips smiled and she held out her ringed hands to him.

"Father." Alvaro strode across the room. "How are you?"

"Well, my loyal son." His father's words escaped his withered lips like the hiss of a ghost. A hand crept from beneath the fine woolen blanket like a pale spider to pluck at Alvaro's sleeve. "And the great Delarentaro? What did he say?"

"The talent is there." He forced himself to hold his father's gaze. "He does not know why it is blocked."

"Enough, this is not the time for family gossip." His mother's lips forced a smile. "Of course, the talent is there. The Requesato is the purest of the Old Family lines. Magic runs in the blood of every scion, undiluted. Sevil, you may serve the champagne now." She smoothed her silk brocade gown. Her glance at Alvaro could have burned through steel as the silent Sevil carried in a tray of glasses.

"To a most lovely and accomplished young woman." La Señora raised her glass.

Alvaro touched his lips to the rim of the glass. "What does your daughter think of this marriage?"

Lord Salvaria cleared his throat, his glance skating away. "Ah, she is young and overwhelmed by this honor."

"Of course, she is overwhelmed by this honor." La Señora broke in quickly. "This is not unexpected." She sipped from her glass, her lips fixed in a bright smile. "Then she will begin planning her wedding clothes and she will count the minutes. Every young woman desires a Blooded husband."

"Of course, that is exactly how it will happen." Salvaria smiled, but perspiration gleamed at his hairline in spite of the breeze through the latticed windows.

So she didn't want this marriage either.

"Ah, girls." His mother laughed and flashed her emeralds at Salvaria. "We all know what they're like. Ice cold one moment, hot the next. Shall we go in to dinner?" She levered her heavy body from the chaise. "The cook has prepared pheasant in a sauce flavored with lavender. It is his specialty and he is famous for it." She fluttered her eyelashes at Salvaria. "The man has magic in his blood. A by-blow of one of the Families, most likely. What he does with food!" She rolled her eyes. "His Royal Highness himself tried to steal the man from me, but my cook is loyal. Ah, even a drop of magic in the blood is valuable, eh?"

Sickened, Alvaro turned to his father. Mama took Salvaria's arm and sailed into the dining hall beside him.

"The talent is there." His father raised rheumy eyes to Alvaro's face. "It will . . . burst forth. Give it time, my son."

"I will, Father." How much time? Alvaro bent to assist

his father to rise and supported his halting progress. He would not use a cane and only the white of his knuckles betrayed the necessity of that seemingly-casual grip.

If only the shadow-demon had torn through elsewhere. They could have summoned help, defeated it with no damage.

Alvaro excused himself early, as soon as the servants helped *El Señor* off to his chambers. He made his pleasantries to his mother and the hungry new lord, left them to their horse-trading and took himself off to sleep. As he climbed the curving staircase to his suite, he saw again the lithe form of the Night Wind as he mastered the mare.

ෆ෬෪෫෬

He went riding at dawn. Geraldo, the stable master, had a tall gray gelding waiting for him, a steady horse without Elena's fire. Alvaro took the path through the olive groves, out to the sheep graze where he could let the gray run. After, he walked the horse to his favorite lookout, a ledge that overlooked the valley below. This morning, the sight failed to soothe him. He wondered how much the lordling had had to pay for the Requesato blood, last night. And found himself wondering if this shipowner's daughter had made the mistake of falling in love.

The sun was high as he headed back to La Casa, so he took a shortcut through the neighbor's grape fields. He didn't like the Duke. One of the Old Families, they had sold their line for generations, until the magic in their blood had grown weak and diluted. The families who worked the soil were bound to the land and the Duke and his sons treated them like slaves. Worse than slaves, Alvaro thought. Below, a crew thinned the long rows of vines. He scowled at the condition of the workers. His father would have died of shame if his workers had looked so thin and underfed. A team of dun mules whisked their tails, drowsing in front of a wagon piled with the cuttings and thinned berries. He saw no sign of a water barrel and his frown deepened as the overseer, shaded by a wide straw hat and carrying a braided lash, paused to drink from a water bottle.

One of the field hands, a skinny youth with long hair bound back with a strip of sweat-stained cotton, swayed and went to his knees, unripe grapes spilling into the dust. The overseer swore and stepped forward, bringing the lash down across the boy's shoulders. The boy choked back a cry, struggled to his feet.

Even from here, Alvaro could see the whip marks on the lad's back. He urged the gray forward as the last blow caught the boy full in the face, then reined in as three horses burst from the trees along the east edge of the field.

He recognized Elena, even as the highwayman charged straight at the overseer. The workers scattered, shouting. The overseer dropped his whip, scrambling for the wagon. The highwayman rode him down and as the man flung himself into the dust, Elena leaped lightly over him. Her feet landed inches from the overseer's sprawled form.

"The sun is very hot." The highwayman's clear tenor carried easily to where Alvaro waited, hidden in the shadows. "Men can die in the sun without water. Murder is murder in the eyes of God. What have you to say?"

"They get water when they're done." The overseer raised his dust-covered face. "They want water, they work for it. They're lazy. . . ." He scrambled backward with a yelp as the highwayman urged the snorting Elena forward.

"I don't think your water flask holds enough for all the men." He nodded to one of his riders, who reined his mount to the wagon and tossed an oaken bucket at the overseer.

The man flinched as the bucket bounced off his shoulder.

"It's a mile to the stream. And a mile back."

"So you should hurry." Ice edged the highwayman's tone. He nodded to the taller of his two men. The man kicked his sinewy little desert gelding into a run and snatched the braided whip from the ground with a skill that made Alvaro's eyebrows rise.

"Santos will help you hurry." The highwayman backed Elena easily. "You will run. Don't spill any water."

Alvaro edged the gray deeper into the shadows. He had complained about the overseer to the Duke, for his wanton acts of cruelty in the field. Now he watched without pity as the highwayman's rider whipped the overseer across the sunbaked field to the stream and back again.

The peasants dared not grin, but Alvaro saw how much they enjoyed it. When the sweating and panting overseer finally stumbled back with the bucket, one of the men produced a gourd cup from his belt and they all drank, offering the first cupful of water to the boy.

"*Señor!*" One of the riders pointed.

Alvaro spied three riders, whipping their mounts. The Duke's men. His eyes narrowed. From his vantage point, he could see another six spurring along the northern edge of the field, out of sight of the trio by the grape wagon.

"Quickly." The highwayman reined Elena around. "Let's go."

They galloped, skirting the woods where Alvaro hid. They wouldn't see the Duke's other men until they dropped down into the draw. Clearly, they planned to cross at the ford and escape into the rough land beyond. They'd be clear targets as they rode down to the ford. The Duke's men were heading into the trees, where they would be hidden. Two to one. The highwayman and his two riders came abreast of where Alvaro hid.

"It's a trap!" Alvaro kneed the gray out into a clear space between two old oaks. "By the ford."

Faster than thought, the highwayman reined Elena in. For a moment, Alvaro's eyes locked with that hazel and jade gaze.

Alvaro jerked his head. "Take this path. It leads to our west sheep graze. Then cut north into the foothills. You can jump the stone fence easily."

For a second, the highwayman said nothing, merely sat the fretting mare. The two men behind him, young, Alvaro noted, looked nervously back as the first trio of riders closed the gap.

With a nod, the highwayman kicked Elena into a gallop. His two riders followed, sweeping past Alvaro. Hooves thudded on the dry forest floor as they disappeared down the path.

Alvaro urged the gray forward, broke from the trees. He pointed north, toward the river, as the Duke's riders caught sight of him. "That way. They're making straight for the river."

The foremost of the riders pulled his lathered bay up so hard that the horse nearly went down. Bocario, the Duke's eldest son and heir. "Did you see him? Why the hell didn't you shoot?"

"I don't carry firearms when I'm out for a morning ride," Alvaro said mildly.

Bocario rounded on his riders. "What are you waiting for? Get him! I want his ears and I want to cut them off while he's still alive. This time, we've got him."

"If that overseer of yours wasn't killing your field crew, he might have left you alone."

"You're soft, Requesato," Bocario sneered. "Your father's magic spoiled you. But no more, eh, he's burned out. *You'll* have to work for your oil, won't you? You could whip a thousand in gold out of those lazy—"

The bay shied as Alvaro shouldered his gray into it hard.

"You will speak of my father with reverence." Alvaro leaned in close. "We don't pay our debts with peasant blood."

"See what song you sing when that filthy brigand burns *your* house." Bocario spurred the bay savagely toward the river.

The Duke's spoiled son wasn't any better than his father. Alvaro reined the gray around, heading for the path to the sheep graze. The Night Wind. He found no sign of their passage at all on the soft dirt of the trail. Frowned. Magic here, yes. This Night Wind—whose blood did he carry and why did he live as a robber?

Alvaro emerged into the sun-drenched sheep graze, shading his eyes with one hand as he searched the rocky slopes that rose to meet the dark pines of the mountain. No sign of the three riders.

A horse whinnied and Alvaro tensed, half-expecting an attack. Elena stood tethered in the shade of the woods, her reins looped over a branch. He smiled as he walked the gray up to her. The horses snorted and blew at each other as he unwound the reins from the branch. She wore a different saddle. He leaned from the gray's back, ran his fingers over the finely worked leather. Nicer than his saddle, ornamented with hammered silver. The bridle matched, made of soft, stitched Seville leather, the headstall and reins decorated with more silver. He dismounted, swung into the saddle and gathered the mare as she danced and fretted, then caught the gray's reins and headed back to La Casa.

සිරිපිරිසි

Mama was radiant at late breakfast in the inner garden, without a single cross word about the hour. Clearly, she had turned out to be a better horse trader than Lord Salvaria. He looked a bit sour, but when Alvaro invited him to tour the stables, his eyes lighted.

"Old Spanish stock," he murmured as he leaned on the stone wall of the paddock, watching the horses circle and run.

"For endurance." Alvaro nodded. "Sultanna Avarre blood."

"I thought so. The white foot gives it away. He leaves it on all his offspring." Salvaria watched Elena kick up her heels, her black flag of a tail flying. "I would pay a lot for that mare. Where did you get her?"

"I bred her." Alvaro sighed. He had sold his blood stock to pay last season's debts. Horse breeding was a rich man's hobby.

Salvaria was silent for a time, his eyes on the mare. "I have heard you attended the University. Did you study with Master Delarentaro?"

"I did." Alvaro kept his eyes fixed on the horses in the pasture. So he had heard the rumors, then, that Lord Requesato's only son displayed little of the family magic. Yet his mother had looked pleased.

"He taught my daughter, Renata. As a private tutor." Salvaria's smile was a bit tentative.

Alvaro blinked. "When I was there, Delarentaro wasn't accepting private students." He accepted no students unless they were Family and highly talented. He had accepted Alvaro only because he had once instructed his father.

"Ah, I met Delarentaro many years ago." Salvaria smiled. "He took her on as a favor to me. Renata stubbornly refuses to understand why women can't attend the university, so he agreed to tutor her." He spread his hands. "Her mother died when she was an infant." He turned away from a moment, his face tight. "Perhaps a father is not the best to raise a daughter."

Alvaro blinked. "I am . . . impressed." Women did not

have magic and Delarentaro therefore had no use for them.

"He said no at first." Salvaria chuckled and raised his eyes to the sky. "I was stubborn. He tells me she is very smart." His expression grew serious. "I hope that you and she will find . . . common ground. She would be the perfect choice to take over my business." He sighed. "My partners will not accept her. She is headstrong. But very bright."

Alvaro's eyes narrowed at the obvious worry in his tone. Another motive for this bit of name-buying? Perhaps it was not acceptance in the drawing rooms that mattered to Salvaria? At least not his own acceptance there? Clearly, this headstrong daughter was not in favor of this bit of horse trading. "I'm sure we will get along." If he didn't know for sure that Delarentaro favored boys only, he'd have suspected. . . . "Would you like to ride out with me tomorrow? The sunset is lovely from the Stag's Leap, where you can look over the valley."

"Ah, I would be delighted." Salvaria looked happier than he had since Alvaro had arrived. "I'm surprised that your family has not invested in the New World. The Duke has invested there." He canted his head westward, toward the Duke's vast lands. "I haul his silver bullion home on my ships."

"I advised my father against that," Alvaro said shortly. "It is founded on the enslavement of the natives. We do not pay our debts with blood."

That was the second time he had said that today. No, he thought with a bitter irony. It was no longer the truth.

"Ethics can be costly." Salvaria's expression was enigmatic.

"Indeed." Alvaro studied a blood bay mare as she tossed her head and skittered across the paddock. "Have you heard of the highwayman who has been preying on the roads hereabouts?"

"The one they call the Night Wind?"

Alvaro smiled as the mare cleared the paddock gate into the far field. "I hear rumors that he steals only from the landowners, that he lets the peasants go." So Sevil had told him.

Lord Salvaria shrugged. "Ethics in a robber? I find that hard to credit. That is not what the Duke was saying. Apparently the brigand burned his carriage house. Everything was lost."

"Did anyone get hurt?"

Lord Salvaria shook his head. "The Night Wind's raiders bound the coachman and his boy and dragged them outside before they set the building alight."

Geraldo cantered out into the field on his big roan, a rope in his hand. Alvaro had a feeling that the mare was going to give Geraldo a chase. "I think I'm going to start that bay mare."

Lord Salvaria looked, chuckled softly. "You enjoy a challenge. I like that."

"I enjoy a challenge." The Night Wind would like that horse, he thought. He'd best be careful about riding her on the highway.

⊗⊙⊰⊱⊙⊗

Alvaro spent the next few days overlooking the business of La Casa. Without his father's web of woven magic, the land was failing. He threw himself into the work, doing his best to compensate with his sweat and muscles. In spite of the exhausting work, the image of jade and hazel eyes, steel thighs and light hands troubled his days and haunted his nights. He had never lusted after boys and his own feelings bemused him. But the images wouldn't go away.

The olives, such as they were, were ripening, but as Alvaro toured the cool, stone storage sheds, he found the casks were in bad repair and the great olive press needed work.

"I cannot replace the casks without planks." Denio looked away.

Alvaro put a hand on his shoulder. "Order the planks."

"The wood-monger wants gold." Denio's face was stiff.

Word was certainly getting around. Alvaro sighed, regretting the fat purse he had so quickly tossed to the Night Wind on his arrival. "We'll have to wait, then. Until after the wedding." Which would take place before the harvest. With luck and hard work, they'd have new casks before the pressing began. If his father had been whole, the staves would be firm as young wood, unrotted, webbed through with magic. Now they were only wood. Rapidly aging wood. As Sevil was aging. Alvaro closed his eyes briefly. Money would not help Sevil.

Alvaro touched the miniature around his neck, a gift supposedly from the daughter, Renata. It was a formal portrait and looked like any young girl, dark hair pulled into a knot, eyes lowered. All the miniature painters used the same pose and all their subjects looked alike. *I hope you will not be unhappy*, he thought as he stepped out of the musty dusk of the storehouse into the hot summer sun. *That's the best I can do.*

Sevil met him as he returned to the house. Alvaro slowed his steps to match the old man's faltering stride.

Sevil cleared his throat. "Apparently the Duke, His Eminence . . . the Duke has . . . aspirations to possess La Casa."

"Not in my lifetime." Alvaro smiled grimly.

"Sir." Sevil's eyes clouded. "Please think about what you just said. You ride alone in the morning. Everyone knows this. You have no magic to protect you."

Alvaro halted in the flagged kitchen courtyard.

"It is something I heard, a rumor only." Sevil's voice trembled. "But without you. . . ."

"Old friend." Alvaro put his left hand on Sevil's fragile

shoulder. "I don't plan on leaving La Casa in the Duke's talons. Even without magic, I am not so easy to kill. Don't worry." But the old man *was* worrying. "I'll stop riding out in the morning by myself. Will that make you sleep more easily?"

"Yes." Sevil sighed.

"You haven't worried that the Night Wind might harm me."

Sevil bristled. "Why would he do that? He burned the Duke's carriage house because he killed a stable boy who struck his son, after that bloated pig assaulted his wife. Excuse me, sir." Twin spots of color glowed on Sevil's cheeks.

"I think Bocario is a bloated pig, too." Alvaro grinned. "I'm glad to hear that the Night Wind is consistent."

"He . . . administers justice." Sevil looked up at the tall peak of La Casa. "Families who have nothing sometimes find a few pieces of silver on their doorstep. Overseers who use the whip get punished. I believe he is a . . . good man."

"I'm not going hunting for him." Alvaro clasped Sevil's shoulder. "And I'll give up my morning rides."

"Bless you, sir." Sevil's pale lips stretched into a smile. "We need you."

It was hard, giving up his morning rides. Elena was difficult to manage without a run every day, and galloping around the field bored them. Alvaro needed to escape the evidence of his failure, visible in every dying olive tree and crumbling building. He began sneaking off while Sevil was overseeing dinner preparations, taking the path along the western edge of the sheep graze to the level land where he could let Elena gallop. No assassin would expect him to ride in the heat of the day.

Today, a few high clouds scudded across the sky, bringing the promise of rain. Elena bucked as they crossed the sheep graze, as if she, too, felt fall in the air. The wedding was in ten days. Mama was in a frenzy of anticipation. The ceremony would take place in La Casa's chapel and everyone with any status locally had been invited. Every person on La Casa's large holdings would celebrate with roast pig and lambs, ale, and dancing. For a day, they could all ignore the ebbing of the manor's fortunes. Alvaro sighed, his heart heavy as he turned the mare's head toward home. Could money replace magic?

He had yet to meet Renata, Lord Salvaria's daughter. She had been indisposed. Then their carriage had had a breakdown. Even Mama had noticed the excuses, although she shrugged them off. After all, what choice did the girl have? Unless she threw a tantrum in the chapel itself, who was going to listen to her?

Elena shied and squealed. Deep in thought as Alvaro was, she nearly unseated him.

Ahead, the dusty landscape seemed to split open like fabric slashed through by a knife, revealing utter blackness beyond. That blackness gathered itself and launched toward them, twin eyes gleaming like hot coals. Elena screamed as black claws raked her haunches. Alvaro fell, rolling, his sword leaping as if of its own into his hand.

A shadow-demon. The thing that had destroyed his father.

Alvaro came to his feet, the tip of the blade weaving a web of liquid silver between them. Delarentaro had forged it and it suited what talent he had.

It was not enough to protect him. Not even his father's magic had been enough for that.

The thing faced him, catlike, those hot-coal eyes flaring, a long, ropy tail whipping. Its blackness was so intense that it seemed to be two dimensional, a cutout of darkness in the bright day. Alvaro flicked his swordpoint toward the eyes and the thing retreated, spitting.

The shadow-demon stalked toward him, circling, hissing and spitting like a grease fire, its eyes pulsing as if they were windows on the heart of a furnace.

Alvaro balanced on his feet and time slowed to a crawl.

The demon leapt, claws reaching for his throat. Alvaro struck, and the shock as the blade went home numbed his arm to the shoulder. The demon shrieked. The sound tore through his brain. He staggered, struggling to hold on to the sword as it was wrenched from his hand. Something struck him and he tumbled in the dust, rolled to his knees and flung himself sideways. He scrambled to his feet, blinking blood from his eyes, clutching his useless arm. A claw had caught his cheek, laid it open to the bone. The demon faced him, red eyes glowing.

His blade lay in the dust between them.

"Requesato." A figure mounted on a nervous bay stepped from the trees. "Contemplate your death before it tears you apart."

"Bocacio." Alvaro stared at him, then at the demon. Understanding twisted like a snake in his gut. "You've sold your blood to the darkness."

Bocacio jerked the bay savagely to a halt. "Our blood is played out, we brought in too many commoners. Good pay, but bad for breeding." He bared his teeth. "The dark power is unlimited, Requesato. Even a weakling like you could make use of it. Too late for that now."

"You invoked the demon that destroyed my father." Alvaro stepped forward, ignoring the demon's sizzling snarl. "Give me my sword and we'll make this formal. You have a decided advantage."

"I told you you're soft, Requesato." Bocacio looked at

the sizzling demon. "Tear him to pieces."

A horse burst from the woods in a flat-out gallop. The Night Wind. The slender rider drove the chestnut right between Alvaro and the demon, leaning out of the saddle to snatch the sword from the ground. Almost, he escaped. With a snarl, the demon flung itself on horse and rider. The chestnut bucked in panic. The Night Wind dove from its back, rolling to his feet, sword in his hand.

"Here!" The Night Wind leaped to Alvaro's side as the demon crouched to spring.

Alvaro seized the sword and his hand and the Night Wind's closed together on the pommel.

The air shimmered. For an instant, everything paused, then an avalanche of sensation thundered through him. He staggered, head spinning. The Night Wind sank to the ground, one arm raised as the demon pounced. Too bright, the light was too bright.

Alvaro shouted. The demon released the Night Wind, half crouched. Alvaro lunged, sword in his left hand. The demon rose to meet him.

The sword tip gleamed with the light of the sun as it struck the demon's left eye. Alvaro nearly lost his grip at the shock of contact. This time, power flushed through him, as if he drew on the very air and light around them. He felt it pour through him and the demon seemed to swell larger and larger, its crackling hiss turning into a shriek of agony that brought Alvaro to his knees, still clutching the sword, still driving home.

With a blink of utter darkness, the demon vanished.

Bocacio's bay reared and squealed, then burst into a gallop, reins trailing.

Alvaro stared at the empty meadow, his ears still ringing. He looked up at the trees. Where he had seen dusty, drought-stricken leaves, he saw green, healthy leaves. Wildflowers bloomed among the meadow grasses. Blinking, shaking, he stumbled to his feet, sheathing his sword.

Magic. It coursed through him like a second heartbeat, flowing through the trees, the ground, the very sky. He threw his head back and laughed, felt that laughter shimmer through the trees, saw the weary, end-of-summer grass brighten.

He turned, found the Night Wind climbing onto the chestnut's back. *"You* caused this. I felt it when our hands met."

Blood showed crimson on the sleeve of the Night Wind's coat.

"You're hurt." Alvaro stepped forward.

The Night Wind shook his head, reined the chestnut toward the woods. Quick as a flash, Alvaro crossed the dusty space between them, grasped the stallion's rein. The horse snorted and half reared. Alvaro caught the Night Wind as the man swayed in the saddle. "Let me help you."

"No." The word came out a murmur and the Night Wind drooped forward, one hand wound in the chestnut's mane.

His figure seemed to blur in front of Alvaro's eyes, becoming more slender . . . different. Magic, he thought. The Night Wind was hiding his true shape.

"I owe you my life," Alvaro said softly. "I owe you far more than my life." He met those jade and hazel eyes, now clouded with pain. "Who are you?"

The Night Wind shook his head. Alvaro reached up, caught the lower edge of the Night Wind's mask. Yanked it off.

With a cry, the Night Wind straightened, snatching the rein from Alvaro's hand. The chestnut leapt forward, the Night Wind swaying in the saddle, to disappear into the shadow of the woods.

Stunned, Alvaro stared at the tail of dust, his head filled

with the image of honey-dark hair, jade and hazel eyes.

A woman. He looked at the linen mask in his hand. The Night Wind was a woman. With magic.

This could not be.

⳾⳾⳾⳾⳾

The wedding was put off, of course. Bacacio had disappeared and Alvaro testified before the King about the shadow-demon and Bocacio's role in the attack on his father. The Duke protested, but once the King sent Delarentaro to the Duke's manor to investigate, the Duke fell silent. What Delarentaro found, he did not divulge. From that moment, the Duke aged rapidly.

Magic blessed La Casa again. It was too late to heal the shriveled harvest, so Alvaro quietly sold the ceremonial sword that the King had given him as a gift on his eighteenth birthday and used the money to replace the oil casks. Sevil whistled when no one was near and looked ten years younger.

Alvaro put off his mother as long as he could, claiming that the King's investigation came first. His father was still failing, but now he smiled and his eyes brimmed with light. Alvaro rode all the way to the capital to talk to Delarentaro. The old wizard merely shook his head. "Nothing is impossible," was all he would say. "Because the magic of this stranger complemented your own, it is no longer blocked."

It was not a satisfying answer. Alvaro had asked *who*.

He could not sleep. That face haunted his dreams, the jade hazel eyes, the high cheekbones, the dark-honey hair. He rode out every morning, took the back roads, scanning the landscape, watching for a flash of chestnut.

No reports of robbery floated on the breath of gossip. Avaro's heart chilled with fear. The talons of a shadow-demon could pierce deeply. His nightmares filled with her crimson blood.

His mother nagged him about the wedding, even though his magic had finally wakened. A contract was a contract, she told him endlessly and often.

Finally one afternoon, Alvaro saddled the gray, since Elena had not yet healed from the demon's claws. The slash on his cheek was mending, but he would bear a scar forever. He ran his fingertips over the elegant leatherwork of the saddle, *her* saddle. Surely, she had not died. He let his breath out, tossed the silver-ornamented reins over the gray's head and mounted. Her hands had held these reins. He kicked the gray into a brisk trot, cutting across the sheep graze to reach the highway.

The oil was safely pressed, the swans flew overhead on their yearly migration, and the last of the hay had been stored in the big barns. The land glowed with golden prosperity. Now he could perceive the strands of sky, sun, wind, and water. Slowly, he was beginning to learn the weaving of them, the weaving that would keep La Casa golden and prosperous for the rest of his life.

And after? He closed his eyes, seeing honey-dark hair and those haunting eyes. A son? A daughter? Magic from *both* parents?

He rode slowly, as the end-of-summer dust puffed up from beneath the gray's hooves. Some dishonesties were dishonesties of the soul. "I would have tried to make you happy." He rehearsed the words for the hundredth time. "It would be wrong to wed you when my heart is pledged elsewhere." His heart and his soul. He hoped that he would see relief in her face, that this was what she had wanted all along. Her father would become an enemy and that saddened him. He would have liked the man as a friend.

Salvaria's little holding had been a neglected property leased out by a local landowner before he took it over. Alvaro noticed the tight barns and neat pastures with approval. The pastures grew green and lush. The shipowner might be a businessman, but he had taken well to owning land. The place looked as if one of the Families lived there.

They did not expect him, of course. So he waited out the flurry of excitement as the surprised doorman took his card and hurried off, as the *mayordomo* appeared, all flustered, to usher him into the drawing room.

"Lord Salvaria is away," the man apologized hastily. "Overseeing business. I will tell the mistress you are here."

"This is a surprise, an imposition." Alvaro smiled to soothe the *mayordomo*. He reminded Alvaro of Sevil and clearly he did not at all approve of this visit. Sevil would not approve either. "I am in no hurry." He strode to the far window, rehearsing his speech once more. She had to understand that he loved another.

The window looked out on a pasture bordering a stream where a half dozen horses grazed. Very nice animals. His eyes narrowed as he examined the fine-boned bays and grays in the field. Desert blood there. Salvaria was the son of a horse trader, after all.

A tall chestnut stallion stood on a low knoll, watching over his harem. He tossed his head, shaking his long mane, and Alvaro's heart skipped a beat.

"The Lady Renata," the *mayordomo* announced a shade too forcefully from the doorway, his tone edged with disapproval.

"Lord Requesato." The cool voice sent shivers down Alvaro's spine. "You are most welcome. I apologize for the lack of hospitality, but you were not expected."

A thread of wariness wove through her words. Alvaro turned slowly, his skin prickling hot and cold. She was tall, although not as tall as he, her dark-honey hair pulled into a simple knot at the nape of her neck, her dress a simple affair of plain blue silk that was not stylish, but suited her slender figure. *You will annoy my mother,* he thought, feeling giddy, *because you will not let her dress you.* "I apologize for disturbing you."

"I am not disturbed." Her eyebrows rose. "I also apologize." She touched the sling of white silk supporting her left arm, still wary. "A riding accident. I . . . prefer horses that are a challenge. But it is almost healed."

He took a deep breath, aware of the maid near the door, the careful chaperone, and restrained himself with an effort. "I . . . came because . . . I believe that it is dishonest to take someone in marriage when the heart . . . belongs elsewhere."

"That is unusual honesty for a man." Renata's lips curved into a smile. "I have heard that you are unusually honest." She lifted her chin and her jade and hazel eyes met his. "Your heart lies elsewhere? Is that what you are telling me?"

"Oh no. It . . . lies here." Breathless, he stepped forward, his hand going to meet hers, her fingers cool and slender against his palm. "I am here to ask, for myself, if you will have me." He heard the maid's stifled giggle. Held his breath, his eyes on those enigmatic pools of jade and hazel.

Light gleamed in them, golden light. "I will have you." Laughter chimed in her words. "I think we have many things in common."

"Many things, indeed." He raised her palm to his lips, his heart pounding in his chest. Mama would be so happy when he told her the marriage could take place any time. Tomorrow would not be soon enough.

"I have a betrothal present for you." He met those jade-gold eyes so full of light. He had started the blood bay mare but she was still a handful. Renata would want to train the horse herself, with her horse magic. "And I wish to return something of yours." His smiled widened because, yes, the elegant saddle suited her. "It was left at La Casa. Quite some time ago. I found it in our sheep graze."

She laughed and the warmth of it filled him with a joy he had never felt.

IN THE NIGHT STREET BATHS

by *Chaz Brenchley*

Chaz Brenchley has been making a living as a writer since he was eighteen. His work includes short stories in various genres, books for children, thrillers, most recently *Shelter*, and two major fantasy series: *The Books of Outremer*, based on the world of the Crusades, and *Selling Water by the River*, set in an alternate Ottoman Istanbul. Winner of the British Fantasy Award, he was named Northern Writer of the Year 2000. His time as Crimewriter-in-Residence at the St Peter's Riverside Sculpture Project in Sunderland resulted in the collection *Blood Waters*. He is a prizewinning ex-poet, and has been Writer-in-Residence at the University of Northumbria, where he tutored their MA in Creative Writing. He lives in Newcastle upon Tyne with two squabbling cats and a famous teddy bear. His website is http://www.chazbrenchley.co.uk/

About "In the Night Street Baths," Chaz writes: "Sometimes books have holes, deliberate or otherwise: spaces where characters have gone away to pursue other interests, and the author can't or won't follow them. While writing *Bridge of Dreams*, two favourites of mine kept slipping off for illicit adventures, and neither the readers or I had any idea what they were up to. Apparently, they were up to this. . . ."

The whistle when it came was sharp as glass, urgent as a whip, compelling as a tug on a pierced ear.

It was a summons, of course: expected, nervously anticipated, very much desired.

Teo didn't—quite—spill the beads he was rethreading. He didn't scramble to his feet on the instant; he didn't yelp or whoop or chatter. As far as he could, he did the opposites of those. He became very still and very quiet, as though cast into the heart of a jewel, rapt and trapped. His fingers and his tongue stopped moving, both together. Only his eyes shifted, to find his mistress and look for her consent.

Perhaps he should have looked for her slave instead, her other slave than him. Mirjana's swift and familiar slap stung the back of his shaved head, knocking his cap askew.

"Finish what you're doing, laze. Then make puppy eyes at a soft heart to beg your liberty, not before."

Mirjana's own heart was softer than her hand, if not much. Under her charge, he'd be delayed, and he might carry bruises when he went, but she was at least safe to let him go. His mistress Jendre was more tender, and more careful. She worried when he was out, enough, sometimes, to keep him in.

Not tonight. Her smile was more teasing than anxious; half-laughing, she said, "Oh, leave him be. He'd be no use to us now if we kept him. Would you, sweets?"

He grinned back at her, and shook his head.

Mirjana snorted. "Go on, then, go. Give your mistress a kiss and come home earlier than last time. And leave your slippers, for I'm not mending them *again*. I don't know where you go or what you do, but. . . ."

Barefoot, then, he scampered away from her perennial scolding. Half his commerce with Mirjana was play-acting for Jendre's benefit, which she knew, and took pleasure from regardless. Unless she was only acting her amusement. Life in the Palace of Tears was a hollow thing, a harem of the widowed, a house without a master at its heart; sometimes he thought it an utter sham, where nothing true or real ever came.

Until Djago's whistle came, and suddenly he wasn't playing any more.

Jendre reached out a long arm, to set the cap straight on his head. Her fingers lingered on his cheek, and he smelled the rosewater he had used to rinse her hands after supper.

"Be good," she murmured. "And be happy, and have adventures, and come back with stories for us."

He said, "Yes, mistress," light and dishonest, which she knew; every time he came back, there was less he wanted to tell them, more to be treasured in the secret spaces of his heart. Then he kissed her fingers and was gone.

CRISTO

Djago waited at the end of the passage, squat and still and monumentally patient. Malevolently patient, since he had discovered—no great trick, this!—Teo's swallowed restlessness. Djago himself had swallowed a rock, Teo thought, to gift himself that perfect inner stillness.

Maybe it was just because he was old. Teo said that sometimes, flung it at the dwarf's big head, but he never believed it. Age didn't bring wisdom, he knew that; he had seen it in Djago's mistress, who was old past measure and baby-soft, baby-stupid. He didn't see any reason why age would bring a devastating patience either. The old should hurry more, should be more urgent, they had so little left to play with. . . .

At least Djago had Teo to play with, when he cared to. When Teo was let run to play. Tonight Teo ran and dropped to his knees, put his arms round the dwarf's neck and kissed him;

and was soundly cuffed by strong stubby hands, and subsided, grinning; and said, "Where have you *been*?"

"About my business," the dwarf said, which might mean tending to his vacant and beloved mistress, or it might mean something entirely other; Teo could never tell with Djago and Djago would never tell until he wanted to. "And now I have a little time, a *little* time that I can call my own. . . ."

And a boy too, whom he could equally call his own although it was not true and did not need saying, being all too obvious to anyone who cared.

෬෬෨෪෨෮

A boy and time together meant this: that they went through a door that was hidden if not secret, into the maze of servants' ways that riddled the palace like rat-runs. Jendre at least knew that they existed, because Teo had told her. He thought perhaps half the women here did not know, the old dead Sultan's wives and concubines who had never given a thought to how they were served or how such a vast house could be managed.

Djago had been forty years in the Palace of Tears; he knew them all. Teo was learning. This corridor, this narrow turning stair was familiar already: along and down, and a door at the bottom of the stair where he reached over the dwarf's head to work the catch because stretching up hurt Djago's joints.

The door opened, the night awaited: a swift step from the heady incense of the house to the brisk sharp scents of a garden after rain, from smoky lights and shadows to a true night sky. Who needed lamps, though, where there were stars and moon and the Shine to come; who wanted the easy teasing comforts of women's company where he could have the stumping, grunting figure of the dwarf to follow; who would willingly stay sheltered within harem walls, when there was a city below to explore?

Nor was it just any city. This was Maras, the glittering eye of empire, the Sultan's own, home to all that was great and terrible in the world. Here in the old palace they stood on a peak and could see it all falling away below them in tiers to the river: tiers of lights tumbling to the broad dark band that was seized by the eerie span of the bridge, tiers that failed entirely within that brighter, stranger glow they called the Shine. That was the city and the empire and everyone within it, Teo thought, caught in a single striking image: safe up high, he gazed at beauty and saw how it was built on the struggle to climb, how it broke apart lower down and was swallowed by despair.

It was no great revelation. His own village had been much the same; he thought the world was much the same. Only that it was brighter here at the heart, everything showed more and mattered more.

Even in a eunuch's life, some things mattered more. Dry of mouth and sweaty in his palms, Teo hung on Djago's heels all through the gardens and down to the wall. It wasn't leaving the harem that made his breath so short, that set a tingle in his skin; he used to run messages for Jendre all through the city, when they lived an easier life lower down the hill, before she was married so high and then widowed so unkindly and so sent here to rot. He loved to be out in the dark, rain on the wind, a dance on the road, freedom under his feet. And he always went home to his mistress, where he belonged.

Now, though: where did he belong now, at her feet or at Djago's heel? He didn't know. He thought there might be two views on the matter, perhaps even two truths. He did know that she didn't inspire this nervous excitement in him, even in her wilder moods. Her maddest exploits were to do with her and hers; he was incidental. These nights out with the dwarf, by contrast, these were all about him, tests to see if he could be trained or broken or delighted. To him, they were mysterious adventures, and the core of the mystery was always Djago, and so Teo sweated.

And thrilled, and shivered with the edgy, sweaty thrill of it; and they came to one of the low guard-gates in the outer wall, and he beat a thunder on it with his fists, because knocking hurt Djago's hands. And because he was young, and was tired of doing things quietly. Djago frowned and said, "A little knock would have done as well."

"Oh, but there is no one else to hear, this side of the wall. On the outside, what do they care? They know that we could knock and knock, and never be answered."

"Until he opens the gate."

"Which he will not do, if there is anyone close enough to see. *He's* not a fool."

Which was true, and an impertinence, and Teo might have suffered for it; but just then there came the rattling scratch of a key in the lock, and the smooth swing of the gate opening; and there might perhaps have been a reason for the sergeant to have a key, so long as he never used it, but it was hard to think of any reason why he would need to keep the hinges oiled.

Except that he was an old friend of Djago's, long since bought and paid for. A simple knock would open this gate to the world, and it didn't seem to matter whether Djago knocked himself or brought a boy along to do it for him.

The sergeant held the gate and grunted a greeting. Djago rolled out on the short stiff legs that gave him that rocking sailor's gait; Teo followed, teasingly mocking it, until the sergeant cuffed him straight.

Some nights this would be as far as they came. Djago and the sergeant would sit against the wall and smoke their *khola*-pipes, and talk of emperors and battles, life inside the palace and far away; and Teo would sit at their feet and talk as much as they let him, which was not very much at all. And it was good because he loved stories and he loved to watch the city and the stars, and he knew that the *khola* eased Djago's pain; but it also made the dwarf melancholy, and that was not so good.

So Teo was just as glad when Djago exchanged thanks and greetings with the sergeant, promised to be back before his duty ended, and walked on into a shadowed alley. Once there must have been a wide and guarded margin around the old palace, as there was now around the new; here no one cared any more—the last dead Sultan's womenfolk, locked up to spend their lives wailing their lost lord: what protection were they worth?—and so the city pressed up close against the wall.

"Why don't you have your own key to the gate?" Teo asked. "The sergeant would give you one, and then he wouldn't need to wait around all night when there's a good comfortable guardhouse at the main gate, and we could come and go when we chose, not just when he had the duty, and. . . ."

Djago chuckled wheezingly. "Oh, you are such a youngling! Listen, brat: it is always, always better to own the man. A key can do two things for me, just the two. It can open one gate, one; and it can betray me. I can be caught with a key. I can never be caught with the key to that man's heart. And because I have that, I can have him do whatever I ask, over and above the keeping of gates. I never have asked anything, beyond a pipe of weed and a night's talk now and then, but I could. What could I ask of a key?"

The old dwarf had the key to Teo's heart, too, of course. And others', no doubt; maybe many others', maybe he collected heart's-keys and kept each one as carefully as these.

He didn't take anyone else out, though, twice or three

times in a week. Perhaps it wouldn't last, but for now, for this while, for tonight—well, it was hard for Teo not to bounce, not to let his legs carry him springing on ahead while his eyes drank in the city's doings all around him and only his hand reached back to Djago, and only then to hurry the dwarf along.

It was hard, but he was good at doing the hard things. Sometimes, he was. In any case, there was no point in trying to hurry Djago. Short legs and pain made for this slow, grunting progress, with as many pauses as there had to be. Teo had learned to follow, to stifle the impatience in his legs and let his eyes have it all; besides, there was shelter in the dwarf's shadow, and he could sometimes be glad of that. Djago was known, he mattered. Teo was nobody, except and unless he was Djago's boy.

Which was, after all, what he wanted: to be with Djago, in reach of his hands, of his voice. They didn't have to be alone, neither of them needed to be tender. He was glad enough just to sit at the dwarf's feet and listen to his stories. Or to shuffle at his heels like this in the bustle of a bright night's commerce, listening to the rasp of his breath and waiting for some biting comment to be tossed back over his shoulder. A woman's dress, a man's habits, a masked face or a sudden scurry in the shadows, anything might induce a little scathe, a fling of words which might be true or might be pure slander, it really didn't matter. Teo would choke up on his giggles either way, and hug himself in lieu of Djago, who was seldom huggable.

Tonight Djago took him unexpectedly far towards the river and the docks, down precipitous stairs and cobbled alleys where soon every step forced out a grunt, pain disguised as effort, fooling neither of them.

Teo had never before been the one to call an end to an adventure; tonight, it had to be him who said, "Djago, stop.

We'll go back. I don't understand why you brought us all this way, you must have known how much it would hurt you . . ."

"It would hurt," the dwarf puffed, "rather more to go back up."

"I'll carry you," which was ridiculous in many ways, but mostly because he was a slender youth and the way was steep and Djago might be small but was certainly very solid. And yet he meant it, which Djago knew; and so he earned himself the whisper of a smile, hidden within the snort and the outright refusal.

"You will not. What, shall I ride like a child on your shoulders?"

"Or like a demon on my back. However is comfortable for you."

"No way would be comfortable for me. Anyone who knew me would die to see it, die from laughing; I would die, sooner than let them see it."

He dressed like a fool still, though his court foolery lay decades in his past; he was certainly a slave; his pride was none the less magnificent, far greater than his stature.

"The further we go, the harder to get back. . . ."

"Not so. Come; not far now."

And on he went, and Teo with no choice but to follow. Djago was cautious down one more uneven run of stairs, even the shallow ones seeming too much now for aching joints by the way he clung to the wall; Teo finally risked the offer of a hand, so he could cling to that. They were well into the Shine now, the bridge's eldritch light that hung over all the lower town, giving them shadows to walk in and shadows of their own.

At last, Djago turned aside, into a narrow lane with little traffic, high walls, no windows. It opened into an unexpected square which must have been lovely when it was a garden in moonlight, before the trees died, before the moon's light was supplanted utterly by the sickly glow of the Shine. Now it was as tainted as the light, as the air, as the water that gleamed strangely in the sunken pool at its heart.

Low steps rose to open double doors, people passing in and out; benches in the square that people should have been sitting on, except that no one wanted to linger in the Shine.

Teo said, "What is this place?"

"This? This is the Night Street Baths. By daylight it has another name, but here, now . . . Give me your arm, lad, up this little last."

That was the first time he had asked. It was a surrender on his part and it felt like a triumph to Teo, even while his mind was swimming. Night Street stories were like the rain, like the Shine: they broke in everywhere that was broken, wherever they could find a flaw, a crack, a breach in the wall.

Privately, Teo thought this whole city was broken, although it was rich and powerful and lordly; he thought the bridge and the Shine had broken it, leaking poison in.

Here was his proof, indeed, just inside the door. Two men—no, two *figures* standing guard, barrel chests and monstrous shoulders, their faces distorted already out of human. Dogtooths, the people called them, for their jutting jaws and fierce canines, but they might as easily have been called bears or brutes or victims. It was the Shine that did this, that thickened their bodies and changed their bones and ground their thoughts to powder. They had lived too long down here, below the bridge. That was all. The city's hierarchies were imprinted on the bodies of its people. The rich and powerful lived high on the hill, above all danger; those who could not climb so high, the poor and the shiftless, lived in the Shine and came to this.

There were none in the harems where Teo had served,

because who would choose ugliness and stupidity to serve them, when they could have the opposites? And in the streets, running errands, he was light of foot and quick of mind, sharp of sight. Those were enough. He'd never needed to deal with a dogtooth; as with so much of life beyond the harem wall, all he had was stories.

He tried not to stare, because stories he knew were like snakes, they could twist around and bite you.

The dogtooths stood guard here, but barely glanced at him. They looked down—far down!—at Djago, and bowed their heavy heads lower yet, as though even the slow and massive could respect endurance where they saw it. And he, Teo, he was passed through on the same nod, insignificant but vouched for. The dwarf's boy, yes. . . .

෮෨ඊ෨

He had seen the greatest baths in Maras, the Sultan's own, in both the old palace and the new; he had seen private baths and public; he had never seen anything like this.

From the grandest to the least, from marble halls to tiled pools to stone-slabbed sweatrooms to caves with steaming springs, all baths are built on the same essentials, a source of water and a source of heat. No doubt this was, too, but its lobby was something else. A marketplace, a meeting-place, of course, all baths were those; but this was also a dormitory, a place to shelter, Teo guessed, a place to hide.

In here were benches as there were outside, as though this wide space was a dedicated substitute for the dead garden. Lamps in brackets made a substitute for moonglow, a better light than the Shine. Most benches held sprawled figures, fully dressed and fast asleep. It was hard to be sure, with their faces hidden in their arms or under a cast of cloth, but he thought most of them were dogtooth, more or less.

Elsewhere, between the benches, people stood about and talked, or stood in silence, or moved from group to group with desperate trash to sell, or sat hunched against one wall or another with everything and nothing in their arms.

"Djago . . .?"

The dwarf had a purse out, and was negotiating with a thin, determined woman. At least, he was offering money, which she seemed determined to refuse. He glanced up and shook his head at Teo, gestured lightly: *You go on in, I'll follow; this could take some time.*

On his own, then, Teo did what he would always do, in a strange bath-house: he looked for the women, which way they drifted.

Following towards an open doorway to the right, he found one woman perched on the end of a sleeper's bench, bent over the bundle that she cradled. Her hair hung down to hide both her face and her baby's, but it couldn't mask the sounds that they made.

The one was a low, heavy keening, the pure sound of a broken heart, the grief of a mother at her child's burying; Teo knew that well enough, he had heard it often and often when he was a child, when he was free, and through the war that had made him otherwise. Likely his own mother had mourned him this way, and never knew what happened to her boy.

The baby's sounds were stranger, unaccountable: a snorting, snuffling whine, broken by sudden high-pitched squeals, like jerks on an unreeling rope.

Everyone ignored the woman, ignored them both. Perhaps the house was used to this.

Teo couldn't do it. He might be outside the wall, but he'd brought his harem manners with him. Unless you'd caused it, you never left another slave in distress; you never passed them by. That was absolute.

He went to her, put his hand on her shoulder, said, "What is it, sister, can I help . . .?"

Of course he couldn't help. He should have known. He was a stranger here, a boy let slip for a night; what could he do? What did he think, what did he imagine he could do?

She lifted her face and looked at him, and he was too startled to wonder what in the world she saw with her eyes so rheumy. What he saw was the twisted gape of a nose, the thrusting muzzle of a woman turned dogtooth, turned so far that she couldn't talk, she couldn't shape words any more. She did try. Her mouth moved, chewingly; he saw the long loose tongue behind the heavy barricade of teeth; he heard the wet and frantic sounds she made, and could not understand them.

She understood him, his unease, his bafflement. Whatever she wanted, she thought she could show it him.

She lifted it into the light.

It was her baby, cast of her body and too long nurtured in her belly in the Shine, too long fed at her breast since, and still kept here under the dull weight of that poison glow.

If it ever had been human, he couldn't read that anywhere in its bones as she peeled its wrappings back. The noises it made were animal, its shape was monstrous; it seemed to have been built for pain, as an expression of its people's suffering.

Most of his own people—if they were his people: those who lived behind the wall, the women and eunuchs of the harem—would shriek, he thought, and turn away, and be appalled that such a dreadful thing could be.

What appalled him—and, he thought, its mother too— was that it had not yet found a way into death. Life is tenacious, but some life ought to know itself better.

He looked around for help, for Djago, but the dwarf was still deep in conversation by the door.

"I'm so sorry," Teo said, then, to the woman, "I'm not the one to help you. You don't need me. You need—"

His voice didn't tail then, it cut itself off dead. He could not say what she needed; only that it wasn't him.

She nodded, and slowly rewrapped her child in its rags, and hunched herself around it, and let her head and her hair fall forward, and began to keen again.

Teo had seen death and dying, a hundred kinds of horror in his own lands before ever he was brought to Maras; he had seen more since. He had seen his mistress's husband, the Sultan, die in agony. He thought he had never seen anything quite so terrible as this, and he was helpless against it.

Nothing to do now but straighten up and turn away, head for the baths, hope to soak these memories out of his brain before they set hard and inescapable—

ദ്രരുഃ

—and was stopped by a voice before he got there, "Hey, you! Pretty priest, where do you think you're going?"

"I'm not—"

"I know what you're not." He didn't quite know what she was: a girl, a woman barely older than he and not noticeably dogtooth, dressed in the shoddy uncertainties that all these people wore, whatever they could find or make from whatever came to hand. Layers of ragged green fabrics, in her case, probably not first meant to be clothing. "You look like a priest, though, in your smart grey robes. And you're too pretty to live, at least without someone to lead you around by the hand. You're going the wrong way. The men's entrance is the other side of the hall."

"I'm not—"

"I told you, I *know* what you're not. And what you are. Which is cute, and cut, and a long way from where you belong. And you're still going the wrong way." And she did literally take his hand, and tug him back the way that he had come.

"We," *we eunuchs,* "we always bathe with the women. . . ."

"High on the hill, I know you do. Not here. Men are men and women are women, whatever's happened. Whatever's been done to them. We do things differently, I guess."

They passed the keening woman with her baby; she didn't look up, Teo's new friend didn't so much as glance aside. He gathered that the woman was known, unless it was her kind that was long-known here, trapped in their helplessness. She could hardly have been the first.

Done talking at last, Djago joined them, unexpectedly taking Teo's other hand; which might have been a signal to the girl to let him go now but apparently wasn't, or was not understood as such.

Doubly escorted, Teo came to the door into the men's bath. There the girl dropped his hand, and he went on with only Djago for company. Which was how he had come and how he would leave and as much as he ever expected, as much as he ever wanted, but. . . .

But he still glanced back to seek her face again, to ask her name, and found her gone, a swirl of green lost in the eddy of bodies that filled the hall. For once, he wished he was taller. Mostly, he thought that he was too tall. His mistress Jendre had said so, from the day he'd overtopped her. To Mirjana, his constant growing apparently gave an excuse for more rough handling, as though cuffs and slaps would knock him back like dough to a sensible height. Mostly, though, he hated the sense of growing away from Djago. The taller he became, the more the dwarf paid in discomfort. Just to tilt that heavy head back to look up was an effort measurable in pain; Djago would never admit it, but Teo saw it none the less, and felt stupidly guilty, and stooped or knelt or found yet another way to aggravate Djago's sharp-witted pride.

Tonight, in this doubled strangeness—a house full of unknowns, and himself caught the wrong side, among full men where he had never been—he might have wished to be shorter anyway, only to attract less attention.

But at least he had Djago, who was no full man either, by any measure; and he had Djago's hand, which was better; and perhaps he wasn't so far after all from where he belonged.

CЯCЯℰ℧℧

Djago's hand had a strength that belied both its size and its deformity, the stubby fingers and the swollen joints. Unless it was Djago's mind that had the strength, and Teo simply read it in his fingers. It came to the same thing: Djago tugged, and Teo went along.

Once, surely, this had been a finer building. It probably could still seem imposing to anyone not used to palaces, but the arched and tiled passageway was grubby and ill-lit. There must have been a time when none of the tiles were broken and none fallen to leave those gaping plaster blanks, but that was long ago. Now the mortar between the tiles was dark with mold, the gutters that ran either side of the passage were blocked and overflowing, the steamy air smelled more of must than soap.

Here was a robing-room, and he could slip off his pristine greys and fold them carefully onto a shelf, top them with his little cap, hope they'd still be there when he came back.

Djago took longer to undress, and Teo dropped down to help him: buckles and lacings were hard for the dwarf, and his costume was heavy with both. This wasn't the first time Teo had fussed at him for clinging so stubbornly to clothes fit for what he was forty years before. Djago only shrugged and said he still was exactly what he had been, he couldn't change his breeding or deny his mistress, and he would wear the dress of her fool until she told him to dress otherwise. Which, as she had lost her words and her sense both long ago, they knew would never happen. He would wear these clothes until she died, that long at least.

Naked, Djago was all the shapes of wrongness, badly made and badly fit together. Between his legs he looked like a damaged woman—no cock, no balls, only a mass of scarring ill-hid by straggling hair—but that was the least of it, the last you came to, if you only came to look.

Teo had seen, though, seen and seen. Tonight he wasn't looking: only clinging to that strong hand like a child grown too tall, while he peered through steam and bad light to see whatever else he could.

One side of the passage offered small rooms, increasingly warm rooms where a man or a couple of men or a group might go to be private. If you could be private, where there were no doors. Teo saw men—and creatures who had perhaps once been men—in ways that might have called for better privacy. Himself a slave whose body belonged to someone else and had been cut to suit, he had no modesty to speak of, but even he. . . .

Finally, the passage gave into a space filled with heat and sound and water, little light. What lamps there were swam in steam like moons behind cloud, announcing their presence but not much more.

No matter. He could have found his way, but Djago knew it. Wooden boards above the floor were slick with scalding water; walking on those, the dwarf headed into the gloom, and Teo followed.

All around the walls, benches rose in tiers. When they found an empty one, Djago stretched himself out upon it with a grunt of ease, as though the steam and heat were already reaching through his skin to find kinked muscles and aching joints, spreading relief all through his body.

Teo dropped to his knees on the boards and felt the dwarf's fingers stroke the sand-stubble on his scalp, heard, "No, not like that. I want you up here."

So he moved, sat on the smooth-worn wood of the bench, took Djago's head onto his thigh. The dwarf's eyes were closed; Teo amused himself by combing out the iron-grey beard with his fingers, feeling how it softened in the steam. "Can we find a razor? I'll shave your head if you shave mine."

"Never mind our heads. That's not what I brought you for."

"Why did you?"

"Hush. Listen. . . ."

Teo listened; and above—no, below—the gurgle and splash of water being poured, the hiss of water on hot stones, lay the constant murmur of voices. He'd known it already, they'd walked into the flow of words as they did into the flow of heat and water. The dark was full of men; of course they talked. He shrugged, and said so.

"Yes," Djago said, "but wait. At the moment, there are two, three men to a bench, and they listen to each other. Soon one man's story will reach further than his own bench; before the night is over, all the benches here will be listening to the same story. When a man talks, he will talk to us all. Then he may be worth hearing."

Before the night was over, Djago and Teo too would need to be back in the harem, behind the wall. Teo was not at all sure how he was to manage that. Heat and steam would soak the pains out of Djago's body, so long as he was here; they wouldn't leave him fit for the long climb home. What did a bath ever do, but leave you drained and sleepy and luxurious?

It dawned on Teo—slowly, because nothing moves quickly in a steam-room, thoughts least of all—that he was worrying about Djago, trying to organise his life; and that was wrong, so wrong. Djago was a fixer, he was the man that Teo came to when he needed help himself. Teo was the flit-bird, unreliable and foolish, needing a steady hand; that's why his mistress welcomed Djago's interest, one reason why. She hadn't said so, but Teo knew.

So no, he wouldn't worry. Djago would have a way to get them home. And meantime they were here in the hot wet half-dark, it might as well be just the two of them because no bench was listening to any other, not yet; and he did so want to talk to the dwarf, if only about helplessness, which seemed to be the tune he always danced to; and—

ᘓᘓᘔᘔᘔ

—and Djago rolled over onto his belly, and his body in the steam might look like a string of ill-formed and hairy sausages, but that never mattered, it was the body that held the mind that held Teo in thrall; and Teo's own body—

ᘓᘓᘔᘔᘔ

"No, stop it, you can't. . . ."

൬൪൪൰

—was his giveaway, his betrayal, helplessness again. Which Djago knew and exploited at whim, but never before where people might see if they wanted to, if they came by, if they cared.

Teo's body didn't care, apparently. More kindly cut than Djago, he still had his cock and it could still misbehave. It was trained to be tame, as he was, but the dwarf's pudgy fingers had a wicked, knowing way to them; these days, just the sound of his voice could set a shiver in Teo's spine and a stir between his legs.

Tonight, Djago wasn't talking; he had other ideas, what to do with his mouth. While his fingers stroked the scar where they had cut Teo's balls away, while his other hand clenched around the root of Teo's cock, his tongue licked at its tip, his mouth enclosed it.

Stiff and gasping, Teo did stare wildly about him, but only for a moment. He caught no one's eye, was aware of no one's interest; people told their own stories, or listened to their companions', or dozed in the breathy heat and listened to no one.

So he gave up his concerns, or turned his back on them all, rather: folded himself down over the dwarf's head in his lap, wrapped his arms around his knees and found them all the privacy he could, as much as they needed, less than he would have liked, perhaps, but more and far more than Djago seemed to care about, which was really all that mattered.

൬൪൪൰

Hot mouths, hot bodies in a hot room, he could be dizzy with it; steam in his head, he could let the world spin away, as it did when Djago let him smoke *khola*, as it had the one time

Djago gave him wine.

When it came back, they had moved somehow so that it was he who lay sprawled his length along the bench, Djago who made his pillow. Not understanding, he lifted his head a little and said, "Have I been asleep?"

"Hush, little one," said the dwarf, his fingers playing at the rim of Teo's ear.

"No, but—are you hurting? You should—"

"Hush, I said," and a firm fat palm closed his mouth while fingers flicked his ear, sharply this time, stingingly.

Teo learned quickly when pain taught the lesson; it was the way he had been trained. He still wanted to talk, but would not; he subsided instead onto the solid comfort of Djago's thigh, and listened.

There was indeed hush out there, all through the dim gathering, except for the sounds of water and a single reaching voice.

Teo lay in the sweat and the steam-rush, yearning for a cold quench but his bones were hollow stalks and his flesh was leaves, he had no strength to fetch it; and that voice was in his head as the steam was, riding his spirit on its giddy circles, taking him somewhere else entirely:

․․․

" . . . This is how it was, that there was a ghost in the well-head and they sent for me to drive her out.

"They had known it for years, of course, that the ghost was there. By the time they sent for me, it was too late for some, almost too late for her. Leave a ghost long enough unlaid, unchallenged, she will inhere to the stone, to the earth, in this case to the water; she will become possessive of it, possessed by it, the two conjoined and deadly.

"Fools, they had tried to fetch her out themselves, it's why they were so slow to come to me. Two of them had climbed down into the well, to feel among the silt and find her bones; they thought if they could find them all and give her burial, she would haunt the well no more. Stupid. What do bones matter? Flesh rots, and so in the end do bones. Even spirit frays, like silk in the wind; but like silk on the wind, spirit will find something to cling to if it can. It wasn't her bones that had to be lifted from that well.

"They learned that, those two fools, too late for them. They went down to her, and she kept them there."

"Did they have ropes?" another voice asked mildly. "Or lanterns?"

"Ropes? What good are ropes and lanterns? You cannot rope a ghost. A lantern will not let you see her face."

"To help them climb out again, I meant. Perhaps they only drowned, diving to find their sister's bones in bitter water."

"No. No, I tell you. She took them, she kept them."

"What good are bodies, to a ghost?"

"Their souls were lost to her fury. She sought vengeance against the living world that had betrayed her. It didn't need me to show her family this; they came to me at last to cast her out."

"And so you did?"

"And so I did, yes. As I learned to do, with fire and water and sounds that spirits cannot abide, with prayers and powers that spirits cannot resist; and so their well is cleansed, and they are safe to drink from it again."

"But not to clamber down into the dark of it, without the good sense of ropes and lights."

"I have said—!"

"Yes, yes. You have said, and we have heard you. You have said nothing about the lost girl, the spirit. Where can she go now?"

"She will fade, and fail. Silk on the wind, frayed and scattered threads. No more trouble to the living."

"And to herself?"

"I don't know what you mean."

"I mean she was the first victim here, thrown or fallen down a well; and for this, you condemn her spirit to utter loss, with apparently no thought at all for her."

"Oh, what would you have me do, beat a vengeful spirit her path to heaven?"

"If you could do that, perhaps yes, I would, if I did not think her vengeful; but you cannot. What you could have done was let her be, tell the family not to disturb her in her well, tell them she was a blessing. Let her do her family good, guarantee them water all summer long. You could have done that."

"She was a curse in the water, and she would have cursed them all."

"So you have said."

"If she had been left in the well, she would have infected the stones that line it and the source that feeds it."

"You have said that too, and that is the only true thing you have said all night. A spirit inhabits a building, as it inhabits the body before death; that is not always an evil thing. It is not often an evil thing. Buildings need spirit as much as bodies do. There was a temple once in Maras, where the priest had bought himself a boy to sing at service. . . ."

☙ ❦ ❧

And so another story, and another; but it was the first that stayed with Teo. He touched Djago's arm and asked him in a murmur which was right, the first voice or the second.

"Perhaps both," the dwarf replied. "For sure, they both

believe it. Every man tells his own truth here, that's why I wanted to bring you, you who love stories about the world. Each man's world is his own, and his stories bend to suit it. Come on now, if you've stopped listening. I've sweated enough here, I am hot all through and I need to lie down."

࿈ ࿉ ࿊ ࿋

They went to one of the small rooms where there was oil waiting, with thin rough towels and a pitcher of cool water, and room enough for both to lie together.

They took turns to play body-slave, each towelling and oiling the other. And slept, perhaps, a little, in the warmth and the ease and the stretch of it, the long night slippery between them. And talked, at least a little, about ghosts and women, water, going home. Not at all about helplessness; Teo was thinking that perhaps he was not so helpless after all.

"We can ride home," Djago murmured, lifting his chin on Teo's elbow, "if we go soon. Soon. Some of these dogtooth men, they pull the night-soil carts that take the lower town's waste outside the walls. For a fee, they will take us clean up to the gate we came from."

"With the *night-soil*? After we have spent all night in the baths?"

"Clean, I said. They have finished their work, and soaked and scrubbed the carts, and now they soak and scrub themselves. But they will take us, if I ask them to. Soon, before the morning."

"You go," Teo said slowly. "You need it. I'll walk up."

"Teo, this is not a time to be nice about your transport. Ride with me."

"No," determinedly, surprising himself perhaps as much as he surprised Djago, *not so helpless after all*. "It's not the wagon. I have . . . something to do, first," now that he had the key for it. "On my own. I'll follow."

"Well. Don't delay. I can't hold the gate open for you, come morning."

"I know. I'll be there. Wait for me, smoke your pipe, talk to the sergeant. I'll come."

಑ಌಕಎಏಐ

He fetched their clothes, and helped Djago to dress, and dressed himself in the sombre grey of his position, body-slave to a widow of the state and eunuch in a great house; saw Djago to the entrance, saw him away in company, the squat rolling figure like a diminutive reflection of the dogtooths who went with him; went back into that broad lobby and towards the women's side, where, yes, the dogtooth woman was still keening over her dreadful child. He knew that: he had heard her at the entrance and on the way to it, he had heard her distantly while he and the dwarf still lay in their little room, not so private as he'd have liked. He'd heard her in his head, all the time that he was listening to stories in the steam and wanting to talk about helplessness.

Straight to her he went, and stood above her hunched misery. He didn't need to speak. As before, she lifted her head, lifted her dull and desperate eyes, lifted the child.

This time, he took it from her.

For a moment she clutched at it, torn, wanting it again; but a voice—not his!—spoke behind him, saying, "Give him the child. He is a priest to us here; he will know what to do."

There was no telling what the dogtooth woman saw, only that it was nothing clear; there was no telling what she thought, though he guessed that the same was true. He stood as straight as he was, as tall as he was, and hoped that his clothing would speak for him, tell better lies than he could.

Her hands fell away; after a little, so did her voice. This was, perhaps, what she had keened for in the end, when she was done with sorrow.

With dignity, with relief, with dread, Teo turned away from her and found that same young woman at his back. He knew that already; he had recognised her voice, although the cheerful mockery with which she'd named him priest the first time had fallen entirely away from it and left it bone-bare, clean and dry and pitiless.

She said, "Follow me. I'll show you . . . where you need to go."

Not what to do. That didn't need discussion, nor direction.

ଔଔଈ

The men's side, the women's side: in the central wall between the two stood another doorway, this one closed. She opened it, and led him through.

Here was the furnace-room, of course, and those who tended it; here a way in from the alley behind, for deliveries of logs and coal and oil. Here were pumps, raising water from the cistern below; here were stairs that took them down to that cistern. It was dark down there and she fetched a lamp, although he wasn't sure she wanted to. He wasn't sure either, but he let it happen.

The stairs led into a broad and man-made cavern, simple but spectacular, a lapping pool beneath a low domed roof. More steps led down into the water, like a summons. He had no resistance, no way to resist; step by step, they drew him in, while his skirts at first floated like lily-leaves around him, and then grew sodden and heavy and tugged him further down.

When the water came to chest-height, it lapped at the baby that he carried cradled in his arms.

There he stopped, breathed, looked down at it without speaking—and took another step.

The child struggled hardly at all, as though this ending were as welcome as anything in its short life: more welcome, he hoped, than the life itself, which must have been swaddled throughout in pain.

He held it until it was entirely still; then he opened his hands, and some current in the water took it away from him. It didn't float to the surface, which he had feared; it was simply gone, into the deep and the dark.

He waited another minute before he climbed slowly up the stairs again, to stand dripping on the lip of the pool.

The girl said nothing. He said, "This house could use a ghost, perhaps," if it were benign or grateful: a spirit that might linger, soak into the walls with all the water and the steam, saturate the stonework and be kind to dogtooths and the desperate, well-disposed perhaps to passing eunuchs whether or not they disguised themselves as priests.

She said, "Perhaps," and took his hand and blew her little light out, so that they stood there for a while in the dark before she tugged him upward.

❦

The woman was gone, who had birthed and suckled it. They had expected that.

What need more talk, now? She kissed him and he left her, left the baths; and trotted up the steps and steep ways of the lower town despite the weight of his sodden chilly dress. So long as he went on upward, he couldn't lose himself. At the height of this hill stood the old palace, the Palace of Tears; and around the

palace stood a wall, and in that wall stood a gate, and outside
that gate sat Djago and the sergeant, smoking, so long as he
could reach them before the sun did.

Which he did, with time enough in hand to let them
enjoy a last slow pipe together, one more conversation about
how short the years became.

"Ah," Djago said, "but I am a short man already,
abbreviated every way I could be. Not the boy here, he will grow
tall and taller," with a nudging boot in Teo's ribs, "but I suit the
years better than he does. We have seen the best of this city,
Master Sergeant; now comes the worst, and as well that it come
quickly. Come on, brat," another toe-poke, "inside for us, before
the sun catch us wanting."

The sergeant unlocked the gate and they passed inside,
and for a few short steps Teo was let hold Djago's hand again as
they walked through the deep shadows of the garden.

෬෬෮෮

The last little way he had to go alone, down the passage to his
mistress's rooms. He sidled in to find Mirjana up already,
with a single light to work by. And made no apology and no
mistake, reading her snort, her gesture; slipping off his robe and
cap and coming damply barefoot to the bed, remembering to
keep his feet to himself as he slipped into the warm place that
Mirjana had only recently vacated, next to the abiding warmth
that was his mistress Jendre.

She was sleepy but not asleep, not quite: alert enough to
reach an arm around him, tug him lightly by the ear, mutter
something about vagrant boys. He took that as the invitation it
was undoubtedly meant to be and nestled close, eager suddenly
for an enclosing familiarity and finding only that his own oiled
body betrayed him, scented strangely as it was.

THE RULE OF ENGAGEMENT

By Sherwood Smith

Sherwood Smith's first ball was in a pink marble palace in Vienna, Austria, when she was twenty. She used to practice sabre fencing on the top of the Gable Building at MGM. She once faced off two abductors using only a switch blade (they were very stupid abductors, or she wouldn't be here to tell about it) but her most courageous act by far was doing the Squawking Chicken Dance in front of a room full of thirteen-year-olds. Her many novels include the popular *Crown Duel* and *Wren* series, and co-authorship of the five-volume *Exordium* space opera. Upcoming releases include *The Trouble With Kings* (Feb 2008, Samhain) and the third book in her *Inda* series, *The King's Shield* (August 2008, DAW). Her website is http://www.sherwoodsmith.net/

Sherwood describes "The Rule of Engagement" as "a duel of wits as well as hearts." It is a story about choice, about honor, about the transforming power of love. . . .

I. Are You Free?

"Are you free?" King Lexan asked, it being the men's turn to choose a partner for the dance.

"I am," Ren Desvransa replied, wondering how many questions underlay those three words. Then she laughed at herself: *And so every single female he speaks to must think!* Lexan Yvansk was not just a king, he was King of Duen Lesc, one of the richest kingdoms in the world. The old saying was that the Lesci rulers did not make war, they seduced their enemies and turned them into lovers. There had never been a homely Lesci king or queen, but Lexan was a throwback to his ancestor, Mattius the Magnificent.

"What is the attraction in rogues?" Lady Tarsa murmured behind her fan as she drifted past a countess.

The countess, a woman of years and experience, murmured back, "You do not like Ren?" Fan in *maladroit* mode, "I thought everyone liked her."

The Blue Moon Masque, on the full moon before harvest season, was traditionally the last spectacular court event before the aristocracy of Duen Lesc, and those fortunate enough to be the king's guests, went home for the winter.

"Liking her is the fashion," Tarsa said, fan sweeping outward to take in the court, who followed Lexan like flowers follow the sun.

Even that languid, black-eyed Cath Lassatar, Duke of Alavanska. Dragonfire blast him.

"I," Tarsa added, fan flicking in *rue*, "am always fashionable."

This year, summer showed no signs of ending. Curiously enough, nor did the social season. In the gallery beyond the crystal lamps floating about in the air on magical currents, the king's own musicians poured continual music into the vast white marble room with its silver-leafed *argan* trees between fountains along the walls, the ice sculpture on the snowy damask-covered table, the tiny blue lamps winking in the trees on the terrace.

Against the wall opposite the ice sculptures, a spectacular fall of water, controlled by magic, sent cool air ruffling across the floor.

Tarsa paused next to Lord Jarvas, who, as everyone knew, had little use for women. "What is the interest in rogues and rustics? Contrast by degree?"

Everyone also knew that Jarvas had been one of Lexan's many youthful follies. Jarvas's folly, Tarsa thought, was in persistence.

Jarvas leaned negligently against the dragon-scale marble carving around a fountain, from where he'd been observing Ren's enigmatic brother, Yvo, twirling an old baroness as competently as if he'd been raised in a ballroom, not in a looming fortress.

Jarvas touched his fan to his lips, then spread it with a dash of the lace at his wrist. "Contrast," he drawled, "to machination."

Didn't he mean—no, he *couldn't* mean—he was just a fool, in love with a king who loved not him. Tarsa curtseyed with ironic gravity and walked on.

All the guests wore blue, their masks either extravagant or symbolic. Ren's gown was necessarily simple, she having not had time to order, much less pay for, something as spectacular as the gown of knotted silk, winking with tiny diamonds, worn by Countess Tarsa of Rezh, the jeweled headdress woven into her pale coronet of braids so elaborate that it resembled a crown.

The music struck up, but Cath Lassatar continued to lounge, idly fanning himself so slowly that not a hair of his long black locks actually stirred. Only Cath, Tarsa thought sourly, had the insolence to employ the mode of *dragon's wing*, which ordinarily signaled an impending duel.

The king had also chosen to dress simply—which Tarsa had not been able to ascertain beforehand, despite hints, teases, and thumping bribes to useless lackeys. To those who led the mode there was extra style in complementing a couple's costumes: she left nothing to chance if she could avoid it. His shining fall of maple-wood hair was tied back with a diamond clasp, his long, slender body mostly hidden by a many-folded robe resembling those in fashion four centuries ago, his only ornament the rich weave of double-chain.

So it chanced that Ren matched the king in her many layers of midnight blue gossamer. Her curling black hair swung free over her straight back and charming shoulders.

To this austere simplicity, thought Cath Lassatar, she brought as ornament her willingness to admire her surroundings, to be pleased with her company. Uncourtly qualities, but far from uncouth.

He had not moved. Tarsa drifted near, moth to flame. He was the senior duke in court: like the king, come to his title during the recent war, when so many of their elders were killed. The war in which Ren's father and brother had played so ambiguous a role. Tarsa wished these fools would remember. Why was justice so drearily negotiable?

"A little late in the season for dalliance," she said behind her fan. "Might it be that Lexan is more clever than I give him credit, and intends the inevitable to be blessedly short?"

Cath lifted one shoulder lazily, so the light shimmered over his midnight blue silk, molding the strength of his arm before he relaxed and the silk whispered into elegant folds.

"Inevitable?" A sardonic shadow bracketed his mouth before he flashed the fan so that all she could see were his heavy-lidded eyes. "One might counsel you to contemplate the evitable," he retorted, his gaze resting on her decorative crown.

Tarsa schooled herself not to flush, to break her fan in a tightened grip, to reveal in any way how loathsome she found his unshakable superiority. "Evitable," she drawled, "it seems, these days, would be the attractions of a climber who'd committed the error of respectable birth."

Ordinarily, she prided herself on her dainty figure, her little hands and feet, all in proportion; the tiny gliding steps of the courtier were ideally suited to her diminutive size. But when Cath stared down at her like that—his gaze resting on her, as on a mouse from a mountaintop—she loathed being short.

"Climber?" he repeated.

"Does a pretty face make you blind, too? No, not blind. Alas. How about witless? In the three weeks she's been here on this supposed embassy, I've seen her flattering the old people who survived her father's duplicity in the war—flirting with everyone who flirts back—and now this stupidity about *us* singing in a play. Do *you* plan to entertain the rest of us by singing?"

"I do not," he said. "I leave singing plays to the professionals."

She smiled, turning her fan over in *wordless* mode.

"But I do intend to be entertained," he said, laying his fingers on her wrist. He swung her into the dance.

ᎠᏤᏍᎣᎪ

Lexan Yvansk's clasp was so light, Ren could have easily whirled out of his touch. While the music lasted, the world and time ceased, and there was only that glory of flesh touching flesh in their joined hands, and the awareness of his fingers through the filmy gossamer covering her back.

It was the same, and yet not the same, for him. Only the lingering sense of necessity, of duty, kept the fire from consuming him altogether.

He said, "My cousin Najad thinks my absence at the

rehearsals of your performance have slowed progress. Is it true?"

Progress. Performance. Ren reached, remembered. "You are welcome whenever you can spare the time to join us. Really, everyone has been so swift in learning their roles, and they all perform charmingly."

"I have held you up, then. I apologize." He glanced across the ballroom to where Ren's brother, Yvo, danced, to all appearances sober and polite, despite his problematical reputation.

"But we've had fun. I think some will even be sorry when the performance is over."

She'd meant it as a joke, knowing that many of her volunteers had agreed to perform out of idleness, out of curiosity, out of a wish to not be out of the mode. Some had discovered in themselves an enthusiasm for being on stage. But wasn't being a courtier a kind of living performance? "I know I'll be sorry," she finished, so he would not take her pause amiss. "I've enjoyed every day."

His smile was more polite than humorous. "You have the remedy to that."

"To do another?" she asked, the implications dizzying. He was never overt, she'd been warned. "What if they tire of me as director? Ought not one of their own be chosen?"

"Do you desire to be quit of your role, then?"

There are two conversations here, she thought.

"They could desire to be quit of me," she said, trusting to the context of the play to mask her real meaning: *Your court is divided, and that hurts you. Can you not see that what hurts you also hurts me?*

"Not," he said as they walked slowly down the room, "from what I see."

From what you see, or what you choose to see? How can

I make the two into one? "Ah, but did we not begin this conversation over duty concerning your missing rehearsal?" She turned her face to the magical breeze as they danced through it, though the warmth was from within, and she did not wish to be shed of it.

"Is that a challenge?" he asked, smiling.

"Come to the next rehearsal, and witness for yourself," she rejoined, laughing. There, that was safe enough.

"I shall," he promised. "But you are evading my question."

"Surely not," she said, winning a quick smile from him.

His gaze went diffuse for a moment, two steps, three. Always at that slow pace, taking no notice of the stealthy glances their way. He was inured to being constantly watched, Ren thought. Thus the formidable mental walls that she would never betray his trust by trying to breach—although she could.

"What," he asked presently, "would you do in my place?"

The implications! Her step never faltered, but her mind sped from one possibility to another, until she realized the pause might become a silence—with its own message—so she resorted to one of her brother Yvo's unloved tricks, answering a question with a question: "Hold up a verbal mirror?"

He laughed, a real laugh. "I should have expected anyone trained as you have been trained would be adept at evasion."

She smiled back, enjoying his deliberate provocation. He was richer than the ten surrounding kingdoms, his family was as old as the First Dragon, he was smart, beautiful, and she'd grown up knowing many future kings and queens, all of whom had talked about the sophistication of the Lesci court, its king most of all.

She had discovered that he was kind.

Are you free?

He was also a king. A crown was nothing but a royal binding.

"Let us make a pact," she suggested. "Each of us must answer one question before posing one of our own, or we'll begin hooting at one another like a pair of owls."

He laughed. "My question stands."

The dance was finishing up. They had reached the vast waterfall.

Trusting the muting effects of trickling water, she said, "Come to the rehearsal tomorrow, and sing, and see what your court thinks of my taste in Duen Lesci singing plays." Her chuckle was sudden, the more enchanting because there was no sense of superiority or of calculation—despite her training having been overseen by the longest sighted person in the world.

The music stopped. His world encircled him again. There was his marble ballroom, and his guests, some watching overtly and some covertly, and the servants who waited on the guests and watched them all for a good chat later. He bowed, let her step away, leaving air between them. Then he looked back.

Ren's body, obedient to the will, had disengaged, but her mind clamored for joining. Through her mind, a thousand trivial questions and comments streamed, to be summarily dammed. This, too, was a common ploy of all his admirers—to keep him by their side, talking. She would not deny his access to others.

The men—all except for Cath Lassatar, but he was watching—closed around Ren. She said something that caused a laugh, covered her eyes with one hand and reached with the other. The fellows gave Najad precedence. Ren was kind to him, Lexan had observed, but he'd swear she never thought of him as a suitor. Her interactions with Cath Lassatar had been far fewer and, from a distance, tense. He could not comprehend her reaction to Cath: he knew, as one does after a certain amount of experience, that what she felt was not indifference.

Ren whirled into the next dance, feeling safe enough with the pleasant, non-demanding Najad to scan the room once.

She saw, with pain, the Duchess Tarsa's pale-faced fury as she rustled, jewels trembling, straight to Lexan's side.

She felt a swoop of warning at Cath of Alavanska's unwavering black gaze.

She did not see her brother Yvo's reflective countenance as he played the role of a model guest, and watched them all.

II. The Contemplation of Rings

The spectacle of Lexan deep in conversation with Ren during that long dance both annoyed and amused Cath. The amusement was caused by Tarsa's increasingly unsubtle efforts to keep them always in view, causing Cath to dance her to the opposite side of the room and keep her there.

When it was over, he stayed away from the eager young lords clamoring for Ren's attention, but did Tarsa take a hint? No. She rushed straight to Lexan's side to claim him before any other lady could, the fourth time this evening. Shaking his head, he began calculating how long before he could be gone.

Tarsa kept her head high, though she watched for Ren to glance her way, eager to see the same anguish in those honey-brown eyes that Tarsa had felt during that long dance with Lexan.

Her own ended far too soon, and Lexan thanked her with a courteous air, so courteous she couldn't think of a way to keep him at her side so he could not ask someone else. He was gone, extending his hand to the delegate from Breis.

She was left standing there, all those jewels pressing on

her head. Her head ached, her eyes ached.

" . . . dance the waltz?"

She felt the touch of a hand on her wrist, and looked up, uncomprehending, into gray-green eyes. It was that strange Yvo fellow: no title, but with *his* history, he didn't need one.

She couldn't speak, but he didn't wait. He slid his hand over hers, and again her body moved, stiff but obedient.

He did not speak. They just danced. Presently, she realized that the slow circles he made, the easy rhythm, were curiously soothing.

A ring on his little finger winked and gleamed like water, no, like silver, only silver seen in a fog or a dream. The ring was carved in a pattern of vines and leaves. She turned her head to watch the gleaming ring on his raised hand that clasped hers in such a cool, steadying grip.

Her eyes ached less, somehow.

"Do you like to waltz?" Yvo asked.

"Yes, I do," she said, grateful that he hadn't spoken until now.

"It's probably the most enduring of dance forms," he said. "Others go in and out of fashion, but this one has persisted throughout history."

"So I learned when I was small," she said. "Do you know where it originated?"

"Ah, that is a mystery. Some maintain it came from another world than ours; others insist we invented it, and took it to that world, where it also persists." He paused, guiding her skillfully between two couples in danger of colliding. "Perhaps it is a form inevitable for humans," he said. "Two people, the entrancing rhythm. The eternal circles, described by each couple and writ large by the group. Rings—" he smiled down at her, "—of promise."

Yvo was one of the oddest persons to come to court. He'd appeared quite suddenly a week ago. No one had known what to expect, as Lexan and his father had been enemies at one time. But he stayed.

"Interesting question that probably no one can answer," she said, feeling strength slowly return. And with it, awareness.

Remembering who he was, Tarsa considered what his words, seeming so neutral, really *meant*. His father was universally cried down as a villain, then lauded as a hero. He involved himself in world politics, not just jostling for rank in a single court.

"Rings of promise? Is that a jab at crowns?" she asked abruptly. "If even a small portion of the stories are true, your father could have done anything. Had anything, at the end of the war. He could have taken over Duen Lesc—I don't think Lexan could have stopped him. Lexan said as much. I was there."

Yvo shrugged. "Maybe true, maybe not. It's irrelevant."

"How so?" Strange, how easy he was to talk to.

"Because my father wanted only one thing, his freedom. Nothing else matters, though he does like comfort if he can get it. His house is very comfortable."

"But . . . to be that powerful, and to give it all up?"

"Give what up?"

Tarsa's mind wheeled. "Rank. Fortune. Influence."

"He never had rank, or not in the world that we recognize. Never wanted it. As for fortune, his requirements were comfort, as I said, and also the wherewithal to carry out plans. Once he judged he had enough for that, the acquisition ceased to be of interest. Influence . . . " Yvo smiled, "he still has that."

"He does? But one never hears of it."

"No," he said, still smiling, and once again steered them

away from possible collision.

"So how can he possibly have influence?"

Yvo paused for a fast-whirling couple to pass. His eyes were shuttered by his lashes, unexpectedly long, then they lifted. "If a hand moves through the still pond, do not the ripples ring out, whether the hand smites the water or dips without a splash?" He smiled again, the same sudden smile Ren had, dimples deep on either side of his strong jaw. "Can we not call them rings of influence?"

She frowned, sensing the proximity of meaning. How could anyone have influence without a position of power?

And what could one possibly get out of it, if one hadn't the privilege of rank?

"Does he get any kind of reward?" she asked after getting no answer within her own perception of the world.

"Yes," Yvo said. "Success."

"Huh." So he implied there was some kind of power outside of rank. Everyone knew that rank conferred power. That was the accepted definition, the universally acknowledged hierarchy.

"Thank you," Yvo said, and she realized the waltz had ended.

She curtseyed to him and watched him drift into the crowd, but her calm snapped away, replaced by anger when she glimpsed Cath and Ren at the far door. They were alone.

Ren! Tarsa felt the corrosive stream of jealousy flood back, then stilled to interest when she saw Ren jerk her arm back from Cath's fingers. Quick as a snake, he gripped her arm again. Ren's chin lifted, her gown shimmered. Was she trying to pull away?

They went through the alcove that led to the garden, and were gone.

Tarsa turned away, smiling. The *garden?* The terrace was for intimate talk; the garden was where the very young retired to steal kisses.

Yet Cath and Ren had not looked even remotely like a couple bent on dalliance. At least, she hadn't. No telling what he thought—ever. Except, of course, to amuse himself by being cruel.

It had seemed, in fact, that Ren did not want to walk with Cath. Was he, by any chance, benefitting her with an excoriating examination of her blatant flirtation with the king?

Tarsa wished her joy of it.

Still smiling, she decided to favor the king's cousin Najad with a dance, since he persisted with that silly crush on her. Najad—cousin to a king, as if she'd ever look at him twice! Cousin to a king was about as close to power as a candle to the sun. At least, dancing with Najad would keep her well within Lexan's proximity, and there was always the next waltz to look forward to.

⊰⊱

Cath of Alavanska had noticed, years before, that the patterns of movement in a ballroom resembled the ebb and flow of sea tides, a curiosity of nature he'd once witnessed while traveling away from land-locked Duen Lesc.

After the midnight bells rang, many of the older people retired. This was just another ball, another diversion in their established lives. It remained for the young and passionate, those whose lives were still unsettled and alive with promise, to dance the night through.

He watched, smiling inwardly, until Lexan was busy at the far end, talking diplomacy. Tarsa was with that strange Yvo. Everyone else drifted after Lexan, leaving the waterfall to plash and thunder unseen, the alcoves unused.

Cath dealt easily enough with the young sparks round Ren, two of whom were drunk.

"Come. Take a stroll, where it's a trifle less noisy," he suggested, loud enough to be overheard.

"I don't mind noise," Ren said, but fell in beside him. He meant to emulate the courtly drift, but must have seemed too purposeful, for Ren reacted, quick as a butterfly. "Why in this direction?"

They were now almost at the extreme exit, far from other people.

"Cooler air here."

"The air is not overly warm in this room," Ren countered. "Nor is it stuffy."

"Ah, but it will be sweeter outside. The gardens, after a rain, have quite a scent."

"They will in the morning, too," she responded, smiling a little.

"But it's better now," he said. "You will see."

Four, three steps to go.

"I would rather walk about in here," she stated, looking down at where he'd taken hold of her hand. She pulled her fingers free.

"But I arranged a surprise," he said, and took her arm. "It will only be a moment." He felt muscle under the smooth skin of her arm.

"Something nice, I trust?" Her voice was dubious.

"Yes," he promised, for he believed his promise.

It was the conviction in that soft-spoken 'yes' that caused her to walk with him, despite the strange intensity of his gaze, his insistent grip, even the way he breathed.

Alarm tingled through her, but she couldn't believe there

could possibly be danger at a ball, not with a hundred couples dancing forty paces away. She walked with him through the alcove and through the open doors into a tiled terrace, potted trees winking with tiny lights. Beyond lay the garden. The scents of woodbine and jasmine and queensblossom perfumed the air. Moths air-danced near the doorway, their wings golden-lit. No one else was there.

Her ears registered steps on the gravel below the terrace, and the soft snort of a horse. She turned her head, her eyes adjusting rapidly, and made out the shape of a horse, and a man beside it, waiting in the concealing shrubs. Not just one horse—two!

She pulled away. "What are you doing?"

He took hold of her arm again, but this time she whipped her arm out of his grip and spun away, almost out of his reach, to discover herself ringed by silent men. Quicker than thought, he closed the distance and seized her more firmly.

It was a quick, desperate fight, for she was very well trained, and knew subtle movements that did not rely on strength or size. Her fragile, exquisitely fitted gown limited her range of movement, and her loose hair got painfully in her way. He was much the stronger and quicker, but he was disadvantaged by his determination to prevail, yet do her no hurt.

Prevail he did. After a silent, swift struggle, he held her gripped against him, one hand round her prisoned wrists, the other covering her mouth. He felt her trembling against his body, and nearly laughed out loud for pleasure and anticipation.

Then came the least pleasant aspect of his plan. He bound her himself. He did not permit his lackey to do it, for he trusted only himself to find that balance between security and comfort, and he would not have any hands but his own touching her.

Silken bonds only, wrists, ankles, mouth. Then he snapped his fingers, and his liveried man silently brought forward his fastest and heaviest cross-country mount.

He carried her himself.

The lackeys ran behind as they trotted along the tiled garden path to the outskirts, between the wide-spaced peacetime guards who watched for trouble from without, not within.

They wound through the gardens to where the paths linked up with one of the main city roads. A turn to the north, away from the few buildings, to the yard of an inn where the northern road crossed the extreme boundary of the palace gardens.

There the remainder of his servants waited with a four-horse carriage. Still mounted, he glanced inside, saw by the single lit candle that all his commands had been carried out exactly.

He dismounted, lifted Ren down, set her unresisting body on the coach seat against the silk-covered pillows, and paused in the doorway, watching her angry eyes above the black sash, gleaming in the light of the candle now held by a lackey.

"We are going to Alavanska," he said.

She didn't blink, just glared at him. No sign of fear, of pleading, of tears. Even when he removed the gag, she said nothing at all.

He shut the door, motioned the lackeys to take their places as he remounted his horse. Waved for the driver to loosen the reins and roll out.

All night, he rode beside the carriage, guarding his chosen lady.

III. The Etiquette of Abduction

Ren saw four opportunities for escape before that first morning.

Each would have involved hurting someone, which—as yet—she was unwilling to do. When the fourth occurred, she cursed herself mentally for not paying attention years ago when her brother offered to teach her that point on the side of the neck below the jawbone that dropped people into unconsciousness. What use would that be to someone who took pride in using wit and good will instead of trickery and brawn?

Men! Except . . . the two successful abductions in her own admittedly strange family had been carried off, both at swordpoint, by women. One, her great-grandmother, was still alive.

Oh well. She'd just have to manage by her own methods.

She thought it all through as the beautifully sprung carriage rocked and rattled northward, pulled by four fast horses. Lexan's roads were very good, she observed. So too were Cath's horses, carriage, and his servants.

The pauses to change the horses were accomplished swiftly and smoothly. At one point, a servant poked his head in, scrupulously respectful of demeanor, and offered Ren a steaming, fragrant cup of hot chocolate.

"No, thank you," she said. "I'll take water if you have it. Nothing else."

The man seemed nonplused. He bowed, and withdrew, telltale red along his plump cheeks.

Ren felt some regret, for the air was chill, and the chocolate would probably have tasted as good as it smelled, but she'd determined on passive resistance, to see what that occasioned.

Cath—blast his twisty little brain—had *enjoyed* her

fighting to get free. Enjoyed it? Well, then, she'd not give him that pleasure again.

The servant returned with a brimming cup of water, which he held to her lips and she drank down. Her headache receded. She thanked him gravely, and he shut the carriage door.

The coach began rolling, and no one came near her again until well on into the next day; with the gag gone, she thought in relief, she could at least use the Waste Spell. But her stomach gurgled fretfully at its neglect.

Noon came and went, with another stop, another offer of food. She accepted only water. She looked out the window at the changing scenery, farmland and well-tended canals giving way to hills, with mountains nearing. She leaned out once, but her eyes met Cath's gaze as he rode next to the carriage. She refused to open the window again.

On the second stop, the door opened once more and this time, it was Cath himself. At some point, he had changed out of his silk and jewels into a sturdy linen shirt under a vest, riding trousers stuffed into high spurred boots. A baldric crossed his chest, to which was attached a well-made dueling rapier.

He untied the sashes round her wrists and ankles. Glad she was to be free at last—obviously they were now deep within his own lands—she gave him no sign of reaction.

"Are you hungry or thirsty?" he asked.

She didn't answer.

"Will you take something? Bread? Coffee?"

"No," she said.

He shut the door.

They rolled on very soon.

Presently, the carriage wound its way up increasingly steep inclines. They stopped more frequently. No one came to the door, and she did not open it, or try to run, for she sensed alert minds waiting nervously outside.

She had decided that she would not involve servants, if she could help it. This duel was between herself and their master.

☙❧☙☙❧☙

She jerked awake when they stopped again. Excited voices surrounded the coach—they must have reached his citadel. The orange flares of torches outside the window shone against the pale blue of dawn.

The coach door opened a moment later. Uneven torchlight outlined Cath's silhouette.

"Will you step out, Ren?" He held out his hand.

In silence she complied, but without touching him. He withdrew as soon as he saw her intention, and waited, still holding the door, until she stood up, shaking out her skirts and fighting against vertigo.

"Please, this way," he said.

She paced beside him without speaking.

Looking down at his prisoner, Cath saw stony control, and the innate grace that informed every movement, even when she stalked, even when she was grubby and tired, and hadn't eaten for two days. Anticipation was heightened by admiration. She did not just have style, she *was* style. Impatient as he'd been, he discovered he did not want her to surrender too quickly.

Ren took in the massive stone lineaments of a formidable castle, not surprising for a border duchy. Clearly, it had been built for defense and to ward off fierce mountain winds, weather, and warriors.

Inside, she found the well-maintained tastes of former generations. Outmoded furnishings amused her, heavy carved chair arms and legs, stylized representations of magical beasts, the court of the First Dragon as envisioned four hundred years ago.

Down a carpeted hall, and into a room whose chill was soon banished by a new-lit magical fire in a great fireplace. Autumn came early to the mountains, she realized.

Two great wing-chairs sat angled toward the fire, with a table between them. Cath indicated one, then bent to augment the light by touching candles to the flames.

He'd gotten rid of the rapier, she noticed. In the golden light, he looked as disheveled as she felt, mud-splashed to the thighs from having ridden the entire distance on horseback. She mentally awarded him credit for his straight back and alert, though narrow-eyed, gaze: he probably had as great a headache as she did. But she permitted no sign of hers in her demeanor.

He sank in the other chair, heedless of his mud. He stretched his booted feet before him, spurs winking in the firelight, and a sigh escaped him.

She remained standing, though she felt her effort in every joint and bone.

"Shall I summon refreshment?" He drew off his riding gloves and laid them on the table.

"Not for me," she said.

His lip curled. "You intend to starve to death?"

"I have not yet decided what to do," she stated in as cold a voice as she could contrive. "Until I do, I've no wish to touch anything of yours."

He leaned back, hands idle on the chair arms. A ruby on his little finger winked with rich burgundy light, a steady wink: his heartbeat. She forced her gaze away.

"What are your choices?" he asked, in the voice of power humoring the powerless.

"Whether to leave or to stay, of course," she said, her

tone one of surprise.

"Meaning?" he prompted.

"Meaning either I cut my way through your people—something I contemplate with distaste—or I remain and dwindle to death, another unpleasant choice."

"I'd rather you do neither," he said, still humoring her. "Though I confess I'd like to see you try the first."

"I know you would," she retorted. "The prospect of killing your servants for your entertainment does nothing to enhance my diminishing respect for you."

"Will it bolster my declining prestige if I admit that I don't think you capable of killing any of my people?"

"You would be wrong." Her steady gaze reflected the candlelight, gold within a ring of black, within a ring of gold, more enchanting a pair of eyes than any art could contrive.

His brows went up slightly. "I'm inclined to give some credence to your claims, judging from how close you came to grassing me in the palace garden."

She remained silent.

"Which one of 'em trained you?" he asked. "Your brother or your father?"

She did not answer that, either.

His fingers drummed on the arm of his chair, but only for a few moments. He became aware of the movement, and ceased.

"Will you consider a third choice?" he asked presently.

"That depends."

"I want to marry you," Cath said.

"Then you should have asked."

"And you would have said?"

"I would have refused. And the present situation is not likely to change my decision."

"Maybe," he admitted, smiling a little. "I was bored with

court, and with waiting on the fools who surrounded you, so I decided someone needed to take action, and why not I?"

Her lips parted, but then she closed them.

He was bemused by her lack of reaction, as she had hoped. She knew that anything else—tears, fury, haughty resentment—would have entertained him. Begging would have disgusted him, but it would have disgusted her more.

"Will you tell me what criteria will affect your decision?" he asked.

"Yes. If you offer me violence, I'll use it back if I can."

"I will not use violence," he stated flatly.

"Then your people will take no harm of me," she promised.

His brows lifted again. He was too tired to mask his reactions, so she saw that he was beginning to believe that she could do what she claimed.

"And me?" he asked next, lips curling.

"You deserve whatever you get."

"So I cannot touch you without leave, but you are bound by no such constraint?"

"I am here against my will," she said. "I see this as a way of restoring a semblance of balance."

"May I defend myself?" The amusement was back.

"Yes," she said tranquilly.

He steepled his fingers. "So you've been trained to strike once, have you? Ah, I'd forgotten the scholarly Yvo. Or rather, your father and his sinister allies, around whom you presumably must have spent your formative years, eh?"

She did not answer.

"Interesting. So the personal risk is mine. It seems fair enough. Very well, I accept your rules." He paused. When she remained silent, he said, "Does that mean you'll take food and drink?"

He spoke in a plaintive tone a shade too obvious to be serious, yet she descried the concern below it.

"Yes."

"I'm relieved." His court drawl was back. "Would you like anything now?"

Her stomach squeezed, but she decided her point was best made if she steeled herself. "No."

"Then I'll show you where you'll stay." He smiled. "Until you choose to change that, too." He rose, and in silence she followed him out.

Of course, it was a tower room. She took a good look at access and egress, not caring if he saw her doing it.

When she was inside, he said, "I wish you a good rest."

She did not respond, for she'd decided that the circumstances obviated politeness. She would not say please or thank you to an abductor. They had a truce, not a relationship.

When he realized she would not speak, he shut the door. She heard a lock engage on the outside.

There was a fireplace—someone had ridden ahead and a clear, warm fire burned—and pleasant if heavy furnishings that evoked masculine tastes. She wondered, suddenly, as she looked at the bookcases, the fine linens on the bed, if this had been where Cath was locked up by his relations during the early part of the war, before he ran away to fight for the king.

She stepped through the cleaning frame beside the empty wardrobe. The tingle of magic snapped away the grit in hair, skin, teeth, clothing. She took off her gown and laid it aside with care, then climbed into the bed. On the bedside table was a water pitcher and glass. She helped herself, drank deeply, then burrowed into the pillows and dropped into sleep.

IV. The Politics of Diplomacy

Tarsa lay in bed, stretching in lazy pleasure.

Ren was still missing, she just knew it. She glanced at the window, and laughed. How often had she woken this early? Not often.

Annoyance soured her mood when she thought of the two long, empty days she'd spent. Everything had begun so delightfully when her silly friend Mrentze bustled in and gabbled out breathlessly, "Did you hear? Ren is gone—and so is the Black Duke!"

Tarsa had seen at once how to destroy Ren Desvransa as a threat, but still not harm a hair of her pretty, empty head. Wasn't that true queenship, to be able to think brilliantly in a moment?

"You don't mean that Ren eloped with him at last?" Tarsa had asked, yawning behind her hand.

Mrentze's face! She'd never forget the sight of those pop eyes, the round mouth, her oh-so-well-born nose twitching. "You *knew*? You knew, and you didn't say anything?"

"That would show so little finesse," Tarsa had murmured, finding her position stronger by the moment. She could just *hear* Mrentze's voice up and down the halls of court.

"What did you know?" Mrentze looked askance. "If you say that Ren told *you* her plans, I say you dreamed it."

Tarsa bit back a hot rejoinder. How dare this mere follower all but call the leader of fashion a liar?

But she had to keep the goal in view. "Tact forbade me say anything last night, when they so obviously wanted privacy, but yes, I saw them go out together, directly from the ball."

All strictly true.

Mrentze scarcely stayed long enough to be polite, leaving

Tarsa laughing as she raced into fevered preparation, so that Lexan, in coming to corroborate what she had witnessed, might find her appropriately employed when he came to seek commiseration. Or even sympathy. She'd give it, because Tarsa always thought of the kingdom first, and not just of her own pleasure—unlike Ren.

She'd whiled away two long days in her rooms, doing artistic things, twice having her maids bring in fresh flowers and throw out the old, while the hired minstrel plunked away in the alcove.

Now she rolled over, looking across her empty bed. How long since anyone had slept beside her in her cotton-silk sheets? An internal image, strong but unwanted, came: Ren and Cath together. Cath's hands, his long black hair, unbound, drifting across flesh, so soft, the scent of it—did Ren twine her fingers through it?

Revulsion tightened her insides. How foolish, she thought, flinging herself out of bed. How weak! One drunken night, long ago, and while it had been good—*very*—Cath was not a king.

She dressed with care, for this would be her first time she'd emerged from her rooms. She'd even decided against attending the concert scheduled for the previous night, because she knew that nothing would be discussed but Ren, Ren, Ren.

And Cath, of course. She didn't want to hear that either.

She sat down to her breakfast just as there came a knock at the outer door. Her chief maid entered and bowed. "His Grace the Duke of Desentis requests a private interview, my lady."

Najad? Well, he'd certainly know what was going on, and she wouldn't have to ask anyone who mattered. Meanwhile, he'd be a fair gauge of the atmosphere of court.

"Bid him enter," Tarsa said.

She had scarcely finished buttering her second little roll when Najad strode in, big, brawny, terribly and tiresomely earnest, dressed in riding clothes.

"Tarsa," he said, without any vestige of the niceties.

"Najad." She nodded regally. "I just sat down to breakfast. Would you care to join me?"

He ignored her gesture at the other chair, and her question. He looked perplexed, compressed his lips, then burst out, "That gabbler Mrentze has spread it all over court that you saw Ren run off with Alavanska."

He hadn't even waited until the servant was gone.

She set her pastry down with delicate care. "Is that still the subject? I am so glad I had a headache yesterday. What of it if she chose to go away with the Duke of Alavanska?"

"Did you really see them?"

She did not like his tone of voice at all. But now was not the time to put him in his place, or what would be his place, when her rank exceeded his. "Oh, Najad," she said in her most lachrymose voice. "The business is too painful to discuss. Why does it matter what I saw?"

He blinked, the stupid dolt. "I'm sorry to upset you," he said finally, slamming his palm against the back of the empty chair before him, thump, thump. Before she could request him not to damage her furniture, he said abruptly, "I'll leave." Turned away without waiting for her answer, and stalked out, spurs ringing on her marble floor.

V. *The Duelists Engage*

Ren faced Cath's wardrobe steward, who had come herself rather than send one of her underlings. "I appreciate your effort, and I shall make certain that his grace knows that you tried," Ren said pleasantly. "However, I will not wear anything but my gown." Ren indicated her blue mothwing, which of course looked absurd in daylight. Wearing it would underscore the fact that she had not consented to be here.

The poor woman glanced up, then down, her mouth working. Ren smiled in sympathy, and spoke again to make it clear that the steward was absolved of any possible blame. "These gowns you brought are very fine, and under ordinary circumstances, I would have liked them very much."

The woman bowed, slowly folded the three day-dresses. She glanced once more at Ren, as if mentally pleading with her to change her mind, and then left.

The door shut.

Ren closed her eyes, sent out a mental feeler, and sensed the enormous armed guard posted outside the door. She repressed a sigh and combed out her hair, then fingered it into a braid down her back. Then she worked through a full set of the unarmed combat drills her brother had trained into her as habit, which left her tightened muscles loose and relaxed.

She'd just finished when a knock came at the door.

"His grace invites you to breakfast, my lady," came a voice.

Outside stood not just the guard in mail and fighting livery, but a sizable herald. Both looked at her with eyes slightly distended, and she suppressed the urge to snicker. Did they really expect her to take them on in a wrestling match? What had Cath *said*?

She was still smiling when she walked into the room with the big chairs, which she recognized as Cath's favorite, and probably the most comfortable room in the castle. Downstairs were the great state rooms, for this was the main residence of the family, but those were vast and, at this time of year, unpleasantly cold.

"You are amused?" Cath asked, rising. "Good morning," he added.

She did not respond to his courtesy, but sat down. "What did you tell those mountain-sized guards? They looked at me as if I'd bite them in half."

"Ask them yourself," he retorted. "I recommend the cheese-pasty. My cook is better than Lexan's, at least with breakfast."

"Now that I can't believe," she said, piling food onto her platter. Not just the flaky-crusted pasty, but fresh fruit and bread that must have come straight from the oven to this table, for it still steamed. A cup of fresh butter stood at the side.

"Have you thought about your rules for how to occupy your time?" he asked, with some irony. "As, I assume, I am still under threat of violence if I touch you."

She matched his tone exactly. "You are. But I am open to other suggestions."

"Well, you can stay here and read, or talk to my head steward. She'd like nothing more than to discuss the intricacies of housekeeping. Or you can ride along with me, for I've a number of pressing matters to see to, not surprising since I've been at court all summer."

"I'd much prefer riding with you," Ren said, "as long as I remain officially invisible. No introductions, no explanations of who I am."

"Shall I arrange for riding clothes?"

"No."

He frowned, rubbed a thumb across his brow. "People will think it odd—"

"They already do," she said cheerfully. "Every single one of them, most likely. They just don't speculate in front of you."

She grinned, and addressed the unspoken question. "I might make a spectacle of myself riding about in a ball gown, but I am an observer, not a participant in your life. Since we have this much of an understanding, I don't intend to go anywhere until you escort me back to Alsais, everything proper and in daylight."

"Ah," he said, brow clearing.

She knew he misconstrued, but that was all right.

He'd find out.

VI. The Politics of Desire

After a week, Tarsa emerged from her rooms to discover that the social season, officially ended with the Blue Moon Masque, had left the palace curiously full of people. So far, it seemed, the only departures had been Cath and Ren. Up and down the guest wing of the palace—Risto Row to the inmates of rank, and the Fribble File to the house servants who had to look after them, although Tarsa would never hear that—doors were still closed, which indicated occupancy. When people left for home, the rooms were opened, aired, and cleaned.

So people were around, but nowhere in sight. Further, no one appeared to have scrambled together delightful parties, or outings, or even concerts or readings in order to pass the time, for no scented invitations had been slipped beneath her door. Was it possible they all waited for Tarsa to take the lead?

Time to survey the field.

She did not bother to check the fencing salle, where mornings found the younger men and the more rambunctious young women. She'd worked hard at swordplay during the war days, but had gladly abandoned it afterward, having decided that a queen did not need to impress anyone with her swordsmanship.

No one in the garden, the card rooms, even the informal dining room. Where were they? Surely not all in their rooms, dallying with one another?

She remembered that stupid play Ren had chosen and its foolish philosophizing. Was it better to be lover or beloved? Her thoughts reached first for Cath and Ren, but she pushed them away. But that left Lexan Yvansk . . .

. . . and the contrast between his neutral, benign deference, on which she had staked her entire life against the gain of a crown, and his behavior since Ren had come. Love? It couldn't possibly be love, just lust for a pretty face on his part, and for a crown on hers. Oh, for his person too, which everyone who had eyes desired. What was surprising was that he had not set her up as a favorite, not even for one of those long, door-shut intervals that had happened so frequently when they were all very young, before the war. He was kind to former partners, but never more than a friend. He had been rumored to indulge in sex in every possible human combination, but he had never once set up a lover in the sense of beloved.

And, despite Tarsa's fears, he had not begun this summer.

Had she misjudged? No, they all had seen his eyes when he watched Ren. *Lust.*

After the noon bells, she went to find out, if she could, where the inner court was. Surely, they were not still asleep!

Rain made it impossible to cut through gardens. She frowned at the gray sky and rounded a corner, then staggered as a figure almost ran her down.

"Oh! Lady Tarsa! I am sorry!"

It was that silly twit, Loria. The girl curtseyed, a court curtsey, her manner so humble and contrite, Tarsa nodded more graciously than she'd meant and said only, "I trust there is no emergency, no fire?"

"No, only I overslept horridly, and now I'm late. Are you coming too? Someone said you were ill."

"Coming?"

Loria looked as blank as that idiot, Najad. "Of course," she said, hands spread prettily. One of Ren's gestures. "You remember: *Love's Favors Lost*. Rehearsing. The king has taken over the direction himself."

Lightning blinded Tarsa, an internal strike of white pain that had nothing to do with the summer storm hissing over the garden. She hadn't forgotten that stupid play, but she'd assumed everyone else had. "Oh, of course."

She followed Loria to the king's theatre, where all the court was gathered, including Lexan. As she and Loria entered, the rise and fall of a man's and woman's voices reached them, along with the strains of a full orchestra, the king's own musicians.

The stage was filled not with professional players, but aristocrats. Practicing, just like paid players wandering the kingdom. Lexan stood in the center, a sheaf of papers in his hand.

At Tarsa's and Loria's entry, most turned around.

"Ah, there you are," exclaimed one of the Zaltans, coming forward to claim Loria.

Najad stood behind his cousin, some kind of prop in hand. He bowed to Tarsa, his expression difficult to interpret; it was a face she'd never seen before. He didn't speak, but walked off with a couple of the fellows, talking in a low voice.

Lexan nodded a greeting to her, and asked if she was recovered?

"Yes, sire," she said, curtseying.

"Thank you for joining us. Your act is just finished, but

we'll review it once more," he said, and turned his attention back to the stage.

Somehow, she made it through the rest of that day, standing on the periphery of that crowd, watching Ren's absurd play being put together, as if it mattered. She simpered and sang when asked to, and pretended an interest.

At the end one of the sillier climbers whispered, "If you have nothing better, a few of us are going into town in mask, for a little diversion."

Although she'd never encouraged the woman's pretensions and had despised people who went to town to seek diversion, she heard herself accept.

In mask. There were no actual masks, of course, hadn't been for a couple hundred years. Aristocrats laid aside their fluttering, embroidered silks and donned ordinary clothing, as worn by the wealthier citizens of the capital. That meant, like the Masques, no claims of rank or precedence. Although one might be recognized, no one spoke of it, but one could not use one's rank, either. A duchess might sit next to a seamstress's apprentice at an inn, but if the dinner was good and the talk engaging, there was a kind of freedom in it, an escape from the fraught consequences of court.

Through the evening she followed the noisy group from place to place, ignoring the music, the laughter, smiling and smiling though her entire body ached with anger, tension, even a kind of grief. She kept wondering why she had even come until, with some relief, she recognized that they had entered the spice-scented House of Stars, the favored pleasure house of slumming aristocrats.

She was never aware of making a choice, but somehow she found herself upstairs, with a tall young man with long black hair, who saw that she did not want to speak, and sensed her need, her very great need, and did his best to assuage it.

Even in the fires of desire and expertly awakened passion, she could not quite rid herself of the vision of Lexan Yvansk on the stage, or of that look in Najad's eyes, the steady and distanced stare of hurt, of sadness, of disillusionment.

And so, although they returned just before dawn, she had gained enough clarity to think ahead, to once again claim her life for her own. By the time the other women had sunk into well-contented slumber, Tarsa was down in the stables, departing alone for the north.

VII. The Perils of Fire

"I was supposed to visit Wyst that year, but war prevented my foray into worldly polish," Cath said wryly as they sat over breakfast that next morning. "Afterward, there was too much to do for protracted absences, so I have that pleasure yet to experience."

"Perhaps we might have met," Ren said. "What an odd thing, to look back and wonder about such possibilities of encounter! My mother and I were in Wyst that year, before she remarried."

"You visited the highlands, of course." He knew it was contemptible, but pride prevented him from admitting that his family had apparently not been deemed influential or worthy enough for permission to see the Dragon Lands.

Ren's lashes lifted in mild query. "We spent the summer there."

He bit back the impulse to repeat, in the witless way he detested in other people, *You spent the summer on the highlands?* "What can you tell me about it?" Cath reached to pour more coffee into his cup.

Ren cradled her tea in her fingers. "What is there to tell? It's big, and vast, and you scarcely ever see the dragons. But when you do. . . ." She shivered. "You remember how small and breakable and impermanent humans are. The other thing is, they are loud. Everything they do is loud. I have a cousin who's a mage, who spent fifty years as a tree. She said we don't realize that we're loud and horrible to creatures tinier than us." She cocked her head, smiling ruefully. "Am I boring you? I'm afraid I was an awful chatterer when I was small. It's still a habit."

"I am not the least bored. I was trying to imagine spending even a day as a tree. Do go on."

She shrugged. "I saw why they'd never let me go to the highlands when I was small. I would have been terrified witless. In truth, I was happy enough to stay in the old city when my mother went to the highlands to study. In the palace, there are so many niches and corners, every one a story! For example, on the sentry walk below the oldest tower, there are footprints supposed to be left from one of the Winged Avengers when she touched down to save the queen's ancestor. The prints are small, and I used to fit my bare toes in when I was about four. The queen told me once they think that story is apocryphal. Not about the rescue, that's in the records, but about her touching down when the Dragons burned the city, and making those prints. I didn't care, it was the palace children I loved. All of them—cook's children, stewards' prentices, princes and princesses—over the centuries, standing just where I was standing. Looking around in wonder at the world." She smiled. "Now I *am* boring."

Cath was not bored. He was unsettled at how easily Ren Desvransa quoted queens. Not conceited or calculating, but with the comfort of long acquaintance. She didn't seem to be aware of the effect, because it was her natural state.

He was trying to find something to say when bells rang

outside, reminding him of the time. And duty.

He set his coffee aside. "Alas. Much as I would like to continue this discussion, I've a Name Day celebration for a liegeman's first child."

Ren waved a hand. "Go on. It seems a good day to sit by the fire and read."

"You do not wish to accompany me?"

"Not the least," Ren said with cheer.

He'd seen that indefatigable cheer when he mentioned social obligations. Since their arrival, he'd been showered with invitations, most of them intimating in the most delicate way possible that if he wished to bring company, he was quite welcome to.

He walked rapidly toward the stable, one of his scribes trotting at his side and reading off the morning's messages, which today were more invitations. To each he said either, "Yes" or "No". At times like this, he thought with a spurt of humor after four *No*s in a row, it was good to have a reputation for a caustic tongue. He went to the ones he didn't feel he could shun; though word had indeed spread, no one had quite dared ask him questions outright.

He would rather have stayed here alone with Ren. Each day he found more interesting than the last, and he would not permit himself to think beyond that.

Ah, the rules governing the civilized abduction!

☙ ⳩ ❧

Ren wandered from the dining room with its abandoned dishes, the abandoned conversation scarcely less palpable but only in the realm of the spirit. Tedium closed in at the prospect of another day alone. Ruefully she admitted to herself that she found Cath the governor, in his plain but well-made riding gear, his attention absorbed in questions of wine trade, root drainage, new bridges, far more prepossessing than she had Cath the courtier in elegant velvet and lace, quoting wicked poetry in the ancient singsong language of old Wyst.

Her heart would not swerve. So far, at least, there was no temptation to disturb her inner harmony. That left her with clear thought and the ability to think beyond just the two of them and to what must be said, and thought, in the Lesci court.

They had not discussed Lexan at all. Though his name came up from time to time, the subject of Lexan as person was tacitly forbidden, as was Cath's motivation. She knew that it was not a matter of unbounded lust. There was in some wise a challenge to his royal relation, one that Lexan had not responded to, though he could have.

They both knew he could have. From brief references, and from the subtle signs of guard and watch round Cath's castle, Ren gathered that Lexan could, and had in the past, exerted his kingly powers, and that he was all the more effective for the rarity and the expertise with which he acted when he chose to.

But no guards in royal livery galloped up to the gates demanding surrender of Ren's person. Nor did Yvo slip tracelessly in and appear at her window, which was the possibility she'd dreaded.

She was convinced of only one thing: the matter must be resolved by her alone. And Yvo knew it. She sensed his presence, still in the Lesci capital, but he made no attempt to contact her on the mental plane, nor did she reach for him.

And so, she whiled away the day, prowling among Cath's books. His servants, obviously resigned to the vagaries of aristocrats, kept a respectful distance, appearing only to offer meals.

ೞೞೞೞೞ

Despite his late return, Cath was at breakfast when she came down in her blue ball gown, her hair in a plain braid. The silvery glow of dawn struck muted color in the fragile fabric. She was thoroughly sick of the gown by then, thought she looked silly in the blunt light of morning, but he found the spectacle quite agreeable. He also knew better than to say anything.

He rose to greet her, as had become customary, then sat down again, frowning over a letter.

"I have to ride up to my vineyards today," he said as she helped herself to fresh-baked oatcakes and berries-and-cream. "It's a long ride, but you might find the area of interest. It's one of the oldest in the kingdom."

"I'd enjoy that."

"Do you know anything about wine making?" he asked, after studying his letter again.

"I've learned a few things."

Probably a lot. But she never enumerated just what she'd been taught, or how much she'd mastered. He discovered things about her through tossed-off references, which just made her more interesting. "You know something about human interaction," he said, neither agreeing to nor denying her claim. "Will you give me the benefit of your observations? This dispute is not an official judicial matter, it touches on personal concerns, and so my judgment might be at fault. I won't say more, lest I prejudice you either way."

"If you like," she said. "I will listen, but not speak before your people."

Very soon they were mounted on cross-country racers, covering difficult ground at the gallop, eight armed outriders behind them. The air was chill in the shadows, but the sun shone brightly, turning south-facing cliff sides pleasantly warm. He discovered that she rode as well as he, so they rode hard and fast, changing horses twice to spare the animals a long uphill dash.

The sun was advancing, casting extravagant shadows, when the long and acrimonious statements, claims, threats, and finally answered questions had been witnessed from angry parents, stubborn young woman, smiling harper, and steady young neighbor whose trade was making barrels. In the distance, clouds piled up over the higher peaks.

Cath told them all to wait on judgment and walked out of the parents' house onto the porch. Ren pulled the rough wooden door shut behind her.

Cath leaned his hands apart on the plank railing. "Well?" He flicked a glance over his shoulder, unsmiling, then returned his gaze to the spectacular valley view before them—and the impending storm.

"My suggestion is to make the first offer a trade that cuts the daughter off from inheriting."

Cath's lip curled. "So you don't believe in a month's courtship either?"

"One person's courtship is another's flirtation—or opportunity for gain," Ren said, her voice steady, uninflected. "A month, a moment, ten years, it's all relative. I do not trust that harper. He grins too much, and he was so busy trying to see down the neck of my gown that he didn't notice how much it hurt the daughter. My instinct is that his words are pretty with no meaning, except as they reveal his desire for personal gain."

Cath grunted. "That matches what I heard."

"I'll wait here," she said. "In truth, I feel for that poor barrel-making fellow. Although he loves her, has she ever returned the favor?"

"Oh, she liked him right fine, until this spring. Just like

he said. Maybe she'll like him again, once she gets the harper out of sight."

Will he like her back? Ren thought, rubbing her hands up her arms. *Does Lexan think I'm here because I want to be? Is a month just moonbeams? Would he have been happier if I'd gone home after my official duties were discharged, and hadn't gone walking in that rose garden with him, and accepted his invitation to stay?*

She turned her hot face into the cold wind; Cath reappeared, smiling faintly.

"All settled?"

"Not yet. But it will be. Soon's our friend the barrel maker caught on, he started in with all kinds of trade proposals—offering the harper good solid work in order to help the couple get started, the only constant being the daughter rescinding heirship to her brother. The harper smiled and smiled, but I swear he was calculating how fast he could be gone. I think the negotiations will last long enough for him to discover an urgent task somewhere down the mountain."

"Poor daughter," Ren said, but softly. A marriage with that handsome harper would be no joy, she suspected.

"Poor daughter indeed." Cath was going to say something more, but just shook his head. "Come on. We've a long ride, and we're going to make most of it wet."

He was right.

The rain started soon after, a drenching, chill rain that promised snow on those mountains before long. The rain lasted as the afternoon light faded and the unseen sun vanished beyond the western peaks. Cath offered her his riding jacket, which she refused, though with an inward pang of regret.

Ren had not had to exert such sustained physical control for a very long time. She managed, forcing inner warmth to kindle, and took no harm, knowing the cost would be tremendous lassitude and a voracious appetite. If she ate well and slept well, she would be fine on the morrow.

Still, never had she been so glad to see lights and civilization as when Cath's castle appeared below them. Round, down, and into the stable at last, the animals were glad to be home, the stable hands rushing to care for them.

Ren could not relinquish her control yet; she had to dismount, and she must not fall, despite watery knees and trembling fingers. Her face had gone numb; as she followed Cath upstairs to the little drawing room, it seemed her brain had gone numb as well.

A fire waited. Its heat drew her as she gratefully stretched out her hands. Slowly the numbness gave way to tingle, and then, at last, to warmth.

"Permit me to tell you," Cath said, unsmiling, "that your point has long been made, and you needn't take such foolish risks."

Ren glanced back. His manner was one of cool reserve, but she saw the concern beneath it. She forced herself to say cheerily, "Oh, I had a kind of wager with myself. I still don't know if I won or lost, but I promise this: no more wintry rides until I recover my wardrobe."

She turned back to the fire, breathing slowly, for the lassitude had hit her, but she would not give in to that, either. Gradually, she became aware of a wonderful summery scent, the precious, rare tea from beyond the Dragon Lands above Wyst.

She hesitated, not wanting to remove herself from the fire, for her gown was still rain-drenched, unpleasantly clingy and cold. The clink of porcelain on wood caused her to turn her head. Cath was within arm's reach, his head bent, his face hidden as he poured the tea into a cup. He stepped back, pulled off his soggy riding jacket, and slung it over a table by the door.

Ren picked up the teacup slowly and sipped, eyes shut, savoring the taste of spring gardens, of summery fields full of wildflowers, utterly unaware of the striking picture she made, the gown molding every subtle curve of her splendid body, her profile outlined against the fire.

Warmth worked its way down to her toes in the now-threadbare dancing slippers, and stayed. She opened her eyes. Realized she'd emptied the cup.

She turned to thank him. The words never shaped themselves; instead she stood there, staring blankly at those steady, intense black eyes.

Warmth. The numbness was gone, leaving her senses with an extraordinary clarity. Each sound, each snap of the fire, the patter of rain against the glass of the windows, Cath's breathing, all took on meaning beyond comprehension. Scents: the summery tea, her wet hair and gown, the faint burning-wood scent given off by magical firesticks ablaze.

She could not look away from Cath. Hazy observations worked into her consciousness: that she had never before seen him as attractive as he was now, sitting there in damp shirt and riding breeches and high, spurred boots. His clothes outlined his lean, strong body, his sharply-etched cheeks flushed with returning color, his long black hair, usually tied back in a neat queue, hanging in wet strands across his brow and over his shoulders onto his chest, which rose and fell with each breath.

He did not speak, or drop his gaze.

The warmth had become a tingle. Not the painful needle-stab of chilled flesh, but the inward, glittering tingle of anticipation, for whatever the masks the mind chose to wear while gambling with emotions, the body's needs were plain, direct.

His gaze shifted. She snapped into intense awareness that her most substantial garment was a ball gown made of fragile gauze, and that it was plastered over her form just as revealingly as was his clothing. The realization, the caress of his long, deliberate gaze, intensified the tingle into desire.

And despite the leap and crackle of the fire, and the rise and fall of Cath's chest beneath his cambric shirt, the world stilled.

VIII. Waiting

In Duen Lesc's royal palace, light gleamed in a tower, visible through cold sheets of rain.

Yvo stood in a window alcove, looking up at that tower.

Lexan Yvansk was perhaps the most oblique subject for observation as yet encountered, if not the most difficult. Yet Yvo was certain that Lexan sat up there in that tower right now, on watch, by farsense, while his courtiers amused themselves in various ways, and his kingdom went about ending another day. He'd been there since sunset, having sent a graceful excuse to Najad, who'd proposed an evening of music and maybe an impromptu dance.

The impulse to let Lexan know that he did not watch alone became stronger as time slipped along its remorseless stream. Yet he felt that a mind-to-mind contact would be a mistake.

Instead, he stood at a window across a courtyard from the base of Lexan's tower. He knew the light framed his silhouette; he lifted his mental shield. Doing so carried its own risks and its fascinations. One suddenly heard, across the unending mental plane, the emotion-charged whisperings of countless minds.

Yvo's father had first shared this experience with him

years ago, explaining what it meant, showing how to sift and sort, and protecting him when a sudden, corrosively fierce intent seared one's focus, like a thousand tortured voices shrieking in one's ear, without the relative limitations of vocal projection, air as conduit, and one's own physical boundaries.

Grief and isolation were no easier to bear.

At least Tarsa was gone, riding swiftly northeast, taking with her that imperfect mental shield. Yvo pitied her, but her presence grated like a fine musical instrument played continually a half-tone out of tune. He'd done what he could, but was not sanguine about how much alteration a few moments' conversation on a ballroom floor could inspire.

Quite abruptly, magic seized him. The transfer was quick.

He found himself standing before a high window, looking through rain-streaked glass over the gold-windowed palace, beautiful at night as it was during the day. And there was the window at which he'd stood only moments before.

He turned around. Lexan Yvansk sat beside a plain wooden desk. He still wore the formal dark green over-robe, sleeves embroidered with herons in flight, which he had worn to preside over state business, but the robe was open over his fine cambric under-robe, the sash gone. These were more signs of human weariness; his long, glossy brown hair was ruffled instead of queued neatly back. More surprising was the half-empty bottle of very fine double-distilled rye sitting before him. No glass.

Yvo took these things in, then met Lexan's ironic gaze.

"You have a lot in common with your ancestors," Yvo said appreciatively.

Amusement banished the self-mockery in that beautiful face. Or almost did.

"The choice in . . . problematical family connections or in anesthetic?"

There it was, the first admission. *Yvansks do not go to war, they seduce their enemies and turn them into lovers.* What about turning them into queens? That Yvo was here at all had already been a confession.

"I'm told your famous forebear, Mattius, preferred Algyran wine," Yvo said.

He repressed the urge to lift his hand, to strike fire-reflection off the dreamstone ring on his hand. Let its influence be felt more subtly; Yvansk was far too sensitive on the mental plane for any overt move.

So. If one cannot be oblique, then be direct. "Ren did not go up north of her own free will."

"So it was you, then, whose prints added to those my searchers found in the garden?"

"Yes."

"I rather thought so. Your pardon. Go on."

"The fact that she hasn't escaped means she's on some kind of crusade."

Lexan said nothing for rather too long; Yvo realized he was listening by farsense, and something was happening. A crisis of some kind. Taking place right then.

A pause to appreciate the magnitude of his farsense—either that or the profound depth of his bond. Even Yvo would have difficulty hearing someone at the distance of Alavanska.

Presently, Duen Lesc's king reached, drank from the bottle, set it down with a frowning precision that testified to the quantity he'd already consumed.

Then he looked up. His eyes were remarkably clear, but his face no longer masked his emotions, nor did he seem to care.

What was he listening for? Yvo fought the urge to

attempt to reach his sister by farsense. His job was here, and his aspect must remain neutral. What he did not know, yet, was whether Lexan had brought him for distraction or for challenge.

"Crusade?" Lexan said, after another swig.

"I know Ren," Yvo stated the obvious to underscore the next: "She'll be tempted to reform your maverick, if she can."

Lexan's fine mouth curled in derision, and for a moment there was a striking resemblance to Cath Lassatar. Kinsmen, then? Probably, but irrelevant at this moment.

Yvo waited for disbelief, scorn, but Lexan's gaze diffused again, for a long space, while rain drummed at the window.

IX. *Grace*

Ren stared for that measureless time at Cath, her nerves singing. Although Cath had contrived her presence here, alone with him in his castle, the choice at this moment was entirely hers. She had only to reach out her hand, and they could embark on an interlude of sensory pleasure for as long as she desired.

So . . . why shouldn't she? There was no fault in shared joy, was there? Everyone back in the capital probably assumed they'd been romping in bed since their arrival.

Everyone? She would not think about Lexan, she would not, and yet even now, with her senses simmering, she remembered the sweet anguish of the very first touch of his fingers to hers.

Be true to yourself before you can be true to the world.

The truth was that the glory she felt was lust. Not love.

She closed her eyes, and now it was possible to think, for think she must. She considered what would happen if she took

Cath's unspoken offer of shared passion. When it ended, she would turn away, because in the long course of her life, it would hold little meaning for her. But it was not the same for him. She knew, after these days in his company, seeing his lands and listening to his people, that underneath the cold court exterior, Cath Lassator of Alavanska was a man of honor—but—*and?*— he was a romantic.

There was no fault in shared joy, but there was, by her own code, in indulgence at the risk of another's well-being. Cath was in love, or thought he was in love, and to embark on an affair would tangle them up in one another's emotional lives with only pain as a result.

And so, she breathed deeply, set down her empty cup, and walked out.

ഇൻഃ

Yvo felt the atmosphere intensify and then, quite suddenly, the tension was gone. Some resolution had been made, some crisis had passed.

Lexan Yvansk looked around as if he did not understand where he was, or how he had arrived there.

Yvo watched comprehension return, and wondered if Yvansk, in remembering his presence, would regret having revealed himself that much. Now is the time, Yvo thought with resignation, for him to ram my father into my teeth as a method of dismissal.

Instead—unexpectedly—there was that self-mockery again, but with it real humor. "I think I've finally solved the mystery of your presence," he said. "Tacit approval from the formidable guardian?"

"My father knows I'm here, but not why." Then Yvo laughed, realizing that Lexan had, in fact, meant himself.

Though he was far from being Ren's guardian.

"So you live in your father's shadow," Lexan murmured.

"Say rather in the light of his sun," Yvo said, and watched Lexan sort rapidly through the implications.

"My own father used to be likened to the moon," Lexan said at last, hefting his bottle and turning it in his hands so that the fire reflected through the liquid, gold, amber, honey. "Appeared infrequently, shed little light and no warmth." He smiled, got to his feet, and with a sudden violent gesture flung the bottle into the fireplace, where it smashed and sent up a shoot of blue flame.

They watched the fire flare and subside.

Lexan turned his head. "Are you sitting on good advice that you simply must impart?"

"No," said Yvo.

X. A Duel to the Heart

Though the annoyance of steady rain after weeks of clear skies made Tarsa cold, her spirits stayed high.

She'd ridden through rain before. During the war days, she'd ridden through all kinds of weather on her missions as a messenger, and the first gift Lexan had given her—well, he'd given them all—was a rainproof cloak that she'd treasured ever since, and wore now. It was a relief to be riding to action again, while warmly embraced by Lexan's gift.

When the capital dwindled behind her, she considered Yvo's words at the Blue Night Masque. The kind of influence he meant might be the rescue she planned out in detail over the long days of her lonely ride.

The pleasure of that image had obliterated the uncomfortable reaction when remembering the disillusionment in Najad's face. Strange, that. She'd never cared a whit for his devotion, but as soon as it was gone, she felt the lack. Adulation was better than scorn from a fool. More telling, it was the possibility of scorn from those who were not fools that galled.

She would be a hero, and rescue Ren in Cath's teeth. Ren, of course, would be grateful. If, that is, she really didn't want to stay with Cath—and if she did, Tarsa would have a different message to take back, and she'd say to Lexan. . . .

She'd say to Lexan. . . .

That part was more difficult to figure out. At least, Lexan would appreciate her selfless act. She would have rescued a rival. Surely that was the action of a queen!

She reached the outskirts of Alavanska, spending the night in a roadside inn as a rainstorm battered the countryside. She set out just before dawn into a rain-washed day. The sky was clear, the air cold. She looked about with the eyes of a countess, and what she saw impressed her: villages, lands, everything well-tended.

Well-tended, and extensive. She hadn't realized just how extensive Alavanska was, for Cath's primary residence was located at the southwest corner of his lands. This duchy might be called a little kingdom. In fact, it was probably the size of some of the smaller western kingdoms.

When she came within sight of the castle, she veered off the road to make her approach under cover of falling darkness. She would slip in, noiseless and unnoticed.

And then!

⊰⚘⊱

While Tarsa smiled with anticipation, Ren was summoned from the library to supper.

She braced herself. Inclination was very much against a

meeting, but she knew that was weakness. The day had passed without any communication between Cath and her. Now it was time to talk.

The amused awareness in his eyes when they met in the drawing room made it clear he felt the same way. While the servants laid dishes and food on the table between the two great wing chairs, they spoke little. As soon as they were alone, Cath sat back with his wineglass in his hands.

Ren looked at that familiar sardonic expression and knew she had the courtier back. "If you're anticipating being entertained by recriminations or protests, you'll have a long wait."

He lifted his glass in a salute. "Recriminations have become a habit."

"I think you thoroughly enjoy your reputation."

He smiled a little. "It has its benefits, mostly at warding off fools. You have no observations to make, then, about last night?"

"I do, if you really wish to hear them."

"Please."

She nodded once, then charmed him anew by thumping her elbows onto the table and resting her chin on her laced fingers. "Denying the intensity of attraction would be as stupid as acting on it."

His brows lifted in surprise.

"It won't happen again," she said. "Now that I know the possibility is there."

"Then it remains . . . an unresolved issue," he said mildly. "Where's the wisdom in that? Certainly no pleasure."

She shook her head. "I cannot speak for you, obviously, but for me it *is* resolved. It's an attraction of the senses only, for we don't really know one another, and although you are brave, intelligent, a good governor—"

"Spare me," he cut in, "the consolatory encomiums."

She grinned. "But they're true. You're also selfish, enjoy verbal cruelty just because you can do it, and you are able to do something like this—" Her gesture took in her presence there, in his castle. "—caring nothing for the consequences."

"On the contrary, I care very much," he said, faint color ridging his cheekbones, and she realized that she had misunderstood his motives: the romantic in him had not permitted him to look past getting her away from the king's dazzle, so that he could court her on his own. In his view, the risk was his own—that if she dusted off, she might very well leave him a laughingstock. He would hate that worse than fighting, even losing, a duel with swords.

She could leave. She had no ties—

Are you free?

She shook her head a little. His brows contracted, but before he could ask a question she would not answer, she straightened up. "I grew up with kings around me," she said, her head tipped to one side. "I learned before I ever had any interest in such matters that kings have two relationships, and the one with their kingdom comes before any relationship of the heart. I never wanted any part of that life."

Silence, except the crackle of fire. She watched him work his way through the several meanings: that she stayed in Duen Lesc *despite* Lexan's title.

That she was in love with the man.

That she was not going to fall in love with Cath, even though she felt the spark of desire.

"I don't think you can prevent it from happening again."

Ren said, "Do you speak generally or specifically?"

He looked wry. "Since my selfish nature is established,

I'll claim only that which pertains to myself. But with this proviso: as for the abduction, I never repeat mistakes."

"I—" Ren's gaze went distant, and for a short time, all the humor vanished from her face. "I dare not say 'never', for who can predict what circumstance will bring? I'd thought, once, that I had suffered the worst temptation of a lifetime, until now. Yet, I think I can sustain this one again, intense as it is, and the outcome will remain the same."

"Your original temptation does not sound recent," he ventured, watching her closely.

Her gaze was still distant as she said, "Oh, it wasn't. During the war." Suddenly she was present again, instead of caught in the past. There was that in the shape of her smile, and the cant of her head, that betokened remembered anguish as she added, "War stories are a bore, so I won't burden you with the details. Suffice it to say that I won, and it was good that I did, for the consequences far outdistanced my little concerns."

Knowing whom she had lived with, and a little of whom she had spent the war with, he suspected that what she referred to was far larger and more important than she admitted.

She drank some wine, then said, "This particular temptation won't occur again because—for me—passion without companionship of the mind cannot last. You and I could become friends, if we work at it. We could be enemies, though I'd rather not. But we will never be lovers." She smiled at last, a bewitching smile full of fun and challenge. "You need someone who will fight back."

He said after a short pause, "You realize it might be to no purpose. Not," he added slowly, "because the wish is wanting, but the exigencies of circumstance."

"I know," she whispered.

He reached to pour more wine for them both, then sat

back again. "It's not your worthiness. I'm beginning to believe that what I'd thought impossible has indeed occurred: that you are, in fact, not just equal to the exacting requirements of Duen Lesc's court and country, but surpass them. But I don't know how much my inscrutable cousin sees. Or why he does not act."

"I don't know, either," she said, relieved beyond measure that he didn't use his verbal claws to rake her heart. He could have, for she'd seen him do it time and again to Tarsa of Rezh. "If our minds do not meet, I'll go away, and none of you will ever see me again."

"That would be a—" A discreet knock interrupted him. He frowned. Got to his feet and went to the door in two strides.

A whispered conversation with a servant at the door, and then Cath said, "You'll pardon me?" The courtier was back, behind his mask of cold amusement.

She raised her wine glass, and he went out.

She was watching the fire glint with ruby brilliance through her glass when the door opened again, and to Ren's surprise, in slipped Tarsa, dressed for riding, a rapier at her side.

Tarsa tossed back a lock of draggled blond hair, then shut the door. Her smile of triumph sagged into surprise when she registered the blue ball gown. Why was Ren still wearing *that?*

Not that it mattered. Tarsa reclaimed her moment of triumph and said, "I fooled the servants into thinking a courier arrived. I'm here to rescue you."

In all her imaginings, Tarsa thought she'd covered every possible reaction. Ren would either storm in helpless anger, or weep in relief, or maybe even act haughty. Disappointment, perchance, that Tarsa came to her rescue, and not Lexan.

But she never pictured what she got: cool amusement.

"Who said," Ren spread her hands, "I needed rescuing?"

Tarsa stared. "You mean you came willingly after all?"

"Of course not. Glass of wine? You must be cold."

Tarsa gave her head a shake. "I don't—"

"Think, Tarsa." Ren rose from the table and came round to face her. "Think. Would you jumble off in the middle of the night, taking no belongings, not even warning your maid, much less sending a note to your host, by choice?"

"No," Tarsa said, furious with her shock-numbed mind. She breathed deeply, then said, "No, I wouldn't."

Ren turned her palms out. "As anyone who cares enough to consider the circumstances would realize."

Tarsa bit her lip. "So it's obvious to everyone but me that you were swept here without your consent. If so, why isn't Lexan here instead of me?"

"I will not discuss Lexan Yvansk with you, Tarsa," Ren said. "You would not accept me as an acquaintance, much less give me the chance to offer myself as a friend, so to share my thoughts with you now would just enable you to use them against me as weapons. Unless you'd like to convince me differently."

Tarsa flushed, knowing it was true. Ren didn't even sound angry, just resigned.

"All right, then. Lexan's response—or lack of it—will remain a mystery. But if you don't need rescuing, then why do you stay? I see no guards or weapons about."

"Oh, we made a truce, Cath and I." Ren, looking at Tarsa, felt missing pieces in motivations, and reactions, falling rapidly into place. The possibilities made her fizzy with hilarity. But she must step carefully indeed, for both Cath and Tarsa were quick, smart, and horrifically sensitive. "Cath would make a formidable enemy or ally," she said at last. "I have been doing my best to work for the second prospect."

And he listens to you? Tarsa wanted to ask, but she knew

the answer: he did. Ren betrayed none of the anguish that Tarsa felt after even a brief encounter with Cath.

In short, he respected Ren.

He does not respect me. Once he did—but no longer.

She backed up a step, her throat tight, her eyes aching. There was nothing to do but leave, then, and concoct a story on the long ride back to court. To pack up, and retreat to Rezh with as much grace as she could muster.

She owed Ren Desvransa nothing. She turned her back and slipped out the door again. Ren did not speak or move to stop her.

Outside the room Tarsa peered about the hallway. No one in sight. Rapidly reviewing her internal map, she slipped past the servants' stairway, finding that full of traffic, unlike the tiled stairway that unknown generations of Lassators had used.

She eased down to the next landing, softly lit by glowglobes. Paused, listening, her senses alert. To? Something, something. . . .

Reached a foot to descend the last stairway, and jumped as a hand closed on her arm. A strong, familiar hand, lace at the wrists, folded cuffs of blue silk.

Her head jerked around, and she stared up into Cath's face. He looked down at her with no evidence of surprise, his most hateful smile instantly kindling her slumbering rage.

Anger, and under it, fear. She fought against the fear as he drew her a few steps into a room just off the landing, then shut the door and lounged against it, still with her arm in his grip.

"Let me go." She tried to wrench free.

"Would you prefer to conduct this interview in the main hall?"

"I don't want *any* interview," she retorted, yanking

harder.

"Did you really imagine you could prance into my land, much less my home, without my knowing?"

She stared, then managed, "Did Ren know?"

"She did not. I was curious. Did you ride all this way just to rescue her?"

"Yes." He had let her go. She crossed her arms. "*Somebody* had to."

"What precipitated this act of altruism?" He smiled again, that hateful smile that never failed to enrage her. "Not, surely, a sudden loss of prestige?"

Heat flooded from her neck right up to her hairline, and he laughed. "Ah, Tarsa, you are so predictable."

Predictable! No one, ever, had accused her of that, in so contemptuous a tone. Reliable, yes, dashing, during the war when she'd risked her life carrying messages in aid of Lexan's resistance to the enemy.

The enemy then had been clear, and was clear now, so clear that the impulse to action seized her with inescapable grip. Too long she'd repressed every passion, every emotion, toward attaining the long goal, which was gone now, forever out of reach, leaving only Cath's lounging, laughing amusement.

Giving in to reckless, glorious rage, she flung herself at him. She pulled her blade free and aimed the point straight at his heart.

He did not wear weapons in his own house, but this was his father's old room, with crossed swords on the wall. He whirled, pulled one down, and met her blade just before it reached him.

Passion is not practice. *Clash, clang!* She tried twice to skewer him and he blocked, then in a whirling bind he caught her blade and wrenched it from her grip.

The weapons crashed on the stone floor. She doubled her fists and launched herself at him. A wild struggle ensued. The room spun crazily, as she cried, half weeping, half gasping, but she no longer cared. Her one desire was to claw the sneer from that face. She fought, and kicked, and writhed, until he managed to catch hold of her wrists and twist them up behind her, holding her immoveable against him, chest to chest, until all the rage died away, leaving her puffing for breath.

Sanity trickled back into her mind, and with it, the awareness of proximity, of the rise and fall of her bosom against his velvet-covered ribs. She threw back her head to see his gleaming dark gaze, and a curious smile on his lips.

"Done?" he asked, tossing his head to shift the fine hair that had drifted into his eyes.

She nodded once, not trusting herself to speak, and he released her wrists.

Rubbing them, she retreated behind a massive table.

"'You need someone who will fight back,'" he said as he righted an overturned chair and dropped down onto it. "That was fun. I wish . . ." He paused, grinning. A twisted grin, not that hateful cold, superior smile. "I wish you remembered as fondly as I do a certain spring night, not so long ago."

"I was drunk," she stated, and sniffed. "Why did you drag Ren up here?"

He laughed. It was so unexpected a sound it caught her by surprise. "To see who would come up here after her," he said. "Fancy that! Lady Tarsa to the rescue."

His voice was unsteady, pitched to provoke, but not to flay. It was not with the intention of doing damage, this time, when she uncrossed her arms and took an open-handed swing at his face.

XI. The Other Word is Communion

When, at dawn, they emerged, they found Ren, still in her blue gown. She smiled in happy welcome. "Come along, my dears. I ordered breakfast, and everything is waiting."

XII. Are You Free?

Word had zapped ahead, somehow, testifying to the interest all three aroused. Not that the most prominent courtiers were as rude as the younger ones crowding the stable yard. A remarkable number of personal runners belonging to older nobles jostled with the young, who would make a fashion of remembering this day.

The three rode slowly through the gates, Cath's entourage somewhere behind. There existed, it seemed, a shared hilarity between all three. Cath Lassatar, Duke of Alavanska, rode with languid grace with a lady at either side. He was impeccably turned out in riding clothes of black. At one side was Lady Tarsa, Countess of Rezh, also in riding clothes, her sun-bright hair bound up in a simple coronet. On the other side, Ren Desvransa wore a ball gown that looked much the worse for wear, though her posture, her smile, transformed the oddity into the glamour of adventure.

Yvo, at the edge of the crowd, took only one look, then withdrew, smiling, to pack for his journey home.

No one noticed him.

Tarsa was thinking: *I wish Rezh were next to Alavanska. On the other hand, it makes a nice inheritance for a second child . . . .*

As the crowd watched, silent in amazement, Tarsa leaned across her horse's neck to address a remark to the other two.

Cath smiled. Ren laughed.

Cath was thinking: *Where are you, Lexan? I need to see your face before I figure out if you were testing me, or Ren—or yourself.*

They rode slowly into the courtyard, pausing only when Najad of Desentis, who was too honest to even think of pretense, dashed up and greeted them all with unaffected pleasure.

"By the Fire, we were worried! What's toward?" he addressed all three.

Ren said in her clear, sunny voice, "Oh, it was a little wager between the three of us."

Najad whistled. "A wager, you say?"

"Can *you* turn down a challenge?" Ren leaned toward him, her manner confidential, her voice carrying. "I can't!"

Whispers rustled through the crowd: *together*, and *wager* being the key words. A wager! An aristocrat could be forgiven anything done on a challenge, especially if it was carried off with this hilarious flair.

Ren was thinking: *Yes, I want you, Lexan of Duen Lesc, and if courting your entire kingdom for the rest of my life is the price I must pay, then so be it.*

The three dismounted and were surrounded by friends, servants, well-wishers, all of whom observed their easy camaraderie. Miraculously, it seemed mostly genuine, though expressed through characteristics typical of each: Cath's faint smile, sardonic at the edges, Tarsa's ceaseless gauging of others' gazes, Ren's ease and delight in seeing friends once again. There was no sign of guilt, or accusation, or even the cold rivalry that splits groups of people into factions when leaders become rivals.

Lexan Yvansk stood just beyond the courtiers who were too amazed to drawl, or semaphore hidden meanings with their fans. They were talking naturally, laughing outright instead of uttering the well-bred court titter, some even lamenting having not been in on the fun.

Presently, the crowd parted, and Lexan moved through his people to Ren's side, offering his arm. People effaced themselves and withdrew to talk, wonder, laugh, drink, rest, or make merry, according to their nature.

Ren rested her fingers lightly on his arm, feeling the tense muscle beneath the smooth linen, then turned toward one of the remarkable fountains with its complicated jets and tiers of fine spray that threw up myriad rainbows.

She sat down on the low rim, and as a stray breeze wafted a mist into her face, she breathed deeply, smiling. "Oh, that does feel refreshing after so long a ride," she exclaimed, and leaned forward to dip her hands in the rilling water.

Lexan sat down beside her, idly running one hand back and forth, back and forth, in the cool water. When he looked up, their eyes met, and he asked, "Are you free?"

She looked at the spray, shards of liquid sun, and at her fingers, dripping with crystalline droplets, and finally at his eyes, so true, like his heart wide and true and boundless as the sky overhead. "No," she said, smiling. And, "Are you?"

"No. As long as I live." Beneath the cool surface of the water their fingers met, laced, and held.

Editor's Note

I began writing fantasy and science fiction in the early 1980s under my former name, Deborah Wheeler. My first professional sale was to a new anthology series, edited by a woman who would go on to become famous for discovering and nurturing new writers. That woman was Marion Zimmer Bradley, and the book was the first *Sword and Sorceress*. Over the years, I learned not only a great deal about writing from her, but also about the special role of a sympathetic, insightful editor.

When Vera Nazarian, publisher of Norilana Books, asked me if I'd ever thought about editing, she offered me a special opportunity to "pay forward" all the help Marion had extended to me, and also to explore a new aspect of my literary voice. I discovered, somewhat to my surprise, that I had ferocious opinions about what kind of stories I wanted to read and how I wanted to interact with my authors. *My* authors.

I have been delighted, awed, and humbled by the literary skill and storytelling excellence . . . the *heart* . . . in the stories I present to you here. I am grateful to everyone who made it possible.

Marion, thank you.

Vera, thank you.

Most of all . . . *my* authors, thank you!

Deborah J. Ross
Boulder Creek, California
October 2007

Publisher's Note

I coined the term "Lace and Blade" sometime in 2005 in an online SFReader.com forum conversation in response to the term "New Edge" proposed by Howard Andrew Jones to define the modern sword and sorcery genre. My original definition of *lace and blade* referred to a kind of elegant and romantic "soft" flavor of sword and sorcery—"where mythic high fantasy has been put in a blender together with strict old-fashioned Conan-style s&s action adventure, and what has emerged is romantic lyrical fantasy with swords and wonder and a bit of 'girl cooties.'" It's a genre within a genre, infused with the effervescent wit of Oscar Wilde and exemplified by dropped handkerchiefs, cloak and dagger intrigue, sophisticated dialogue, stolen glances, fiery passions, and such gallant swashbucklers as Zorro, the Scarlet Pimpernel, D'Artagnan, the prolific lover Casanova, and Cyrion, the beautiful, deadly, and charming hero created by Tanith Lee.

However, *lace and blade* in my mind has now come to mean so much more than sword and sorcery, but the whole oeuvre of exotic and beautiful high fantasy and period fantasy, including fantasy of manners, ancient historical fantasy; where duels of sharp wit and steel are as common as duels between the sheets; where living jewels flash in earlobes and frothy lace defines the curve of wrist and the hollow of throat; where erotic tension fills the perfumed air with frissons of anticipation and romantic delight; where hearts are broken and resurrected by true love, dangerous liaisons decide the fates of kingdoms, and courtesans slay with a kiss.

The need for such stories is urgent, as so many of us

hunger for beauty, elegance, and classic style. And so, I've asked my friend and wonderful fellow writer Deborah J. Ross to edit this annual anthology series of elegant fantasy, *Lace and Blade,* the debut title for Leda, the new romantic fantasy imprint of Norilana Books. Not only did she do a brilliant job but, somewhere between inception and completion, a rare kind of true magic happened, and the book became more than either one of us expected; it came *alive.* I hold it now in my hands and I am in awe. I am overcome with giddy champagne delight, because I can almost feel a pulse, a fluttering, delicate movement of breath . . . a hint of passion coming from each and every story. There's an aristocratic feast within these pages—thank you, Deborah, and all the marvelous authors within, for this exquisite pleasure.

At last I must acknowledge the glorious and inimitable muse of our time, Tanith Lee, and her body of work as my primary inspiration for this literary sub-genre or movement, and hence this anthology. Award-winning and critically acclaimed author of the Flat Earth books, *The Birthgrave, Cyrion, Lycanthia, Kill the Dead, Sabella, The Silver Metal Lover, Sung in Shadow, The Wars of Vis,* the books of Venus, and countless others, she has filled most of my working life with inspiration, with visions of beauty larger than life. And now, she has gifted this anthology with a story.

Thank you, O Muse, Tanith.

Vera Nazarian
Los Angeles, California
November 2007

CPSIA information can be obtained at www.ICGtesting.com
Printed in the USA
LVOW04s1732220615

443396LV00017B/1551/P

9 781494 488161